D0674015

YOU CAN LIVE
FOREVER

You Can Live Forever

Julie Maxwell

Jonathan Cape
LONDON

Published by Jonathan Cape 2007

2 4 6 8 10 9 7 5 3 1

Copyright © Julie Maxwell 2007

Julie Maxwell has asserted her right under the Copyright, Designs
and Patents Act 1988 to be identified as the author of this work

First published in Great Britain in 2007 by
Jonathan Cape
Random House, 20 Vauxhall Bridge Road,
London SW1V 2SA

www.randomhouse.co.uk

Addresses for companies within The Random House Group Limited
can be found at:
www.randomhouse.co.uk

The Random House Group Limited Reg. No. 954009

A CIP catalogue record for this book is available from the British Library

ISBN 978 0224080439

The Random House Group Limited makes every effort to ensure that the
papers used in its books are made from trees that have been legally
sourced from well-managed and credibly certified forests. Our paper
procurement policy can be found at: www.randomhouse.co.uk/paper.htm

Typeset by Palimpsest Book Production Limited,
Grangemouth, Stirlingshire

Printed and bound in Great Britain by
Mackays of Chatham Plc, Chatham, Kent

for Marius, with love

Chapter One

Alice's life had been in peril from the very beginning. But she became fully mortal in her twenty-second year. Her father, William, was a part-time arsonist. He knew himself a man of cunning who placed his faith in two sayings. The first was, 'It's not an exact science.' This applied whenever petrol and a match were posted through the wrong letter box. The second was, 'I have it down to a fine art.' This applied whenever the same items went through the right letter box. William spoke often, with dazed satisfaction, of all manner of burnings. People say there is a connection between madness and arson. But it need not be arson solely. William told Alice he would happily dispose of a corpse in his incinerator – DIY or valet service. Five grand if the murderers used the incinerator themselves, ten grand if they wanted him to do it for them.

'Many people take you up on it?' Alice asked one afternoon, sitting in the passenger seat of his Ford Mondeo with its scratched grey plastic interior. William said not, but he was hopeful. Not long since, a car with mirror windows slewed to a halt in his yard, its three occupants asking for him. The yard was a site of greenbelt opposite a military airbase. As it happened, that day he wasn't around.

'Will be next time, though, I can tell yer,' he boasted shyly, as if the intention of criminal activity amounted to an accomplishment.

Alice waited for him to unchain the gates. Red, rusted metal sheets bending at the corners, they gave access, through the wild hedgerow, to the business yard. A brick building, in the style of a 1930s Underground station, commanded the centre. A gravel road encircled it like a moat. Bare black trees leaned over like candle wicks. On the grass verges, two caravans were perched on bricks. Green fields stretched in every direction. William owned four acres. He parked up beside some heavy plant machinery – a couple of long green cranes, seven stubby once-white mini-excavators with concrete breakers, three new muddy yellow JCB 3CXs.

'Anyway, whaddyer think of my new machines? See the signwriting?'

Alice turned to look.

'Environmental, isn't it?' he asked.

'Very,' she agreed politely. The slogans were forest green.

'Well, I'm doing all right, yer know. I'm gettan there – even if yer mother doesn't think so. Did I tell yer I made Henry a director of the company?'

Henry G. Shepherd, as his bank accounts, bank statements, credit cards and mortgage agreements designated him, was a dog. If anyone rang looking for him, William said, 'Henry? Well, yer see, the thing is, he's a bit tied up at the moment.' And so he was – his tangled brass chain lay in the diesel dirt of the workshop floor. Henry's fellow employees included, according to the tax returns, Tom Thumb, R. Sonist and Billy Shakespeare. Alice wondered why no one at the tax office had ever cracked any of these jokes.

Now she asked her father what was so special about nitroglycerine. He'd been keeping a small store of it cool and motionless, stowed away carefully in the yard. He had a plan for it that very afternoon. His eyes, the brown of strong tea, held her as he rehearsed the details. He was going to release a few of the volatile oily yellow drops, by pipette, into the engine of an 804 excavator. Finally, he explained the particular brilliance of nitroglycerine: it left no trace. The fire brigade had heat-searching light, able to probe a raging fire and determine where it was started. Clever arsonists would start a fire in several places, but the heat-searching light was not fooled. Nitroglycerine, however, was different. Also, it was not a substance they would expect anyone to use nowadays.

How had he got hold of the stuff? Alice wanted to know. Old contacts, he explained, made when he infiltrated IRA cells for the British police. Done it for years, and never whispered a word of it to a mortal soul. The immortal ones he talked to, she knew about already.

'I can see them now,' he said, looking obviously delighted. 'Firemen, forensics, not a hope. I'll tell them – if they really want to know, they should try talking to Henry G.'

So, nitroglycerine, no trace. A few drops in the right places, her father said. They'd be well clear when the blast occurred, triggered by his mobile telephone. Listening to all this, Alice had her usual sense that her father had something crucial missing. As though one half of his brain had been sawn off, roughly, like a log, while the other half was modelled on a cockpit – full of neurotic dials, smart-clicking switches, nictating red lights.

'You know me,' he said. 'I have it down to a fine art.' William was always a great lover and praiser of himself.

'But – "it's not an exact science"?'

'Exactly. Yer've got it now.'

He got out of the car and told Alice, 'Whaddever yer do,' to wait for him there. A panicky person as a rule, Alice sat stringently calm. Her mind began to float at the pleasant distance from reality it managed whenever she had to open her mouth for the dentist.

Several minutes later, she watched as her father made his way down a chalky track to the old water tank, which served as an underground garage. He walked with the limp that he rehearsed for hours. In company, it gained him sympathy. Alone, he took pity on himself. Hanging from his left hand was the black plastic briefcase with the worn corners that he carried everywhere. In his right, the metal canister containing the liquid explosive. He had the little pipette (he'd shown it to her on the way over) in the pocket of his grey navy anorak. Parked inside the tank, alongside the 804, were several other old machines and his bridal-white Bentley Mulsanne. Alice loved the Bentley. It had tiny, diamond-shaped mirrors set in tortoiseshell on panels above the back seats. You flicked a black switch at the bottom of the mirror's frame and a light came on. Suddenly she was mourning – to think of the cool 'champagne' leather blackened, the sparkling paint fried to matte, the bodywork a skull of scoured metal, the shrivelled rear lights like sun-dried tomatoes.

She felt compelled to get out of the car. She shouted urgently across to her father, who was limping rapidly into the blackness of the tank. 'Are you quite sure about the Bentley? Can't we save that? Especially as we know about Mum now?'

'Will yus stay in the fuckan car!' her father shouted back. 'And what do we know about yer mother anyway? That curse-it woman could have anything wrong with her at any time!'

When everything was over and the tank cooled down, he

4

intended to haul the Bentley out with the lorry. Then he would leave the metal carcass, like a sculpture, in the grass.

'Just get in the car!'

So she did. Then, just as Alice was visualising what was going to happen to the Bentley, she heard a loud explosion. Her father was gone in a bang. William was bold and cautious, vengeful and philanthropic. It was the combustion – quite literally – of his conflicting sides that had got him in the end. A couple of seconds later, Alice saw a clod of earth flying towards the windscreen. After that, she saw no more of anything at all. And there was an end of it. Dust she was, and by the dust of the earth she was returned. In the Year of Our Lord 1997.

Chapter Two

William gave life with no less enterprise than he took it. Alice had personal reason to be grateful: she was the by-product of a condom he sabotaged. Her mother, Oonagh, thought the Pill was making her ill and fat. William saw his chance and seized it. One Saturday afternoon she went out to the Church of the Worldwide Saints of God with her young son Peter. William waved them off, full of admiration for Peter in his three-piece tartan suit. Then he went to the bathroom. Taking a pair of tweezers from his wife's yellow, quilted make-up purse, he smiled to himself at this trespass. The first incision cut the small piece of tape on the back of the box of condoms. The second punctured the individual foil wrapper. The third created life. William held the condom up to the light bulb with satisfaction.

There was no need to unfurl it. He was not a Roman Catholic who would have made the hole safely away from the tip – salving his conscience about the use of contraception because the intention to procreate was still (just about) there. No, William made his hole right through the tip, like the scheming, paternally-minded member of the Church of Ireland he was. Then he put the condom back in the box and bided his time.

He feigned displeasure when the first split occurred. 'Sure Christ, the English can't make nothan.'

It seemed to happen on each occasion thereafter. Sometimes William made just the single hole, sometimes he turned the rubber tip into a pepper pot or a flour dredger with the aid of a cocktail stick. Not one, but two pregnancies resulted. Oonagh became suspicious. After the second pregnancy miscarried, she began to defend her womb with multiple forms of contraception that included a more rigorous abstinence.

'You wouldn't be without her,' William would observe of his daughter.

'The ends do not in any sort justify the means,' she would reply. 'Just remember: one day, when I am a goddess, I shall come to Judge you.'

The child born of this parental deceit was compensated, however, by the Plain Truth. Her mother made sure of it, with the help of William P. Pope, apostle of the Worldwide Saints of God, who published a bimonthly magazine called *The Plain Truth*. Oonagh licked her fingers to turn its thick shiny pages.

She admired its candour because, long before, she had lived in trembling and evasion. She came from a tiny seaside town in the north-east of Scotland. A blear grey-blue world of rusting iron and wet slate. There was no beach. On the large pebble sea wall, the local children blew on their red hands and discovered their native tenacity. The chill wind was reliable and the rain drove at aggressive right angles, darkening the blondest hair and pasting it to the skull. There was a choice: harden, or dissolve. At first, Oonagh thought she could simply take shelter. Everyone called her the mouse because she hid under the furniture and never spoke.

But the hiding and the silence only brought her the notice of one of her uncles, who took her to the cinema, touched her in the dark and got her to touch him. He would never have touched Oonagh's sister: she was too plump, brazen and curly-haired to seem vulnerable. Whereas Oonagh looked as vulnerable as she really was – with her straight shiny satin bob and thin little legs. As the uncle calculated, she would not speak of it. Not even when the police took her home from the cinema in their car with the armrest.

For a while no one went to her grandmother and aunt's house, where the uncle lived. When the visits resumed, it was the uncle's turn to hide and the turn of the grandmother and the aunt to be silent, to pretend nothing had happened. Whenever the children went to visit, Oonagh could hear her uncle making the floor creak as she sat downstairs with the old ladies, eating shortbread. She took her teacup firmly by its ear and refused to let her hand shake. She began to toughen up, to learn the lesson of the rain. She told herself the Scots were hardy people.

Oonagh moved to London when she was seventeen and lived with a deaf woman. She did window dressing for a clothes shop run by a Jewish couple who resented her for being taller than them. Obliged to shout in the ear of the deaf landlady, she found a voice at last. Obliged to make the window displays look pretty and looming helplessly above her employers, she found herself an identity. She decided she could be a tall beautiful woman as well as a hard one.

Then she went one step further. She wanted to be a goddess.

The means arrived in *The Plain Truth* and more especially in Pope's book, *The Unbelievable Potential of Human Beings*. By this time she was married to William.

The night he met Oonagh, William thought she was remarkable already. He could have wept; she looked so thin and beautiful in her only black dress. She had been living for two weeks on a packet of Jacob's Cream Crackers and a bottle of salad cream. Over the dress she wore a short black cape with three big silver buttons at the top and diamanté studding on the collar. Like a velvet cardinal or a camp copper, he thought to himself, as he sent his brother to approach her across the varnished, sprung floor of the Kilburn dance hall. She was invited to go to the seaside on Sunday with the brothers. William had calculated correctly the flattering effect of this ambassadorial approach, and Oonagh behaved with due majesty.

At Brighton, they spoke without intercession. Standing on the pier, he asked if he might buy her an ice cream. She assented. Queuing, he smelt seaweed in the breeze and saw it in the tangle of her hair as the wind blew it around. As a boy he had gorged on seaweed, until his mouth hurt with the salt, because the sea did not charge him for it. Learning, halfway down the cone, that her parents lived in a council house, he countered with the news that his parents had always owned their own cottage. With his pale brown eyes he saw that she had green ones. He explained he had his own house too, although you had to be twenty-one to get a mortgage and he was only nineteen. He had pretended to the English bank manager – who took a gentleman at his word – he was twenty-one already.

'It makes yer fear, don't it?' he suggested.

'Fear what?'

'Why, for the native. I fear for the native of this country, truly I do!'

William loved to call the English 'the native', as though they were the colonised. There was, he explained, only one way the English had ever had anything. They used Irish generals in the wars. The English, they were just the grunts, cannon fodder.

William imagined he was on safe territory here, with a Scot.

But then Oonagh said, 'My mother is English. Personally, I was born in Portsmouth.'

'I see.'

They began to walk along the shore and William watched the froth as it ran up the beach. To a man in love (or a very bad poet) it looked like a bride's lace shawl. Thrown down for an instant, it was withdrawn just as quickly. William did not hesitate. 'Will yer marry us?'

'I don't think so,' she laughed. 'I'm going to marry a Swiss gentleman.'

'Any in partickler, is it?'

'Oh, yes. It's one in particular.'

William said nothing, but then, near the end of the return journey, he pointed out the window. 'See that?' he asked his passengers.

Oonagh did not deign to look. William's brother saw a telephone booth.

'Not that. The bridge over yonder – I built that.'

William, then labouring on construction sites, believed verily that he had built by far the greater part of London. Whenever he looked at roads and bridges and buildings in which he might have had the most menial share, he said, 'I built that! I built that in 1962, so I did!' What if he *had* come from nothing – plenty of people had. He reminded his brother, for the benefit of Oonagh's ears, that he was going to drive a grand white Bentley by the time he was forty. Own at least ten houses. Have at least ten sons and ten daughters.

'Oh, aye. Are yus?'

'Yes. And I'm gonta call messef a typhoon.'

'A what?'

'A typhoon. Yer know – not a tycoon.'

A typhoon – because then people would think the tycoon was simply ignorant, and marvel all the more at how well he had done for himself, and not realise it was actually the better description. In short, he was going to be as rich as Job – but not as religious, for then he might avoid the inconvenience of being stricken by Satan with a malignant boil that went from head to toe.

'Are yus, by Christ?'

But Oonagh, sitting in the back seat, had found these same arguments less than immediately persuasive. She'd always had shoes on her feet as a child and was not the sort to run about with country lads who had not.

When Oonagh told William she was no longer seeing the Swiss man, he proposed again, with equally unsatisfactory results. Then it turned out she was lying. She was seeing both men. The third time a marriage proposal came around, it was Oonagh who got down on her knees to William. She had her reasons, expressed one night and then secreted in the same hole she had put the mouse. She said she wanted to propose a deal.

'Yer a woman of the greatest beauty,' William replied. 'I'll listen to whaddever yer haff to say.'

She explained that the Swiss man was no longer going to marry her. He had wanderlust. She was tired, disappointed, compromised. A fallen woman who, while she could not offer William her heart, was entirely willing to part with a new set of saucepans. Directly she opened up a large canvas bag she had brought with her and showed them to him. He would not have love, but he would have Tefal. Scots were straight and honest people, she said. She was just telling him it like it was.

'Thanking yer kindly,' he said, with the ziggurat of saucepans in his hand. 'I think that's grand now.'

And it might have worked, except – it didn't. Things had just continued badly.

'I'll look after yus, yer know,' William said, his voice brisk with love as he took in her suitcases. 'I'll do my damnedest.' Halfway up the stairs, he stopped. 'I'm not so late.' Meaning he was a worldly man who didn't miss a trick.

'I make no accusation about your timekeeping,' she replied coldly. These were not the sorts of things the Swiss man would ever have said to her. William stared at her fiercely from the top of the flight. He *was* too late, or too early. At any rate he knew he wasn't Swiss. On their honeymoon night in the Croydon B&B, they shared corned beef sandwiches by a dim lamp and still she did not love him.

For several months in the first year of her marriage, Oonagh sat on a green corduroy sofa reading Pope's book, *The Unbelievable Potential of Human Beings,* and a Bible with a maroon cover. She sipped tea and contemplated further metamorphosis. A big-bang patterned carpet of green and blue nebulae swirled under her feet. The wallpaper was sombre and frenzied. A television in the corner was turned off. Another maroon Bible lay on the hearth. Oonagh held back the hard navy covers of the slim book.

Earth, wrote Pope, was soon to be the new headquarters of the universe. God would come to earth. Then the members of the Church would become gods themselves, create life on other planets, and rule over them as well as the earth. Oonagh liked the geocentricity of the arrangement very much. She had never been able to see the point of going to heaven. It was one reason she'd never got on at the Protestant church. They were very big on heaven.

'Who'd bother with it?' she would ask herself aloud, as she turned another of Pope's pages. 'With heaven and all that dying? When you can just stop here for all eternity. Stay young and beautiful and live forever.'

William argued that he'd married a member of the Church of England, that she couldn't just go and change herself into a goddess or anything else. But Oonagh dreaded the sorts of changes that might come if she left things too late. The mosquito net of white hair, inch-thick glasses, the mottled, crumpled skin put on in preparation for the coffin. Insolence, indifference, incontinence – she saw no point in a life beyond fifty. Bicentenarians might as well be put down, before things got any worse. Periodically she placed her drained cup of tea on the low, tiled coffee table. There were great green swirls on these tiles too, and into them she gazed.

The evidence against old age was compelling. She'd seen the liver spots that appeared on the back of elderly hands. Then there were the soiled pyjama bottoms – a contour map, a desert drift of stains – drying on radiators. The pink blancmange on the plastic spoon that missed the mouth. She wanted none of it. She decided to be an immortal earthling instead. Whenever Alice asked her mother how old she was, she always got the same reply. 'Twenty-one,' the last birthday Oonagh ever celebrated – because birthdays were pagan, wicked and also untrue.

The Plain Truth made everything possible for her. The Plain Truth stood to reason. And, perhaps most importantly, the Plain Truth was extremely moral too. It was not merely a way to get godlike and immortal and achieve universal domination. It was *the right* way to do it. In the pages of *The Plain Truth*, no lies were ever told. Alice learned that other children were told there was a person called Santa Claus who came down the chimney and left presents for them at the bottom of trees. Or there was a tooth fairy who paid good money for the milk teeth deposited under pillows. Or they would one day grow up and go out into the world – get jobs and have children and grandchildren of their own. Die, if they were lucky, in contented old age.

Alice and Peter were spared all these lies. They were told the Plain Truth. And the plain truth of it was, the planet was on the verge of the most astonishing change. Before earth became the universal HQ, three and a half years of tribulation were coming to it. The faithful would be taken to a place of safety – protected from the abominable sights but still able to hear the faint screams of the sinners and the muted pounding of their fists as they begged to be let in. Then the Lord would arrive – that all flesh might not be entirely destroyed – and establish His Kingdom. It would probably happen before Alice was old enough to go to school. It would certainly have happened before she was old enough to leave. God was giving everyone fair warning. In America, Pope had a radio station as well as his magazine. In Britain, he had Oonagh – who was, while not unduly concerned about what happened to William, always pleased to share the plain truth of things with other people too.

Then Alice began to pass on the knack of living forever too.

Then Alice began to lose the knack of living forever too.

Chapter Three

One Sabbath Alice walked to the church, with twenty-one uncelebrated birthdays to her credit. Behind her mother, forty-eight. Ahead of her brother, twenty-nine, a deacon in the church, and his wife Maria, who was Spanish and exquisite and wore a mink stole. Alice carried a black Bible, a blue cloth notebook and a folded copy of the latest *Plain Truth*. Also a bag too small to hold any of these items. It had other virtues. Chiefly the definitive contours that were – Alice put it to herself, trying to keep her mind busy – so often lacking in baggier bags. She felt nervous. A few seconds later, she'd made it, to the nearest row in the left-hand flank of seats.

There were three seats. Oonagh sat closest to the aisle, her bag sat in the middle, while Alice sat closest to the wall. Oonagh always arrived twenty-five minutes early, so she and her bag would be sure to have those seats. She said she was agoraphobic and did not want people, including Alice, crowding her beauty. Alice compared it to the way her mother would never even drink out of the same cup as her children, as though they might contaminate her.

Peter put his briefcase down in the adjacent middle aisle. As there were still over twenty-three minutes to go, Oonagh and Peter and Maria were up and about, talking to other punctual Christians. Alice hung about on her seat, for a few moments, trying to look preoccupied rather than uneasy. She sneezed and welcomed this routine favour from her nostrils with gratitude, for it allowed her to spend another couple of minutes absorbed by her bag. A tissue obtained and the blowing achieved, it then became difficult to make sitting still look like a taxing and purposeful business. She hoped for another sneeze. Quite often she had whole fits of them. The perfume and hairspray people wore to the church helped with that. Tissues themselves often contributed generously to the vicious cycle: bits of their fibre drifted up her nose and created further irritation. But this time the body said, 'There are *limits*, you know.'

An elderly lady called Mabel Day took a seat two rows ahead and Alice went to chat, trying to seem animated and pleased. As though she were a marionette in stilted competition with the real believers. Where possible, Alice preferred to talk to the old, the sick, the downhearted, or the children. As they were speaking, a young man of twenty-three called Jude came into the church by the back entrance. He turned two paces to the right, stopping beside two book racks that occupied a recess. He began leaning against the wall as though he needed its support.

Alice made her excuses to Mabel. She got up and walked over to him, head down, failing not to hurry too nervously.

'Going to sit down today?' she asked him, looking from his alert brown eyes to the swarf of copper on his chin.

'Maybe,' he said, smiling. Most people took Jude's failure to sit down in the church for a sure sign he was, like his father, Athenian and mad. They said it ran in the family. His great-grandfather had been a poet and revolutionary.

'You going back to Oxford tomorrow?' he asked. She was a joint honours student – English and Fine Arts – at the university.

'Yes.'

'How'd you get there?'

'With difficulty.'

'Coach?'

'Yes.'

'Want a lift?'

'To Oxford or the coach stop?'

'To Oxford.' He seemed surprised at the question.

He would pick her up at four o'clock. As the first hymn ended, she saw him sit down and felt slightly victorious.

There was not much to look at in the church. When Alice was younger, some of the building's original features had still remained. Now the high peaked roof and its beams were hidden. Purified out of sight by the white plastic of the tiled Artex ceiling, whose other chief task was to stifle the air. Two curving white wooden alcove seats at the back were also gone. Effort had gone into making the church appear as little like a place of worship and as much like an office suite as possible. In the ceiling there were fluorescent tubes of light and regularly spaced fans, as though God might be found in a hole punch. Or perhaps in the photocopying machine sitting on the bay window in the back left corner. There was no ecstasy or holiness here. No possibility of floating to heaven. No icons or paintings whatever.

No reminders of the dead either. Except perhaps the nylon geraniums on the stand in the left corner of the stage, and the false red tulips in a blue vase on one of the right-hand sills. No plaques of passed-over worthy Worldwide members adorned the walls. There were two clocks telling different times. Funerals were sometimes conducted here, but the real business was done in the local crematorium. There was no burial ground outside the church, only a designated car parking area. All Alice could see, apart from the other Worldwide Saints, were windows with mismatched panes, Hessian-covered walls, rows of hard brown seats with low backs, a speckled carpet, thick fawn velvet curtains. The pastor stood on the slightly raised stage area, behind a carved rostrum with a fixed microphone. He wore a pale grey polyester suit and tinted glasses that made him look shifty. To his right there was a table with a projector and a white screen between another set of the fawn curtains.

Alice tuned her mind to the pastor's voice. The suction of his tongue against the sides of his mouth was picked up by the microphone. It made a continual clack-click-clacking sound, as if he had swallowed an entire flamenco *artiste*, castanets and all. Today the theme of his sermon was, 'Science – Why It Has Not The Answers.' Scientists doubted the occurrence of Noah's Flood, he was saying. They put its effects on the earth's crust down to the Ice Age. But they were ignoring, he argued, the human cost of the Flood. Did he mean the people who drowned? (Alice's first thought.) No. He did not mean the people who drowned. He meant the increase in illicit sex everyone could see in the world of mankind today.

Why did God bring the Flood? he asked. Sex, he replied. Some angels flew to earth and materialised in human bodies, so they could make love to beautiful women. These women bore them a race of murderous giants, who filled the earth with bloodshed. Then the Flood came and washed them all away.

What were the effects of the Flood? he asked. Sex, he replied. The angels, no longer allowed by God to materialise, became voyeurs. It was why there was now so much illicit sex in The World. It was all for the viewing benefit of these minor devils, who treated it rather like a porn TV channel.

Alice unplugged her ears and looked around her. To her left, her mother nodded. To her right, Peter gazed ahead blankly. To Peter, the plain truth of it just *was*. Like marmalade, or the Grand Canyon. Undeniably there. In front of her Alice saw other people she knew also nodding and taking notes. She wondered which bits they were writing down.

She wondered if she was the only one to find this all a bit crazy.

Sitting on the chair, Alice began to be really preoccupied.

What the pastor said was nothing new to Alice. It was strictly orthodox. Her thoughts moved from the frustrated demons to the vilified scientists. The comments against them, like the comments about everything out there in The World, were so vehement it began to seem suspicious. Everyone in the church said everyone in The World was a drug baron or necrophiliac, or something of that order – so you could be glad to know the plain truth of things and be spared their company.

Twenty minutes later, she watched the pastor get down from the stage to a burst (she unblocked her ears again) of applause. The seventy-eight members of the church stood for the hymn. The pastor stood beside the projector, a recent innovation that threw the lyrics up on to the screen and made the old hymn books redundant.

Four minutes and three verses later, everyone sat down again. Alice heard announcements about the celebration of the forthcoming Festival of Joy. She concentrated on not flicking her hair or rubbing her nose. These nervous tics might be misinterpreted as her hand going up to make a remark. She often did make remarks, but not today. Today she wasn't even inclined to listen to anyone else's remarks either. She listened instead to stifled coughs and babies taken out to wail. A small girl, making happy humming sounds, got *sshhed* and *tssked* in return. A car outside protested its unwillingness to go anywhere. She listened to the wind and saw it stir the weeping willows she could see through a windowpane patterned with tiny palm tree shapes. It sounded like the rustling of a silver paper grass skirt she used to have. Next she found she was listening to herself sneeze, again and again. Typical. She tried to blow her nose as inoffensively as she could.

Playing with the used tissue in her hand, she began to think about what she might say to Jude. In her imaginary conversation, she held, not a tissue, but an imaginary cigarette. She didn't smoke. Never had. Never would. It wasn't allowed. But the imaginary cigarette calmed her down. Gave her a certain conversational coolness, a cinematic grace, she was otherwise unlikely to have. She liked particularly the way it punctuated her most pleasing sentences. Good sentence here – and a definitive flick of the ash followed. Excellent sentence there – and she might even boldly stub the cigarette out, halfway through. Just because she could.

'Jude's taking me back tomorrow,' she told her mother on the walk back home.

'Is he? Why?'

'He just offered.'

'There's something I want you to do for me.'

'What?' said Alice, a bit crossly, expecting unnecessary instructions about conducting herself with Jude.

'Type a letter.'

'Beware of Greeks bearing gifts,' William said, when Alice came into the living room and repeated the same information to him. 'The lad's not quite right, yer know.'

'Why, what's the matter with him?'

'Have yer met his father? He's a nice enough lad, Jude, don't get me wrong. But. It was that spell he had in London that really did it, I would say, messef personally. Whaddyermecallit, that place? St John's Wort?'

Alice tried not to think of the turquoise velvet hat with the gold trimming she had once seen Jude wearing in St John's Wood. She closed her ears to her father's speculation that Jude had 'gone funny' at this point because 'some arse-bandit' had more than likely had his way with him in a public lavatory.

'Oh, Alice,' he added with a sigh, 'if yer only *knew* what they did.'

It was a fiction preserved between them, that she did not know – had still not got things sorted out from the time when, during the Aids scandal of the early 1980s, she asked a dinner lady if girls who wore netball skirts over tracksuit bottoms were 'homosexual'. She had been genuinely bewildered by the gender implications, but the dinner lady was furious.

'Alice?' her mother called. 'Can you do the letter now?'

The letter was to Peter. He owed Oonagh a long outstanding £200 and she thought the formality of print might accelerate his conscience. There were certain rebuking and threatening phrases in the letter that Alice did not relish – 'a deacon of the Worldwide Saints ought not to be a debtor', and 'if you do not pay I shall be forced to approach the pastor' – but she was only the typist.

The next day at four o'clock Jude turned up. He sat down on the sofa with William, and cupped his hands behind his head as he spoke. Alice saw her father willing homosexuality into his every motion.

'This child is my first and eldest and wisest daughter,' he told Jude. 'So drive carefully or I'll cut yer balls off.'

Jude drove carefully.

Chapter Four

In the church Jude was famous, not merely for his mad father and Parnassian great-grandfather, but for his secret love affair, as a boy of eighteen, with a woman seven years his senior. She was Italian and exquisite too, having spent some time with Alice's sister-in-law. Then there had been some sexual misdemeanour, whose details Alice did not know but would very much have liked to. She made enquiries and was told to 'use her imagination'. Alice's imagination brought a manikin Jude to a manikin Italian lady, got stumped on the decision about which one would undress the other first, and could go no further. Evidently, Jude could. People began to talk. The pastor found out about it and suspended Jude from his duties in the church – doing (free of charge) their accounts, which involved some complex tithing arrangements, and stacking the book racks. Again Alice did not know precisely how this exposure came about, but applied one of her father's cautionary sayings to the situation – 'Never confess: most murderers get nailed on their own confession.'

Whichever part of the advice contained in the church manual, *All About Dating and Courtship Leading to Christian Marriage*, Jude had ignored, the Italian lady came out of the debacle with impunity. Disgraced, he moved to St John's Wood, away from the church of his childhood and the Italian lady in particular. His hair fell out with the shock – of losing her and God at the same time.

Now he was back, and refusing to sit down in church as though he wanted to make a point. To say he wasn't getting involved with this lot again. Or perhaps, Alice thought, it was just a better watching post. How much time did he spend each service, she wondered, on the Italian? Or the husband who'd had no qualms about taking her swiftly off Jude's hands? There was no getting away from your history here. You had to watch it flit in front of you twice a week at least.

Alice found the facts of this particular history, which went unmentioned between them, both fascinating and comforting. In particular the widely reported fact that he still loved the older woman. The scandal fixed the perimeters of their own relationship. It drew the line firmly at an old friendship with lust stirring under the surface. And yet there was also, Alice realised as they chugged down the A40 in Jude's Fiat Punto, another fact to be considered.

The automatic presumption of Alice and every other member of the Worldwide Saints was this: if two people of the opposite sex, single or at least unmarried to each other, were alone together in a room for any more than about two minutes, there was a high risk of sexual intercourse taking place. It was simply a fact, whether lust was writhing under people's surfaces or not.

The fact weighed on Alice as Jude parked at the back of the college, and they began walking up the sloping cobbles towards her room. The main door to the block, painted French navy, was like a wardrobe, with two separately opening halves. One of them was ajar. Alice walked through it, Jude following, then up a short flight of steps. She turned right through another door, took out her key, and told Jude to stay where he was, outside the door, while she dropped her things off. He could consider himself lucky, she indicated pleasantly. It was a nice door. It was worth looking at. It was white and wooden with large attractive panelling. It was even located in a heated hallway.

The caution seemed necessary. She was not being rude: she was avoiding a high-risk activity. It was true she had been reliably informed, by some of the worldlings she had known at school and among whom she now lived at university, that two people in a room need not add up to sex. They said there were many occasions when this did not happen in The World. They added that men and women of The World generally would be astonished to be told seduction was really supposed so *easy*. Even Casanova, it was pointed out to her, failed at times. On the other hand, she cited the rules and regulations of the William Pope Seminary, founded to train youngsters for the ministry of the Church. If a man had a woman in his room, he had to leave the door wide open. Even engaged couples should not be on their own at any time. Alice knew cases of Worldwide Saints who married 'simply,' as they said, 'so we could have a conversation in peace and quiet at last!'

To Alice this prompted the question: why was it permissible for two men or two women to be alone together? Why were the corridors of the William Pope Seminary mainly filled with young men sharing bedrooms, two by two? A dangerous number. There was not the dormitory risk of being caught out. But the homosexuals-in-a-room problem was not hers to solve. The heterosexuals-in-a-room problem was, and she had done it in the best way possible. Locking the door behind her, she asked Jude if he wanted to go for a walk.

She took him a few paces to the library. It was a grand affair, like a wedding cake. Marzipan sides in sandstone, white eaves piped, like icing sugar, in a complex pattern. She leaned against one of the white neoclassical pillars and said that sometimes she felt like Samson.

'Push it –' she suggested, 'and this whole theatre of wickedness may come tumbling down.'

'You're joking.'

'Of course I'm joking.'

'Your mum's still unhappy, then, about you being here?'

'Yes. Breaks the bargain, doesn't it?'

'What bargain?'

'You know: don't do anything with your life because The End will be here soon. Of *course* it's coming soon. We all know that. But you've still got to live, haven't you, in the meantime?'

Jude looked amused. 'Wasn't what you used to say to me. As I recall, we were at the pub once and I said why didn't you just apply and you looked completely appalled.'

'I probably did. Well, they're all appalled now. I remember when I got an interview, Peter saying to me, "Don't worry. You'll get a place: *Satan will make sure of that.*"'

'At least your dad's pleased.'

'Yes. He said, "If yer get a place, I'll give yer a lift to the coach stop, yer know."'

'Generous.'

'He doesn't want to appear too enthusiastic. Especially in my mother's hearing. Thinks it might put me off. Reverse psychology, except that I know about the reversal. It's like when I was younger. He used to forbid me from going to church. Now he says it was the making of me, why I'm such a good Worldwider.'

'You are, aren't you?' Jude agreed, in a way that didn't exactly sound admiring.

They descended the library steps and continued walking through the college, leaving by the main quadrangle that looked like a giant sandcastle. She didn't take him to the cathedral, because she was afraid of it. Besides, she didn't know what his position was on that sort of thing. They walked through the streets of Oxford and then left them quite behind. They took a turn over Port Meadow, where the horses ran wild.

'You know the sermon yesterday?' she said.

'Yeah?' Jude hadn't been listening too closely and had little recollection of the contents.

'The funny thing is, what the scientists say isn't too different.'

She'd been reading Richard Dawkins, because she wanted to know what the much-maligned intellectuals had to say for themselves. She did not tell him precisely how, at home, she was managing it: in the bath, or behind the large door of her wardrobe, which collided handily with the door to the room when anyone tried to come in.

What Dawkins described, behind the door or as the bath tap burnt Alice's toes with unexpected hot drips, was just like the devils materialising in human bodies before the Flood. Except his devils were called genes. Genes created living bodies so they would have somewhere to shelter, to reproduce themselves. Our bodies were merely hosts for these ancient replicators. Devil angel or devil gene, then? What was it all about? It didn't sound too damn good either way.

'I wouldn't worry about it,' Jude said, laughing.

They walked further. Jude kept pausing and looking across at her, not saying very much. The minutes passed. She felt embarrassed. Now he was all charm, while she was all difficulty. Didn't she think they should spend more time together? She said she didn't have a whole lot of it to spare. He said he'd gone to the cinema with Peter and Maria and some others on Valentine's Day and where had she been? She said it was a pagan festivity, as he knew. He said he didn't want to distract her from her work. She said, with a short laugh that tried to be hard and knowing, there was little chance of it. She had an essay on Wordsworth and Coleridge to write for the following morning and they had better be going. Then he put out his hand, but it was like trying to catch a butterfly.

'Alice,' he said in the end, 'I'm going to try harder. See if I can get the pastor to give me my duties back. I doubt he's making a good job of the accounts himself.'

'But you've only just begun to sit down again!' she said, conscious of absurdity. 'What's all that about, anyway?'

'Nothing really. I do want to get my privileges back.'

'Why?' she pushed.

'Alice, I've been . . . Well. Here it is.' Jude paused to take breath. 'Do you think you might – go out with me?'

Shit, thought Alice. What had happened to the fascinating and comforting fact of his undying love for the Italian lady? It was as well she had trusted in the consequences of the other fact and not invited him to her room. She'd pushed it with him, and now . . .

'I don't see what that has to do with the church accounts,' she began to say, scurrying a few paces ahead of him and shouting back the words. 'And anyway – what about our friendship? We might not be friends then. I wouldn't like that.'

The ancient replicators Jude's body was hosting told him sternly to fuck friendship.

'Are we friends?' he asked, catching her up.

'I thought we were,' she said.

They began to walk back the way they'd come.

'What about the Italian one?'

'What about her?' He sounded surprised at her question for the second time that weekend. 'I mean it, you know, about getting my duties back.'

'Well, don't do it for my benefit.'

They stopped. Jude was silent, looking at his feet. She tried to make it up to him a bit.

'Because it doesn't really matter, you know, what the pastor lets you do. Just be a good Christian. That's what counts, isn't it? It's my advice, anyway.'

'But I feel like a moron. I can be responsible for handling millions of pounds at work, but there – it's, like, I'm not worthy of stacking a rack! You know what I'm saying?'

'Oh, the racks!' she said, laughing and thinking of their sacred mysteries. The pastor was particular about arranging the books by cover colour and piling them right up to the edge of each shelf. 'Yes, I know what you're saying.' She repeated it to herself in her head.

But a walk, even one in which you knew exactly what you were saying, could not last forever. Alice took him to the back of the college where his car was parked. At a large cast-iron gate they said goodbye. She leaned forward to kiss him on his cheek. To Jude, this was a dismissal. To Alice, it was the very height of whorishness. A sign that could not possibly be mistaken. Indeed, she quite wondered, as she walked back across the cobbles, at her frank boldness in the matter.

The next day she had a letter. 'Hope I didn't mess up your essay too much,' the letter said, optimistically. And added, 'Two modern masterpieces await you.' Alice spent the week impressed by the efficiency of the postal service and also wondering what Jude would mean by a masterpiece.

Chapter Five

Peter was holding a tiny brass nail. He felt full of possibility. Deacon Peter Stransky. The surname came from a Polish forefather of his Spanish wife Maria. Peter had adopted the name eagerly. He told his bride he could trace ancestors to the Isle of Harris, yet with a name like Stransky he might be a vampire count of Eastern Europe with emphatic canines and suspicious lip gloss. Or a celebrated vodka maker, the owner of a distillery, rubbing his wealthy hands like a conjuror palming a coin.

In fact, his fantasy profession of choice was assassin, the mercenary murderer. Stransky. Surgical, impersonal, photogenic – with, every morning, a different death in a different city after a different woman had wrapped her spaghetti legs around him. Morally indifferent Stransky.

The career began before he was born.

Peter imagined he had seen off a rival twin in Oonagh's womb. Leaned on him, crushed him with his weightier, bloodier placenta sac. As his twin wilted and shrank, he watched without emotion and coldly smoked his thumb.

Aged sixteen, he stood at The End of the World and challenged the ocean, at a distance of sixteen feet, to drown him.

'A foot for a year and a year for a foot,' he chanted, biblically. It was only him and the ocean now, he said. Again he was victorious.

At the same time, Peter was the nicest and most charming of men.

He was absolutely the sort of person you would want to share a biscuit with.

He stood in front of a mahogany dresser. Soufflés of mould floated in coffee cups like Monet lilies. Sun brought a Lichtenstein *ZING!* to the smiling rims of two wine glasses. Dust sparkled, appropriately *pointilliste*. He was considering his portrait head, done in pastels. This, certainly, wasn't an art historical masterpiece. Peter's face had been reconstructed as if by a zealous mortician after a disfiguring accident. The pinks were too carmine, the rigid smile, showing teeth, tensely holding its pose. He was wearing a white shirt with a black sandwich collar. *Deacon Peter Stransky* was engraved in italic script on a tiny brass plaque. For the fourth time, he tried to nail the fiddly thing on to the gilt frame.

'There,' he said.

(Names. Maria had a relative whose first surname meant, in Spanish, 'Little One', her second, 'Big Ears'. Her two forenames were 'Maria' and 'Solidad'. Try that at school.

'Mary the Sunny Little One with Big Ears?'

'Present, Miss.'

It was worse than Dances with Wolves.)

Peter put the hammer down on the carpet and wandered about the bedroom. His portrait sat propped on the dresser. Originally commissioned by his father, when he married, it had trailed out of the family home after Peter, like a non-identical Siamese twin. Embraced eagerly by his wife, she tended it twice daily. Peter turned round. She was at it again. A white cloth, ironed and doubled over, prevented the frame from slipping on the wood. The rich butter lace *mantequia* she had worn on their wedding day was draped provocatively around the side of the picture. Maria had a gift for popery and an admiration for Madonna. It looked like a shrine to the dead. 'Oh, Pedreeto,' she complained at the painting, then patted the lace.

It had taken Peter some time to discover that Pedreeto was 'little Peter'. He did not consider himself that little. Nor that dead. She might have ambitions for an elegant widowhood – in Prada black with a single strand of grey Tahiti pearls. He was not willing to help advance them.

'And why you wear this shirt?' Maria pointed accusingly to the painting. '*Es – grosso.*'

He needed no translation. 'It was him, not me. The one I was wearing was blue with a white collar. He said the black looked better against my skin.'

'But joor skin – *es grosso* also. No, no, I think he laugh at joo.'

'How'd jer mean?'

'He say – joo are not the réal preacher.'

Peter feigned indignation. His raised eyebrows locked in battle like a pair of butting chamois. He stuck his chin out.

'Why joo always make joorself so ugly?'

Peter relaxed. Then Maria explained what she meant about the picture. The colours of the shirt and its collar were surely an inversion of clerical habit. The Worldwide Saints disdained, as pomp, the simple black cotton clerical shirt with its blank white sticker around the neck. And she wanted to know what this was called 'in the Ingerlish'.

'A dog collar?'

'A doggie? A doggie like a bow-wow?' Maria spurted laughter. 'You so silly boy, sometime.'

She had something special to show him, she said. Peter congratulated himself anew on his choice of bride. If Maria remonstrated with his picture, she saved her treats for him – the arrangement seemed entirely right. Wagging a departing finger at the portrait, she left the room. He stood, slippered and full of plans, at the foot of the marital bed. His eye rested hopefully on an old moment of teenage transgression – a prefect's badge on the bedside table, spelling LUST in thin gold letters. Their marriage was one year and nine months old.

Three minutes later Maria re-entered the room clutching a cage containing two guinea pigs. Peter's pupils dilated. Setting the cage down on the floor and taking one of the guinea pigs out, she explained this was how he would learn to love small living things such as babies. The portrait was good preparation for a Pedreeto. But a pet was a better one. Till then, it hadn't occurred to Peter that the portrait was more than a shrine. To Maria, it was an imaginary cot. This was particularly the effect of the floor-length swagged curtains behind the dresser – framing his inflamed, newborn complexion, the painter's apprentice plastic surgery.

Peter kissed his wife on the tip of her Ingrid Bergman nose and stroked the guinea pig. She looked down fondly at his cupped hands.

'It is like having . . . no? I think joo always want one, jes?'

'Yeah – when I was a kid.'

Why was everything always about twenty years too late?

'And this one – for joo.' Maria indicated a letter lying unopened on the dresser.

Peter pressed the warm guinea pig to his heart where it hung like a bean bag. His free hand burst the envelope with difficulty. He began reading his mother's unpleasantries. It reminded him that his genius was fecund in ways other than fatherhood. Fratricide in the uterus, for one.

'God damn her.' He couldn't think what else to say. He was not a verbal pyrotechnician. This covered the principal point. He put the guinea pig down.

'Hey, hey, Pedrie.'

'No,' he repeated, 'God damn her. Have you seen this?'

It wasn't easy being a Saint. Especially when the other Saints got so tough on you. Conscientiously, the guinea pig's mobile nostrils hoovered his slipper.

'I'm not speaking to her again, I can tell you that much.'

Maria looked impatient. 'Oh, jes? And what happen, hey, when she is in the accident? Eh, what you say then, eh? Then – is too late. In the hospital, is too late.' Her tongue somersaulted triumphantly on the *l*. She raised her chin and shook hennaed curls out down her back.

'She doesn't believe in hospitals. And neither do I. And neither should you, *chiquito*.'

Sickness and death were spiritual diseases. Pagan operations could not possibly help. Maria shook her head again.

'Me, me – I believe in the hospitals. I have sin them. I know they are there. In Espain, we have the most beautiful hospitals with the toilet floors so clin and so marble joo can even *eat* from off them.'

'Well, baby, that's just as well,' Peter replied drily.

Eating off the hospital toilet floor would be permissible to a Saint of the Worldwide Church. It wasn't a form of medical treatment.

'Listen, when joo –' The door buzzer gave an abrupt snore.

'Expecting anyone?'

'Noh.'

It was William. Maria invited him in 'For tea, jes?' and told him they had just got guinea pigs.

'*Did* yus? Why was that, then?'

'Pedrie he always want one but his parents, they say *eh – no.*'

'Did we? Sorry, lad.'

Peter raised an undisgruntled palm.

'And we were just talking as well about the medicines, are they allowed, or no. I like to know, what joo think?'

William explained that he thought like any normal person. It was one thing he'd never been able to stand, the way 'the Pope lot' were so against everything. Against wealth. Against entertainment and sport. Against doctors.

'Christ, next yer'll be against breathing God's air. Extremely fuckan negative. What's it all in aid of?'

Maria snorted. William smiled at his argumentative prowess.

'Yus talk about how bad the world is, how much worse it's always getting. Yer mother winds on and on about it till I'm near as damn ready to dash my brains out on a stone. Well, it's a lot fuckan better than the old days, when yer'd get knocked out with a hammer for an anaesthetic. Yer've no respect at all for what's been achieved, so yus don't. The way I –'

'Mum sent me a letter,' Peter interrupted. 'She –'

'Oh, Christ, don't tell me. She's been on my case about it on a continual basis. I tried to tell her, she's up that church five times a week, doing a hard-core training course in Christian fuckan kindness or whatever it is, and she can't even get on with her own bleedan son. She never gives up.'

'Well, anyway. She wants that two hundred quid. And I haven't got it.'

34

'Don't worry, son. I'll sort yer out. You know yer old dad is always reliable.'

William pulled a bap of notes from his back pocket.

'Cheers.'

'No bother, lad. Anyway, I was wonderan. You two – fancy coming for an Indian tomorrow night?'

'With Mum?' Peter objected, suspecting a trap.

'Christ no.'

'Just as long as you're sure she won't be there,' Peter agreed.

'She won't be there.'

William and Maria continued celebrating the marvels of modern medicine. On the sill in the living room, a small book rack tilted its contents like washed-up plates. Maria sighed as her husband picked out the first volume of *The Chronicles of Thomas Covenant*, leper, by Stephen Donaldson.

'Pedrie, will joo just make the tea, pliz?'

The Covenant chronicles excited him. He reread them annually. Peter had long considered himself a theoretical leper. It might be that everyone loved him and wanted to be with him all of the time. But in his heart he had himself down for a leper. On his face there were red ampoules of acne.

Lepers couldn't speak to people or be near them. (This seemed handy now.)

A leper could be cursed and avoided and blessedly detached from everyone – especially his mother.

As his wife and his father lauded Lemsip, Peter was practising the words 'Unclean, unclean!' An audible inaudible mutter.

'Just like his mother,' William whispered to Maria. 'Melodramatic. Y'ever see *The Phantom of the Opera*?'

'No.'

'Well, there's this phantom in it, right, who keeps screechan on and on whenever he can't get his own way. Then he starts killan people with a chandelier. *Pe-yoo-er* melodrama. Lecherous bastard, too. Drags a woman down to his den and tells her he loves her. She swallows it, a course. That's what women are like – not you, love, a course, but yer know what I mean. Most girls are dead thick. And the thing is, with them two,' William leant forward, 'Peter and Oonagh, it's just the same phantom blood runs right through them.'

'Joo think . . . he *kill* me?' Maria's excited black eyes flashed.

'No, no, nothan like that. But overreaction. It's their middle name. Jer know what Oonagh said to me when I took her to see it?'

'No.'

'I jerst couldn't believe it. She said, "It's not really as *passionate* as I expected." I mean, fuck it, how could it be any *more* OTT than that? Anyhow, sorry, my love. That's just the way they are. And sadly – we bear the brunt of it.'

William sighed noisily down his nose.

'Joo are right. We do,' Maria sighed back, delighted with this introduction to the way her life was really. 'Pedrie?' she called sharply.

Peter came back into the room with the tray of tea.

'What about the vet?' she asked impatiently.

'Oh, a vet's fine,' Peter replied. 'Animals haven't got immortal souls. Doesn't matter if they see doctors or not.'

'So.' Maria *humphed*. 'Let me see. Because the animals they are less important, they get more and better treatment than the peoples?'

'Sounds more like Animal Rights than a religion to me,' William observed. 'Anyway. I'll be on my way. See yus tomorrow. Seven thirty at Mahfooz's.'

Before he went to bed that night, Peter slotted his mother's letter, like an apocryphal epistle, into the centre of the Donaldson volume, and decided to behave as a leper. There were other possible responses to a request for £200. Dismay. Prompt payment. The depositing of the money you'd just eased off your father so you could write a cheque out to your mother. He was ruling none of them out. But leprosy was the choice that really caught his imagination. His powers of self-determination were well trained: whenever he did good it was always in the knowledge that he could have chosen evil, and this gave him a great sense of decision.

The Festival of Joy offered an excellent opportunity to start his career in leprosy in earnest.

Chapter Six

Festivals of the Worldwide Saints were times when the Plain Truth got still plainer. Frills dropped away, satin clouded into cotton, shoulder pads were stripped off like epaulettes of the dishonoured military – till the uninflected silhouette of truth was before the assembled believers: flat-chested, waistless gooseflesh drably dressed.

Alice felt uneasy from the moment when, waking, she flipped over in bed. With her sudden movement, the bed talked back. It did not creak. It spun and clicked, like a bicycle chain set briefly in motion. As though the sounds were part of its job. They informed her that she must be in her bed at home, in Westwood, not in college. Her body sensed a general constriction of space: lower ceilings, a pine desk footing the bed as though it were an overgrown blanket box, two bin bags ready with clothes for the Red Cross, a bookcase, a red velveteen chesterfield armchair, quilted like a strawberry. This was a large grand house on three storeys, but she had the smallest bedroom.

Alice leaned on to her right shoulder and three spots pricked like drawing pins. She raised herself slightly to draw the curtains and the bed bicycled again. The window was filled with waving green leaves. She put a finger in the hole of the nearest bedpost where the metal joiners had entered, originally, when the bed was one half of the bunk set she shared with Peter. She pulled out her finger and it made a pleasant popping sound. She repeated it three or four times more.

Here at home things still continued ordinarily enough.

She could hear her parents discussing suicide in the kitchen below. William, already a martyr on the stake of marriage, was equally unhappy about the failure of his businesses. He'd invested and lost a quarter of a million pounds in Pretty Polly shares. It had seemed like such a sure bet. He liked their stockings very much. He assumed other people must as well.

'Fuck it,' he lamented, 'yer can't even count on people to be *kinky* nowadays.'

'Would you mind not being so rude.'

As Alice listened, familiarity bred anxiety. She felt less self-possessed than the kiss she had given Jude suggested. In fact she felt panicky. Her feet kicked about. She started biting her nails before she even got out of bed.

Her finger ends were puffy, hooded. The embedded nails had ragged untidy white edges and resembled boiled eggs at breakfast. Splinters in the corners burrowed painfully into her. She caught one of them between her teeth and pulled a nail out like a nail. Then she pushed it between her front teeth. The top layer of another nail had been pulled right back but still hung by a hinge. She could lift it up and down like a desk lid. Alice decided not to rip just yet. Instead her tongue felt for the nail between her teeth. The movement wedged it into her gum.

What if she could never, ever get it out again?

She could wiggle the very end of it with her tongue. She took – in the absence of any nails – two finger stubs to the gum, and made an implausible attempt to grab hold of it. The nail-biter is pitiful in many situations. Picking chickenpox, removing price tags on fruit, winding the knobs on watches, finding the end of the Sellotape – these are skills beyond them. It is a wonder they survive at all. She would have to borrow her mother's tweezers.

And then what if she swallowed them in the process? Fear death by tweezer. She felt anxious again, her heart suddenly taut, caught like a kite in a gust.

It was true that, should she meet an untimely death before The End of the World came, she could still live forever. God would simply resurrect her. He kept everyone's details in his memory. In church they said it was like a video. Alice felt sure someone would tape *Coronation Street* over her. So it was better to be vigilant. She continued panicking.

The trouble with mornings was that Alice had enough energy to get really terrorised. As the day wore on, there was a good chance things would get better. By late this afternoon, she estimated, she might be tired enough, or simply bored enough, to stop panicking. Phlegmatically panicky. Then she remembered it was the Sunday of the Festival.

'But I'm not being rude,' she heard her father protest. 'See what I mean?' he appealed to himself. 'Yer can't even *say* the word, in actual fact, before yer nuts are strung up in a bag for the birds. I tell yus what. I think I'll do it messef, actually, soon enough. You'd all be better off without me.'

He pointed to a piece of the wall just above a spider plant in a hanging basket.

'There will be a time,' he prophesied, 'when yer'll come home and find me hanging off that pot hook.'

'That hook wouldn't support you.'

'Who'd miss me?' William asked the air. 'Who?' he challenged the eye-level grill and the beige tiles with the blackberry motif. 'I'm used to this, right? Everything going wrong. Having to do everything messef to put it right.' His own thoughts were more interesting than anything anyone else could possibly say. His conversation was interior monologue on speaker-phone, his stream of consciousness in spate. 'My wife, she's about as useful to me as an ashtray on a fuckan motorbike. Oh, sorry, love – didn't see you there . . . It's like bin bags,' he began afresh, as he saw Alice coming down the stairs. His face shone like a lemon with sweat. 'Yer can't call them *black* bin bags any more. Now they've started making these grey ones. How'd jer suppose that makes the old people feel? And the pigeons?'

He cited it as 'a well-known fact' that all the muggers in the UK were black. The worst offenders were the 'young black bucks', all rapists who abandoned their children.

'They should be *put down*. And their children should all be aborted. But I suppose,' William sneered, 'next thing yer'll be telling me abortion's wrong.'

Oonagh did not reply. William did not need her to.

'*Wrong*? How would it be *wrong*? Are yer tellan me that if Alice was ravished by some young darkie – no, don't look at me like that. You may have all yer happy Congo faces in para-dise in the whaddycallit – *The Plain 'Credible Truth* – but have y'ever seen a black woman, with a couple of babies in the pram, who actually had a husband? No, didn't think so. And it's a shame, because they're decent women mostly. So that if that was Alice, and the baby was going to come out black or half-black or whaddever –'

'What about Dr Sulakahn, then?' Alice countered. He was William's doctor, brown rather than black, but William's grasp of the distinction was shady.

'Oh, yer can't be counting *him*. He's what I call a white black man.'

Dr Sulakahn wasn't a sexual menace to society, so far as anyone could tell. William was extremely fond of him, told him everything, fancied his turbaned head throbbed with anxiety at each mention of pain. Many diagnoses went wrong, William believed, simply because patients pre-selected the information they felt relevant. Consequently William was full of stories of persons who had failed to report ticklish coughs and died of throat cancer a fortnight later.

'Should I fart three times in the night,' he hypothesised, 'I'd tell it to Dr Sulakahn. Could be me bowels, could be anything. He says I'm under far too much strain at home. Trying to do everything for everyone . . . Need a lift, love?' he added.

'Not from you,' Oonagh replied shortly.

'*Some* people, yer know, are so fuckan miserable I can't understand why they would even *want* to live forever. What's it going to be, I'd like to know? Misery for all eternity? I thought that was hell.'

'Some people aren't going to get the chance to find out.'

'Don't you *get it*? I don't want to live forever. If I had to look at your miserable fuckan face for all eternity, I'd fuckan top messef.'

So far, so ordinary. Her parents' marriage was still a cold war of continual unpleasantness that no one was now willing to end. Sometimes Alice could scarcely believe she was the product of it, but the evidence seemed indisputable.

They left for the Festival, around an hour later, to the tune of her father telling himself, 'Live forever! I'm only human. I'm only a human being. That's what they never seem to understand.'

Chapter Seven

Festivals were anything but festive. In the sombre staircases of the hall, sombre-suited Saints trailed up and down, chains of marching ants, in search of seats and conversation. Women wore polka-dotted navy summer dresses and straw hats under the heat and the glare of recessed 60-watt bulbs. In the crepuscular foyer, young men with cold hands and lips chapped to glacé cherries sold protective plastic covers for Bibles. Programmes listed the order of sermons but not the speakers. It was beyond the bounds of Christian modesty to name the speakers in a small pink paper programme. Alice prepared for two days of mental desolation. She was not disappointed by the opening speech.

'Brothers and sisters, friends and visitors, Saints of God's only true Worldwide Church, we are happy to be gathered here together, are we not?'

Applause clicked around the auditorium like rows of falling dominoes in a world record attempt. There was much beaming, Oonagh's mostly in the direction of Alice.

'We rejoice, do we not?'

More applause, more dominoes.

'We thank God for it, do we not?'

Alice's hands were beginning to hurt. And the nail was still stuck between her teeth. She took some comfort in stabbing her tongue punitively against its white spike. Soon she would hurt everywhere. The bottoms of the seats flipped up fiercely when people stood, and were unable to maintain right angles when sat on. Alice was stuck in a foetal position, knees drawn up by the rise of the seat at the front and her arse continually threatening to slip through the gap at the back. Oonagh turned her legs, with a roominess Alice envied, out into the aisle.

Towards mid-morning the deacons began handing around a newsletter and asked everyone to read the editorial. There was a two-minute silence. This had never happened before.

The editorial explained there had been a New Idea about The End of the World. William P. Pope was no fool. Others had named a date for Armageddon – 1867, said Isaac Newton, 1843, said W. Miller and, when the event passed uneventfully, 1844.

William P. Pope learned the lesson. Calendar-shy, he had always avoided a precise date. It would happen now-ish. Somewhere in the last quarter of the twentieth century. Ish. Because now things were very bad: there were wars and food shortages and earthquakes and iniquity and disobedience to parents and excessively long tailbacks on motorways. The editorial said, however, that even talk of an 'ish' period was 'dangerously presumptuous'. Only the Father knew the day and the hour and the season. Of course The World was still extremely dreadful. Of course The End was still coming. But it might be some way off yet, a little further than previously suspected. Then again, it might just as easily be tomorrow, so everyone had better stay prepared.

And there was a text in the book of Habakkuk that proved all this: *Even if it should be tardy, still it will not be late.*

Alice opened her Bible. She flicked through the India paper pages and put on her glasses. The red satin marker lay in the gutter of the Good Book like a long thin fuse already alight. In this translation the text was gobbledygook, comparable to 'the latecomer isn't late'. She closed the Bible, and realised the end of things would not happen at all. It had been one thing to doubt. It was another thing to have all her long cherished doubts confirmed like this.

In mortal anguish Alice took off her glasses and cast her eyes up to the ceiling. The miniature spaceship of a fire alarm blinked its red landing lights back at her. Her gaze washed down the powder-blue walls and reached the raspberry floor. Cynically Alice suspected the Church leaders were revising their theology only because this was 1997 already, and the century would soon be over.

What angered her most was the way the editorial was phrased. The dishonesty of it. There were no apologies. No admissions that it was William P. Pope who had formulated the 'ish' theory in the first place, and repeated it insistently on every suitable occasion. The editorial was signed by an anonymous Church Writing Committee. It said that some Saints were far too enthusiastic for The End and had 'even' tried to calculate it to around the last quarter of the century – as though this had not been the orthodox practice of the Church of William P. Pope itself, till this very moment.

'Were such speculations helpful?' the editorial asked rhetorically.

'Not in the least!' the editorial replied breezily.

Alice read aghast. Few disappointments compare to the loss of eternity. Nothing ever came close to eternity. That was why it was called eternity. True, Alice knew kids who read Enid Blyton and complained, when they grew up, that the world was not full of adventures. Ginger pop and rugs laid by Anne and the whiff of smugglers in Cornish coves – all close rivals to immortality.

People said the figure 8 was like eternity. It went on and on without a break. Lack of the number eight was much like the loss of eternity. Without the number eight, things would get awkward. When there were supposed to be eight in the bed and the little one said, 'Roll over, roll over,' no one would fall out of bed. There would be enough room. No one would take over the chorus. The song would end in embarrassment all round – again, just like not living forever.

With any other disappointment, just so long as you can still live forever, you have forever to get over it. Faced with other difficulties, there is forever to prepare. Whereas Alice might as well have been told she had just months to live. Days. Two minutes, in short. She began to feel distinctly out of breath.

In the intermission she was surprised to find she could still stand up and walk down the shiny steps without slipping – then last the length of a considerable ladies' queue for the toilet. In the mirror over the basins, she appeared smaller and paler. She was atrophying. She managed to make it back up the stairs, to sit down again, to reach into her bag, even to unfold the tinfoil-packed lunch that was sustaining her short sojourn in this world of woe. It contained a bacon roll and assorted lunchtime treats.

It was Waitrose between her and death.

Cadbury's fending off the Grim Reaper. Kettle's versus Kryptonite.

But eternity wasn't just about time. There were things Alice had been promised. Things which she felt she'd a perfect right to. Global paradise, for instance. In paradise on earth – or any other planet of her choosing, William P.

Pope's illustrated literature said – Alice would gorge on untold fruits that grew directly into unwieldy wicker baskets. She would ride on the backs of lions and stroke the skins of snakes without fear – two advertised activities she found puzzling, unless you were phobic about public transport as well as snakes. She would grow beautiful, she would dip her hand into clear pools filled with sweetie-wrapper fish. Everyone would eat the healing leaves of riverside trees and thus reach states of physical and mental perfection. No one would ever look or feel any older than thirty. Indeed, they would have no problems of any sort: no war crime pollution speed-cameras hatred sickness. They would have all pleasures of every kind: love shelter hoeing radiance. All the Saints loved each other. All the Saints would live together and forever in this harmony. In fact, to the right way of looking at it, they had begun living forever already. Paradise was to be an endless extension of their lives, affording them all the time they needed to grow carrots and keep rabbits. To build simple white wooden houses that revolved, all day long, with the sun. Many of the dead, who had not seen their way to becoming Plain Truthers before, would be resurrected and given a second chance to get it right with God. There was mercy as well as a lot of fresh fruit involved in paradise. And there would be enough land for them and for everybody else who would be born for all eternity, because deserts would bloom, mountains fall flat and seas recede. Mountaineers would find other hobbies. Piers would be extended. Paddlers could get a lift from the lion. The whole universe would become a prairie swaying with wheat dinners. No one would have a gluten allergy. She'd seen the pictures in *The Plain Truth* and *The Truthful Children's Book of Bible Stories*. She'd watched the church movie. She'd been told, so many times

47

as a child, that it was coming soon. She thought her mother meant tomorrow.

Tops, about two weeks.

And now, nothing. Only to die, like everyone else who'd ever lived. It wasn't on.

'Hi.'

It was Jude, grinning in a Boateng suit. Alice started to stand. 'No, don't,' he insisted, as he crouched beside her chair. 'You look nice.'

'Thanks. So do you.'

'You didn't reply to my letter.'

'No.'

'So when are you going to invite me to Oxford?'

'I don't know. You can – just come, can't you?'

'People like to be invited.'

'OK, you're invited.'

'When?'

'Whenever.'

Alice hated how hostile she sounded, but didn't know how to yield. Jude began to retreat. 'Listen.' He pretended to check the time on his watch. 'There's something I have to do. But – maybe later? Or next week?'

'Yes,' she replied vaguely.

Alice stood up again and took her lunch packet to the designated eating area, where she could get herself a hot drink. A drinks dispenser choked into life like the tube that vacuums away the saliva of dental patients. Alice selected chocolate. Finding a seat, feebly she attempted a slice of cake, but it was a cliff edge, eroding perilously with each bite. She felt un-environmental. She felt like Adam. God told Adam that if he ate the forbidden fruit, he would die. But Adam ate the forbidden fruit – and did not die. Well, not immediately, anyway. He begat a son at the age of 130, and lived a further eight hundred years. Not immortal, then, but not a bad innings.

Yet all the same, Adam died the day he realised he was mortal. Alice's thin hot chocolate was definitely ageing, evaporating in front of her eyes.

'Oh, *there* you are,' she heard her mother say. 'Shall we go for a walk?'

As they walked Alice tried to put far from her mind the idea that her life had just been shortened by millennia. Her eyes read the seated rows of Saints, the queuing Saints, the simply milling Saints. There were about a thousand in all. Small children ate ice creams or hunched over their felt-tipped drawings of the auditorium. Two glamorous grand-mothers with bright dyed auburn hair displayed themselves: eyelashes rough with mascara curtsied and lifted, beautifully coarse above depressed clericals.

Oonagh was magnificent too. Her red hair swayed like a great conifer. Her fine peach lips communicated a brave bright nervous smile to onlookers. There is a nervousness so author-itative it induces greater nervousness in everyone else. Oonagh had this in good measure. She had majesty. She also had sex. Her navy jacket swung heavily open like an old door, but the side split of her skirt was ajar with the weight of her thigh. She was illicit and autocratic. Appropriately, but uncon-sciously, she wore a replica Mrs Simpson brooch on her lapel. She had a dozen of them. Today's was a ladybird, pinned down from flight as though its glazed tin wings might otherwise have managed it. After two flights of stairs, they saw Peter.

He was in the foyer practising his leprosy. Behind him there was a mirror wall and two punk rock ferns. He turned his head away pointedly as his mother and sister approached. Oonagh stopped and tilted one of her high heels. Her eyes were green marble. Peter turned his head slowly back and held his Bible firmly against his thigh. They stood there as if someone had pressed *pause* on the remote.

'What's up with him, then?' Alice asked.

'The letter worked, that's what,' Oonagh replied without taking her eye off him.

'Oh? Paid up, did he?'

'I had a cheque two days later. And for the full amount. It just goes to show.'

'Show what?'

'He *could* have done it any time. But he chose not to. And it's not as though I have money of my own. It's not as though I work.'

'No.'

'As a matter of fact, I work very hard. Bringing up that man's children –'

'We're *your* children too,' Alice protested, as she always did.

'– keeping his house clean,' Oonagh continued without a pause. 'Not that anyone notices.' Then, remembering the original subject, 'They obviously aren't happy they've had to pay up.'

'They?'

'One less Louis Vuitton handbag she can buy, isn't it?' The liner on Oonagh's lips crinkled.

'I suppose. Will you tithe it?'

'The £200? Of course.'

Alice had expected some specious excuse – money elicited under sufferance, not good enough for the church coffers ... Oonagh's housekeeping allowance from William wasn't pure enough for this purpose, after all. According to the Plain Truth, Oonagh shouldn't have loved money, or showy display. But she did. Alice was consistently amazed by her mother's mixture of eccentric religious convictions and ordinary materialistic grasping. Paradise and pelmets for the curtains concerned her equally. Carnal and astral, today she was perkily concerned with things of the flesh. She got away with it in church – where even the prospect of living forever failed to mitigate jealousy – by saying the wealth was her husband's. Oonagh had been repeating the same thing for as long as Alice could remember.

She rehearsed all the familiar phrases, she gathered the glib, the facile old friends.

'King David was rich. And just look at Solomon. You don't imagine he kept two thousand concubines in frillies without some cash, do you? Of course people don't like it.' Today, though, there was a newcomer among the time-servers, the stale stalwarts. 'It's just as Oscar says: *Few men can bear another man's prosperity.*'

'Oscar? Oscar Wilde?'

'Of course Oscar Wilde. I thought you studied English Literature. I thought you were supposed to be a clever girl. No?'

Alice winced.

'They have it all wrong, anyhow,' Oonagh swept on. '*We* are not rich. It's your father who's rich.'

It was William who had brought them into the state of superabundance. It was William who was beginning to take them from it. It was William who had better get them back to it. Pronto. But if it were down to her, Oonagh implied, they would all live simply enough – in a caravan, perhaps.

'Doesn't know she's fuckan living,' William always said. 'Can yer see her on the can? Can yer see her on a fuckan Elsan? Or tootling off to the communal khazi? Can yer? Doesn't know she's fuckan living.'

'You know, Dad says you don't know you're living,' Alice said, pleased to be able to retort under the protection of indirect speech.

'Such is the way man thinks,' Oonagh intoned. 'But man – he is very, very limited.'

She went back to the letter. 'Peter wouldn't even look at me on Friday night. Embarrassed, no doubt. Resentful, probably. You know what he said about you?'

'About me?' Alice's heart shuddered like a washing machine on its last cycle. 'What've I got to do with it?'

'I don't know. I suppose he thinks you knew about it. I think I may have told him it was you who typed the letter. I really don't recall.'

'You did *what*?'

'Anyway, what he said was this – *Tell her not to call me her brother any more.*' Oonagh pronounced the phrase triumphantly, as if she'd coined it, then recoiled into herself, a yo-yo refusing to play.

Chapter Eight

There were times when Alice yearned to select a mother by mail-order catalogue, or, preferably, take her straight off the peg so there could be no further mistakes. She wanted a plump happy placid dimpled *Erdemutter* whose chief delight was to extend her ample arms around the whole world. What she had instead was an embittered twig. You could, perhaps, admire the pretty greenness of the moss around the bark, but there your comfort ended. Sometimes Oonagh sulked for days in bed on the grounds that Elizabeth I had also commandeered her couch when things were going badly. Brooder, not broody, Oonagh brought forth sickly brain children: perverse interpretations of the family saga, self-dramatisations of her potential responses.

For instance.

By the next day, Peter would have paid her back 'only out of spite'.

By the end of the week, Alice would have 'forced' her to dictate the letter in the first place and thus be responsible for the whole dismal affair.

How she would rebuke her children! How she would assert her rights! 'Peter, how dare you impose that two hundred pounds on me. Alice, how dare you write a letter instructing your brother to impose that two hundred pounds on me. Oh, I shall tell the pastor all this. Oh, how I shall.'

Of course, she never would.

For these endless self-fashionings could be achieved far more comfortably under an oyster silk duvet cover than anywhere else. Sometimes Alice pitied her mother, sometimes she wearied of her, but most of all she felt unsettled by the continuous rewrites of her over-acted and under-motivated melodramas.

When Alice retraced her steps and peered at Peter, he was wearing a grey herringbone coat and a plain grey tie, satin with dirt, which hung like a gutted fish. His grey suit was shiny too. On his face red boils glistened. He was a missionary leper from Albert Schweitzer's Lambarene.

Peter purposely ignored his sister. He lavished attention on other Saints. He seemed deliberately to be choosing ones she didn't like. It hurt her to know that he didn't like them much either. Jude's ex-girlfriend, the Italian, Isabella, waved a bouquet of fuchsia nails. They smiled like rival toothpaste advertisements. Then he seemed eager to be crippled by the hilarity of an exchange with her lumpy husband.

Alice was about to walk away when she realised how much braver she was in this situation than she would be normally. She was near as damn on her deathbed, after all. They both were. They had better make things up quick.

'Come *on*,' she said, pushing past the Italian. She felt like an old lady in a bread queue. There just wasn't time for politeness. 'What's all this? Please can we make it up?'

Peter hesitated. 'It's not that straightforward, Alice.'

'Why not? We can just decide –'

'No we can't.'

'But you're my brother and . . .' Alice went as far as she knew how to. 'And I love you.' She had never said this before. This would solve everything, surely. She'd kept it in reserve for her whole life. 'What more is there?'

'Words are easy,' he replied, using easy words.

Alice felt exposed. She fumbled for another way. 'Is this about Maria? Is she upset? Shall I apologise? I can do it right now.'

'No it isn't about Maria.'

'That's *it*, isn't it?' Alice insisted desperately.

'This isn't,' Peter repeated with annoyance, 'about Maria.'

'So how can we fix this? What can I do? *Please?*'

'I don't know,' he said, and shook his head. He was about to leave. She needed to say something.

'What did you think of the New Idea?' she asked quickly. Momentarily, she didn't care about the New Idea. But at least she had him talking.

'It made sense,' he replied, seriously, after a pause. 'Everything seems much clearer to me than it did before.'

'Really?'

'Yes. Doesn't it to you?' he said, walking off without waiting for her answer.

This was, Alice discovered, the pattern.

Theologically, for her, the New Idea wasn't just a U-turn. It was a U-turn on a motorway and the consequences were fatal. She sat through the afternoon sermons, half weeping for the loss of Peter, half weeping for her dying self. Everyone else, though, seemed delighted with the new and plainer truth of things. Alice was disconcerted by this. If you believe everyone else is mad, then sadly you're likely to be the one who's nuts. Oonagh reasoned thus with her daughter in her Golf Clipper convertible on the way home. She did it by posing a series of

Steering Questions. William P. Pope always advised their use. Steering Questions always steered the way to the clear truth of things.

'You remember when some of Jesus's disciples were disturbed by the things he was saying? He said they would have to eat his flesh and drink his blood.'

Alice remembered. It was all too much for them. They were Jews. They didn't eat pork or prawns. So cannibalism was way out there. No wonder people were bewildered. Jesus hadn't actually meant cannibalism. He had meant the symbolic eating of bread and wine. But he didn't explain. It was a test. Love me – eat me, drink me. Alice could sympathise. She had trouble eating gingerbread men.

'They decided to stop following him,' Oonagh continued. 'They were stumbled. You remember?'

'Yes.'

'You know what St Peter said?'

'Yes.'

'What did St Peter say?'

'He said, "Lord, where shall we go? You have the sayings of eternal life."'

'Alice, the Church of William P. Pope is no different. It has the sayings of eternal life. It is the instrument God is using in our times. So where shall we go, if we leave the Church of William P. Pope? These things are tests. Will we be loyal to the Lord's organisation? Will we be loyal to the Lord, no matter when The End comes? Only He can give us eternal life. Perhaps this change has been made to see if we'll still stick around. To weed out the time-servers.'

Theology as *bluff*? Alice thought it dubious. Then she remembered Martin Luther and John Calvin and their idea of Justification by Faith, not Works. You couldn't improve your rating with God by doing good works, because the chosen were already chosen – and the damned, damned. You might have been chosen or you might not. You just had to hope for the best and hang in there. Theology as bluff.

Oonagh was capable of believing the most extraordinary things. Or disbelieving them, as the need might arise. And this made her superior to Mother Teresa, or anyone else of charitable ilk.

'This is all Martin Luther's fault,' said Alice, who really did not know very much about Martin Luther, but wanted desperately to take the argument somewhere beyond her mother's scope. The Saints were generally ignorant of their theological heritage. They imagined William P. Pope had thought of everything.

'I really don't see what civil rights –'

'Not him. Martin Luther the Reformer.'

'It's so easy,' Oonagh continued, ignoring this, 'just to walk the other way, into Satan's world. The hard thing is to stay. And trust me, there's nothing good out there in The World. It's all murder and misery.'

Chapter Nine

Alice was reluctant to contradict Oonagh. Her mother's experience was persuasively black, pervasively black. Maybe Oonagh was thinking of her incestuously abusive uncle. Or her brother Vic. Vic lived with her until he committed suicide in the early seventies. There were several previous attempts, but the last time he made sure of it. There was an argument about the washing-up rota. Vic threatened Oonagh and William with the bone-handled carving knife. Oonagh defended herself with the unwashed butcher's steel. William parried with the carving fork. The police were telephoned. But the police were unable to proceed without bodies, suitably knifed. When Vic holed up in his room for a day or two, William and Oonagh left him to rest in peace.

In the end, William had to break in the panels of the newly painted door.

Things got worse after that. It was a year of deaths and disgrace. It was worst for Oonagh's parents.

There was Oonagh's infanticidal sister. One wintry August day, the telephone rang. Oonagh let it. Then she thought it might be important. It was. Her father quietly said hello. He had been an officer in the navy. In his civil career, he did very precise things – assembled transistor radios that arrived in the post and made the machine parts for National Cash Registers. The parts had to be manufactured to within a thousandth of an inch. A lesser man would not have managed it, Oonagh always said. That day, though, her father said he was struggling with his latest radio. Bits were strewn all over the house. 'I'll no be ebble to do this one.'

'Why, Dad, what's wrong? Is it because of Vic?'

Dead Victor. The banshee in the night. Whose hands were tied with crêpe bandage to the cot sides to stop him scratching his eczema. Whose weeping skin dried to garnets and parchment. Whose small body was racked in a tug-of-war between the grandmother and the aunt who housed the paedophile uncle. Everyone always told Vic he was too tiny. But he was entirely optimistic about the issue till he went to work on trawlers and got buggered by men bigger than himself.

'It's no Victor, no,' Oonagh's father said. 'It's your sister. I was at the trial today.'

Oonagh's sister had moved away from the tiny seaside town to Glasgow, where she met a man, married him and had a child by him. The child, a boy, died aged two, of multiple injuries inflicted by one or both of his parents. No one could say for sure what had happened.

'Why didn't you tell me there was a trial?'

'I didna want to worry you. But now, with what's happened – I thought you might see it in the papers. I thought I should say.'

At the trial, her father explained, Oonagh's sister testified her husband was to blame. The husband said nothing. The prosecution pointed out that the boy's body had sustained injury over a period of months. Bones had been broken and healed in faintly contorted positions. The right wrist in repose resembled a spinner bowling a googly. Forensics found old blood in the child's belly button. There it had lost its liquidity, given itself up to a fine brown dust. People said there was no way a mother could not have known. If she was not responsible for the fatal damage to her child, she had done nothing to prevent it. Nor did she look as though she had been battered herself.

'You know what the judge said? He said – he said –'

Oonagh's father began to cry. In the way it falls to judges to find the words others will take away, the judge pronounced Oonagh's sister *amoral*. She was worse than immoral – you could say that, after all, of a fornicator. What she had done was beyond the limits of the judge's morality to quantify. Several times Alice had looked the word up, in *The Oxford English Dictionary*. *Amoped, amorado, amoral*. There it was. After misery and love.

The word had begun life as a description of the situation to which ethics do not apply. Which was more right, the eating of an apple or an orange? (Production methods and all other things being equal.)

Now its meaning was less tidy. It applied to people without any sense of right or wrong. To people without morality. Which was more wrong, infanticide or cannibalism? (Unwillingness of the victims and all other things being equal.)

Amoral: what a rebuke. Oonagh's father stopped crying and said the word three times on the telephone. Thereafter he repeated it often, sadly, to himself. He was a man of scant conversation who kept the Decalogue. He had never told a lie, stolen a morsel, done a deliberate harm. He was appalled when the church asked him to collect money for handicapped children – then decided the proceeds (so much better than anticipated) should fund the construction of a new roof.

'We canny be askin money for the kiddies, and then be geein it to something else!'

He walked out of the church more briskly than usual and did not return for three years. But he continued paying, all the same, the monthly contribution that 'kept up' a family pew. And now there was this. It was hard to stop thinking about how long, and how badly, the child had suffered. It was hard to understand why it had ever happened at all.

Oonagh felt guilty because she could not now remember the murdered boy's name. And she could not ask.

'Just murder and misery,' she repeated softly to Alice.

Suddenly sprightly, she added, however, that the New Idea didn't change anything fundamentally. The End was still coming, bang on God's schedule. Living forever remained the plan. So did life on other planets. There were many aliens who would be saved, many more who would be created so they could be saved. If Alice was 'stumbled', Oonagh said, then it was her own fault: Alice was 'stumbling' herself. She was strewing banana skins in her own path – and sk-skidding on them deliberately. That was what she was doing and it was perverse.

Home again, Alice took it slowly.

Her father asked if he could carry her handbag up the stairs to her room. It wasn't heavy.

'Listen. I've got something to ask yer,' he said, easing the door confidentially shut behind them. 'Peter speak to yer mother today?'

Alice watched curiously the shutting of the door. She could not work out why this should be a matter of especial secrecy.

'Don't think so.'

'Good.' William seemed relieved.

Alice couldn't understand this either. '*Good*? Why is it "good" if a mother and son aren't on speakers?'

'I mean bad.'

'Why are you so pleased about this?'

'Pleased? I'm not pleased. I'm aggrieved. I'm upset. In actual fact – ' William set out his synonyms. He seemed to be lying, but Alice was too weary to enquire further. 'I'm outraged. What's the point, I'd like to know, in yus going to all these Festivals and then knockan on people's doors askan them to join yus, when yus can't even agree 'mongst yussef?'

'Not now, Dad.'

'Something wrong?'

'No. I'm fine,' she replied impatiently. She wanted to get back to her worry.

William left. Alice sat on the edge of the bed and concentrated on breathing. She inhaled with deliberation and exhaled with reluctance. A novice at mortality, she hung on to air as though it were cigarette smoke. She opened all the windows and looked across the fields behind the garden. All those trees. All that oxygen. She thought she would take a walk. A walk was good for the mortal heart. Next she ate an apple. Finally she drank a glass of water.

Clearly it wasn't going to be easy.

She wasn't her mother. Oonagh had had some practice in being mortal, from the time before she became a Saint. She'd known sexual abuse, suicide and infanticide before she hit twenty-one – so was not easily daunted. Added to that, her belief that the world was a satanic charade, imminently about to collapse, made her awfully hard to fluster. Her faith in the shakiness of the temporal world was unshakeable.

But how did you learn to be mortal? And how, without delivering a diatribe, did you sit, week in, week out, among a churchful of people entirely persuaded they were not? Briefly Alice considered throwing the whole religion thing over, right there and then. If she was fearful, she was also extremely cross. She was probably going to die – and all because someone had changed their mind about an 'ish'!

'Dear God,' she began to pray, 'tell me how to have a mind and yet –'

No, she couldn't say that. '*And yet stay in Your Church?*' That would be insulting. That would imply that His Church was mindless. He must know it too, of course, but there were things better left unsaid.

She tried again.

'Dear God, tell me how I am to be saved from The End of the World when –'

Alice cringed at the unavoidable conclusion. '*When I'm not sure The End of the World is really coming now?*'

The answer came to her in a bolt. Why couldn't she give up the Church?

Because of superstition. Because of Sod's Law. If she gave it up now, then it was bound to turn out to be true.

Because of Pascal's Wager. Presented with the choice of believing in God or not believing in Him, you may as well try and believe. Because, if you believe, and God *does* exist, you have something to gain. If you believe and God *doesn't* exist, you've lost nothing and gained nothing. Whereas, if you disbelieve and God *does* exist, you're damned.

And, finally, Alice couldn't give up the Church because of her mother. Oonagh was her sister's antithesis. Her sister murdered children, more or less directly, while Oonagh tried to arrange for hers to live forever. You couldn't say it wasn't more thoughtful.

Chapter Ten

'Fancy a quick drink?' William asked his daughter airily. He was driving her to the Oxford coach stop. His half-timbered, pebble-dashed local was around the corner. He swung into the car park. It was raining hard as they got out. In the early dusk, as if at a signal, two Taylor & Walker lanterns over the pub doors flickered, faltered, then burst irrefutably into bloom. Entering by the nearest door, William walked across to a table on the left of the bar. Alice followed. A small woman stood up and William kissed her on the cheek. It was apparent to Alice that their meeting was prearranged. She felt unnerved. The woman wore a belted cream linen jacket over a black shift dress. Her hair was a carefully trained hedgehog – a pointed pelt of highlights, without a parting. Alice was conscious of her unlaundered jeans. Rain leaked from her hair.

'You must be Alice,' the woman said brightly, holding out her hand. 'I'm Jill. Lovely to meet you at last.'

'Yes,' Alice echoed uncertainly, as they shook hands, 'lovely.'

What could she mean by *at last*? Alice looked to her father for guidance. He seemed amused to find her so disconcerted. Taking a seat on the red leather banquette next to Jill, he squashed against her affectionately. Alice balanced on a stool opposite. William and Jill held hands. Then his fingers began to paddle in her nape. He kissed her cheek and gave it a pinch.

Jill was embarrassed. Alice was embarrassed. William was delighted.

'Isn't she beautiful? Didn't I say she was beautiful? I was telling her,' he told Jill, 'all about you on the way over. Wasn't I?' he demanded.

Alice lied politely. 'Yes.' She tried to make her eyes say, *You bastard.*

'Oh, William!' Jill tapped him, mock-reproachfully, on the arm. She got up and said she would be back in a minute. The Ladies' door swung open and shut, open and shut, a diminuendo behind them.

'*What is all this about?*' Alice demanded in a whisper which could have been engraved on the air. 'You didn't tell me you were meeting someone. Have you any idea how *embarrassed* I feel?'

'Sorry, love. But I wasn't meeting her. How was I to know she'd be here? It's a public house.'

'Oh, come on. Who is she? What are you doing with her?'

'I'm telling yer the God's honest truth. Anyway. You know why she's out there?'

He nodded his head backwards in the direction of the toilets.

'Needs the loo?' Alice replied drily.

'Weak bladder,' William confided. 'I met her at Dr Sulakahn's on account of that bladder. But whaddyer think? Beautiful woman, huh?'

Grimly Alice said nothing.

'She's beautiful,' William insisted. 'I know it. You know it.' He paused. 'Nothing in it, mind. She just does a bit of book-keeping work for me, from time to time. She's very good with figures. And she's got a husband,' he pronounced, as if that settled the impossibility of adultery.

'But,' Alice protested, 'you looked so –'

'The thing is, Alice, what yer've to understand, right, is that she was an orphan. Her parents abandoned her. She found out she was adopted the day she was six. She cried all day. She never got over it. She needs support. I give her confidence. I'm a friend. It's all very well for you, yer've *had* a mum and a dad and yer know who yer are. Yer don't know what it's like for her. You imagine – finding out that yer dad and yer mum wasn't yer dad and yer mum after all – how heartbroken yer'd be.'

'Mmm.' Alice was non-committal.

'She needs the affection, yer see,' he emphasised.

'What about the husband?'

'Not up to it. Nice guy. But. Too shy himself. You get the picture? That's the thing about you, Alice,' he flattered. 'Yer've got great understanding and insight.'

Alice swallowed uncomfortably. 'Yeah, me and Mahatma Gandhi.'

'Not like Peter,' he added.

'Peter?'

'Yeah. I took them all out, Peter and Maria, with Jill, last night. It was a very nice meal. In the Indian. Ahmed Mahfooz's. We had poppadoms. We had everything. You know that stuff with the yogurt and the mint, whaddyercallit?'

'Raita.'

'Yeah. And they do a very good vindaloo. It doesn't cost an arm and a leg either. I was asking Mahfooz what he recommended and he said –'

'So what happened with Peter?' Alice cut in.

'Oh, *him*. He just wouldn't say a word to Jill. Got completely the wrong end of the stick about it. I was never so embarrassed in my entire life. It was a terrible thing he did. Poor old Jill. She wondered what she'd done wrong. She went to the toilet so many times. I tried telling him. But. Limited mentality, isn't it. Not like us.'

'All I'm saying is –' Alice persisted weakly, 'it might *look* suspicious. It's all very well *you* knowing it's innocent. But you've got to think about what other people think. I mean, I thought it looked odd, didn't I? What will other people think? It could get back to Mum.'

'How?' William asked scornfully. 'She never goes to pubs.'

'Someone might tell her.'

'Who? Only you. And you understand.'

'What if Peter tells her?'

'How would he tell her?' William retorted impatiently. 'He hates her. Not even talking to her, is he?'

Now Alice knew why William was so pleased that Peter and Oonagh weren't talking. 'Might be a good reason for starting.'

'Nah.' William flicked off the possibility like a small fly. 'Never mentioned any of me women friends to her before.'

'You've done this *before*?'

'Had a wee lady friend? A course I have.'

Jill approached the table. The conversation would have to wait. Alice watched as William put his hand over Jill's. Jill gulped and put the other hand, affirmatively, over his. A club sandwich. Her eyes sought Alice's approval, half shyly, half defiantly. Alice smiled back, radiantly neutral.

'So you *were* pleased,' Alice pursued, an hour later, 'when I told you Peter hadn't spoken to Mum. You – lied to me.'

'No. It's like I told you. I'm very upset.'

William turned with a fierce look that commanded her credulity.

'But it's to your advantage,' she said.

'It's not that simple. It's not like that.' William always covered illogic with alleged complexities.

'So what *is* it like, then?'

William sighed. He started dialling on the car telephone, switching it to speaker mode, so that Alice would be able to hear the conversation.

'So what did yer make of Alice, Jill? I just dropped her off. She just got the coach. Lovely girl, isn't she?'

'Lovely, William,' Jill replied. 'I had such a lovely time.'

'She told me how much she liked yer. She was admiran yer, no end. Her exact words were, "I wish I could be more like Jill." Anyway – yer breaking up – can't hear yer . . .'

'No, the line's fine. I wasn't saying anything.'

'Yer breaking up, love. I'll call yer back in a minute.'

He turned to Alice. 'It'll give her a lot of confidence, hearing that from you. Especially because you're at Oxford.'

'But I didn't say it,' Alice objected.

'No. But she's not to know, is she? It'll give her great confidence. It's a great thing yer've done for her, there.'

Chapter Eleven

William was so mired in lies and half-truths he made Satan look like a misprint of Santa.

Flattery in exchange for credulity was the trade-off he imagined with Alice. Told that she was 'insightful' enough to 'understand' baloney, she was then bound to believe it. Alice calculated the entrance price for her admission to her father's world rather differently. She knew his love and acceptance were conditional on her seeming to be persuaded by him. Peter knew it too. The more improbable William's story, the more he enjoyed requiring Alice to believe it. Or to say she did. It was a test of loyalty.

And it reminded her of something.

'There's yer coach, love.'

William strained his cheek towards Alice – his seat belt was fastened – and she kissed it. She got out of the car quickly. The coach door opened slowly on large hinges with the crudity of a child's toy vehicle. The driver hole-punched Alice's return ticket. She put on her seat belt and settled herself under the blast of an overhead fan that refused to shut off.

Alice pondered the family saga. By the time the coach drew into the high street, she had it sorted. Keen in her own mind to absolve her father of infidelity – mainly so that she would not have to tell her mother about it – Alice could see a way. She knew he had behaved altruistically in the past: hadn't he, for instance, married her mother when she needed it, after the Swiss gentleman jilted her? William always said he was the only one who'd ever looked out for Oonagh. He'd been doing it since 1964. So perhaps he deserved a little selfishness, if it made him happy, now. Alice suspected that Jill was merely mercenary. But had her mother been any better? No. Alice felt quite proprietorial on this point. She imagined she was composed almost entirely of her father's genes – unfortunately diluted by whatever she had of her mother's. That was why she was loyal to her father and not her mother. She and her father were one. Then these women came along and tried to snatch their property.

All the same, the idea that her father had a love life was something new and startling to her.

As was her own.

For a few days more, Alice did not reply to Jude's letter. She liked to pretend this was because she was waiting for another one from him. Each morning, she found her mailbox empty and tritely instructed the absent Jude, 'Faint heart never won fair lady, mate' – as if it were Jude and not herself who quivered mortally. The mailbox was not located on the door, or near the door, or anywhere excessively convenient like that. It was a five-minute walk away, in the Porter's Lodge. There was plenty of time for Wisdom.

On these occasions she told herself the good thing about being mortal and perpetually terrified was that it levelled everything. When every moment you thought you might self-combust, in the event of such a thing actually occurring, you'd confront it with, well, equanimity. Nothing, as it were, out of the ordinary. When every conversation felt like a job interview or first date, then job interviews and first dates themselves were not too bad. *She* would not be caught short of the right emotions – dread, anxiety, panic, shock. In the big crises, she would be very proficient.

It was things like walking down the road that she really couldn't manage.

And of course, *anyone* could walk down the road.

Few people could get so unnerved by it. She dropped her head, as though shortly expecting collision with a lorry. It would be more sensible to raise her chin, she knew, and not tuck it away like a prize-fighter. Better a busted chin than a busted brain. And better a clear-sighted view of the worst than this wary glance from under her gathered eyebrows. She folded her arms in front of her as she walked – like a surgeon after scrubbing up – in case her innards might fall out.

In the meantime she cheered herself up with the idea that anxiety was also an indicator of genius. All that chemical imbalance in the brain was bound to set things off.

A week after the Festival, another letter had arrived after all. Alice jogged up the short narrow flight of stairs that took her inside the Porter's Lodge. The mail was held in a grid of pigeon holes. And she could see that there was – there was! – another envelope for her. Ordinarily, Alice held envelopes with trembling. They might be life-changing, even when their signs of origin – blue letters saying the *Times Literary Supplement*, the librarian's scrawl on a small brown envelope concealing a demand for the return of books – gave hints to the contrary. The first letter from Jude she had not recognised. This time she was certain and steadied herself with particular care. She suspected that falling in love was a physiological hazard for the generally terrified person like herself. Whose pulse rate did not require raising. The massive overreactions of the person in love – supernovas of joy at the tiniest glint of hope, epics of melancholy from a couplet of disappointment – were quite a lot to manage on top of her routine inflation of every situation. She gazed quietly at the pastel clouds on the front of the card.

Inside, Jude simply asked when he could visit again.

In the greater safety of her room Alice considered her reply, pen poised on high, so the ink rushed, like blood from the brain, back inside the cartridge. Rococo, doctor's-prescription swirls of ink informed Jude that she might be able to fit him in one Friday night, somewhere between Lord Byron and P. B. Shelley. That was three weeks away. Nothing too hasty. Falling in love was one thing, tripping was another. She didn't want to rush it.

The second hand stuttered and the hours hesitated. She opened books, she listened to her fridge, she inspected with her usual fascination the imprints left on her skin by her clothes. Pulling her socks down revealed fine-tooth combs, and old broken rail tracks on her shins. When she wore tights, the seam sometimes left on her belly an elver. Nothing perma-nent about this damage. That was why she liked it. If anything it was the measure of young sprung skin. The fascination had begun in early childhood. She remembered Peter, when they shared the bunk bed, his face indented by the lines that the sheets had left overnight. 'Oh, get off, will you!' he would say, as she examined them curiously. As time went on, she developed certain rules about the hobby. Marks should not be deliber-ately induced. Sitting wilfully on a zip and waiting for another rail-track mark to arrive was not the idea. The whole pleasure lay in the discovery of unanticipated marvels. The griddle-panning of her rump – after she had sat for a long time on her slatted desk chair – might have happened before, but the degree of cooking was always different.

On Friday afternoon she pulled her knickers down and twisted her rear in front of the mirror, absorbed by her sudden transformation into a Jasper Johns American flag.

Meanwhile Jude practised the grey arts of accountancy all day long and then drove with precipitous keenness down the A40. It was three years and four months since his last proper kiss. It was five years since his last love. His twenties were, so far, untainted by knowledge of a female and he thought it very, very possible to underestimate the virtues of haste. And besides, there was a jacuzzi of passionate Athenian blood pumping through him.

Like many people, Jude wanted not to be like his parents.

Like many people, he was at a genetic disadvantage in this respect.

At six o'clock, just as Alice draped her hair over her left shoulder as though it were an evening scarf, his feet flew, at a sensible height, over the cobbles, now buttered like sweet corn by the early-evening sun. She picked up a small brown leather bag and, since the hyper-heterosexuals-in-a-room hypothesis remained unchallenged, stood waiting outside the door for his arrival.

Four minutes after six they were exchanging awkward shy *hi*'s.

Chapter Twelve

A lot can be done in four minutes. You need not live forever to get things done. Peter dipped a finger deeply into a family-size tub of Sainsbury's live natural yogurt.

'Joo are thinking I can't see what joor trying to do?' Maria demanded. 'Hey? Joo think –'

'All right, all right.' Peter felt hustled. He would be very surprised if she *could* see, actually, since he was trying to insert the yogurt into her backside. Because prescriptions and over-the-counter products from Boots the Chemist's were equally forbidden to the Saints, Maria had devised ways of soothing her own predicaments. For skin complaints she sat in the bath and added salt to the water. Then she felt as queasily English as jellied eels. This time Peter had offered to help. Maria was spread across a self-assembly pine kitchen table from IKEA.

The bio-cultures of the yogurt were curative. They worked very well on cold sores and thrush. But it was the first time she'd dabbled with them anally and the first time he'd been permitted to assist – so far without success. He thought he must be very careful. He did not want his finger to rupture her.

Then, suddenly . . . he was inside. It was not at all as he had thought. He was taken by the sphincter's grip. Absorbed. Charmed. Gripped. Never mind Maria – he felt he would be lucky to escape with a finger intact. His finger was not especially large. He began to think his wife must be rectally challenged. How wrong you could be.

'Mind you,' he remarked pleasantly instead, 'I can't see a great deal myself down here. The sun shines so brightly out of your backside, *chiquito*, I just can't see a thing.'

Maria was unfamiliar with the expression. She had other concerns now than English idiom. 'Hey, hey, no, no,' she said firmly, wriggling away and sitting down. Peter checked his finger, then looked at his wife enquiringly.

'What about the yogurt?' he asked.

'*Joo bastard,*' she responded fiercely. 'I remember now, there was an Esaint in Espain who divorce his wife for something like this.'

'Oh, *that,*' he said. 'You mean . . . ?'

'Joo know what I min, joo bastard Ingerlish Esaint.'

Maria meant marital sodomy. Divorce was a complex issue among the Saints. But Peter was the expert in the legal chicaneries. When it came to the Bible, he knew it all – how many ephahs of flour were in a poor woman's guilt offering, how many coins she had to lose from her dowry chain before her husband could divorce her. (One.) The dimensions of the Second Temple, the four words for love in *koiné* Greek, the pivotal dates from secular history that confirmed biblical chronologies. He knew when the 1,260 days were ended and when the two prophets who had dwelt in all the earth were killed. Inside the pimply brown plastic covers of his study Bible, the pages bore a complex system of markings. There were wriggling underlinings in red, neon yellow and neon green scorings, square bracketings in a black biro that leaked tiny sticky flies. Enough annotations to write a small exegetical book. Well-loved passages on the sanitation regulations concerning lepers were marked up with stars or flowers.

And he knew about adultery too.

Until 1981, adultery was the only permitted grounds for divorce in the Church. Jesus had said it. It had to be right. The Jews of Jesus's day used to divorce their wives for all sorts of trivial reasons. A badly cooked meal. So Jesus told them to stop all the footling around. It was adultery or nothing.

Of course it was awkward that the word Jesus had used was 'fornication' not 'adultery', but fornication meant, well, what? Well, it meant adultery.

But then, in 1981, the Lord gave unto William P. Pope a New and Plainer Understanding of what Jesus really meant by adultery. Adultery wasn't so much about *who* you were doing it with, as *what* you were doing. You could do adultery with your own wife. You could do adultery with your own husband. It could all be done in the safety of your very own marital bed. The way Saints managed it was through oral or anal sex. (Or, Maria feared, a natural cure for piles – the insertion of a yogurt-smeared husbandly finger.) These were all versions of Do-It-Yourself adultery, and hence legitimate grounds for divorce.

'But sodomy isn't grounds for divorce any more anyway,' Peter said. 'Pope realised it was a mistake. He retracted it in a later issue of *The Plain Truth*.'

'Why, what happen?'

'People say he only did it to get divorced himself. You know – he was like Henry VIII, and bent the Church rules to suit himself. But that isn't true. Pope made a mistake.'

'I know him. I know this Henry that ate. See – he divorce a Spanish wife too.' Maria *humphed*. 'And a *mistake*?' She repeated the word dubiously. 'How? If God tell him every-thing, then how he make the mistake?'

'Well, he was reading Milton, the English poet, you know? It led him astray. But only temporarily. God put him right.'

William P. Pope was addicted to plagiarism. Every time he read something new, he was itching to copy it up, with flourishes, for the next issue. And people had had so many fabulous new interpretations of the biblical grounds for divorce before.

The poet Milton, for instance, in the seventeenth century.

His first wife left him after a month and he had a lot of explaining to do to himself. So he wrote a pamphlet called *The Doctrine and Discipline of Divorce*. Adultery couldn't be *the only* valid reason for divorce, said Milton. Because that would make sex *the most* important thing in marriage. And it wasn't, was it? Because that would be too base.

'So there is this Meel-ton. And what happen then to the people who make the divorce for the sex in the bum?'

Those in Pope's Church who had divorced their spouses on these grounds did not have to return to them. They did not have to suffer those injustices against the flesh again. Those practices were still wrong. Only you could not now get a divorce for them. And if this logic was good enough for God, it ought to be good enough for everyone sat in the Church of His Worldwide Saints.

'Me, eh, I take no risk. Me – I would prefer to have itchy in the bottom than not a husband.'

One minute, you had piles. The next minute, you had the divorce papers.

'No, no, no, *no*. No thank you very much.'

'But *chiquito* – this is ridiculous.'

Inserting yogurt wasn't anal sex. That would be like

comparing the use of a tampon to vaginal intercourse, Peter argued. And tampons weren't wrong. True, no tampons were mentioned *directly* in the Bible. Peter was willing to concede that. But they were in use among the ancient Egyptians. They could have been included in the Ten Commandments if God had been so minded. And there were six hundred other rules besides the first ten. There was more than enough room for a prohibition.

Maria looked suspicious. Her red rectum was not about to be wooed by false and worldly reasonings.

'Joo frustrate me now. Joo are so clever that joo are – be*yond* cleverness.'

'Really? I like the sound of that. Do you think you could just say that again?'

'Be*yond* cleverness.'

'And one more time?'

'So. We have the baby very soon, jes?'

Together they agreed to put the yogurt back in the fridge. Within a minute, Maria was on the toilet, discovering that all that colonic fingering was the perfect natural remedy for constipation.

Within another minute, she was on the telephone.

Chapter Thirteen

Alice glanced surreptitiously at Jude, Jude at Alice, as though they had somehow met by accident and the meeting had not been arranged by Sheaffer fountain pen the better part of a month before. In the pause, someone could be heard coming into the corridor, talking to a mobile telephone. Alice felt the fear of being discovered doing nothing wrong, and rummaged weakly in her bag for her key. They recognised the voice.

'Don't worry yussef about him. I'll sort him out. Tell yer what, if it comes to it, *I'll* give yer a baby messef, no bother. Yeah, not a bit of trouble to me, love.'

The voice stopped in the corridor. 'I'm easy, me . . . All right, then, I'll love yer and leave yer.'

William came through the door. His cheeks were lacquered Chinese lanterns. 'Hello, love. Oh!' He was surprised to see Jude. 'Lad,' he acknowledged.

'Who was *that*?' Alice asked, referring to the telephone conversation.

'Women,' William replied sighingly, as though it were the whole gender that plagued him. 'Can't get away from them.'

He was still regrettably popular with a great many of the

most beautiful. Another one had been after him, only the day before, at the bank. It was the eye contact when she stamped his cheque stumps, and the glance away when she pinged the elastic band around his passbook. The plastic screen presented no real barrier to their passion. Their breaths mingled through the guichet. And she was only nineteen.

'Nineteen!' William repeated, shaking his head. 'Can yer just credit it?'

Alice raised her eyebrows. Jude gave a long low whistle. All this before they learned that the nineteen-year-old's manager 'had the eye' for William too. William liked his tales of sexual conquest to involve some conflict with authority.

'So the manager said to me, "What's wrong with Clare?" Clare's the nineteen-year-old. "Don't you think she's pretty?" I said, "Oh, she's pretty all right." So then she wanted to know what would make a difference. I said she'd have to be in her twenties. Then I'd see.'

'One year would do it, then?' Jude asked drily.

'It's not the year, lad. It's *the decade*. If she was in her twenties, well, sure she might as well be twenty-nine, then.'

'Or twenty,' Alice pressed.

'Or twenty-nine. If a woman's in her twenties, she's as good as twenty-nine. That's the way I would be looking at it, messef, like.'

'I'm twenty-one,' Alice said.

'I know. I was there at the time.'

'I'm nearly twenty-four,' Jude offered.

'I don't fuckan *care* how old you are, you dirty wee bugger,' William laughed at him affectionately. 'Yup, I can pull nineteen to ninety, me,' he boasted grimly. 'You don't think Peter would've ever pulled Maria without me, do yer?'

'Well . . .' Alice interposed.

'Cos yer silly if yer do. Just look at Jill – she'd jump at the chance of having me, if she thought she could. Course there's nothan in it. We're just friends. But I don't understand it messef, even, why all the women are so mad about me. Mother always told me: *You haven't the looks, boy.*'

'Well, you're not –' Alice began. Her father shrugged mystified shoulders. He raised palms innocent of sexual prowess. The disclaimer was gleeful. There was an endearing comic modesty in these claims of extraordinary success. Alice reached for less wounding terms. She took into special consideration her father's cropped, grey rabbit-fur hair, which he was now stroking with his hand and which she rather liked.

'I wouldn't say you were exactly – *bad*-looking.'

'Alice, I'm A Dog.' He said it without self-pity and she giggled at the honesty. 'So,' he continued. 'Are yus coming in or coming out, then?'

'Out,' Alice replied, too quickly. 'Jude's just arrived. This very minute. I was waiting for him outside the door.'

'Relax, child.' William could sniff misdemeanour and this wasn't it.

'Didn't you see him?' Alice pursued, all the same. 'You must have been right behind. Which way did you come in, then?'

'Usual way. Front.'

'Oh, that would explain it. You used the back gate, didn't you?' she said, turning to Jude.

'C'mon,' Jude replied. 'Let's all go out. Where shall we go?'

'I don't know – the buttery?' Alice suggested.

They waited for her father. He bent over to tie shoelaces already double-tied and to hitch up fully hitched socks. The socks were black. 'Mother always told me: Navy is a sign of poverty. Wear black socks and you will go far.'

William's Reebok jumper and bottoms were navy. Wasn't that displaying a larger surface area of poverty? Jude enquired.

'Also useful,' William replied, unperturbed. 'Old ladies give me ten pees at the bus stops, then.' He made his way back slowly to *homo erectus*. 'And I get twenties when I've the anorak on me.'

The floor in the buttery was ice cream stone. A barred window, high up, cut through a yard of an ancient wall. The hearth was deep and unlit. Jude's eyes skated about admiringly and he asked the room's history. Alice had no idea. She said she didn't think it *had* one, separate from the college. Cunning reply of the ignoramus, she thought. It saved her for the moment.

'The college, then?' Jude suggested helpfully.

'Can't say,' said Alice. 'Talking about it is considered –'

She was going to say, 'bad luck'. But luck could not be mentioned by a true Saint of God. There was some dim allusion to an Aramaen deity, the God of Good Luck, in the Bible. So luck, whether good or bad, was an evil and pagan thing – not to be invoked under any circumstances. This was all very well until someone was going for their driving test, and said, 'Wish me luck?'

Now she said, instead, 'There are issues of confidentiality . . . tell you the truth, I'm not confident I can remember when the college was built.'

The historical details, had she ever known them, were quite beyond her recollection. She didn't have the mind for it. Jude didn't believe her. She was simply being modest. She must have a store of beguiling medieval anecdote and was simply afraid of intimidating her listeners. But her father nodded.

'Never had any sort of general knowledge, this child. For some unknown reason.' He compensated by insisting, fiercely, 'But yer know there are a *bullion* Chinese. A bullion! Can yer just imagine?'

'Is that right,' Jude replied flatly.

'Time's up,' the buttery man announced.

'That's early.' William sounded disappointed.

'Yes,' Alice replied, omitting to mention that, while the buttery closed shortly after seven, the bar was open all night.

'Well, I guess that's that, then,' she said, as they walked towards the main entrance where her father's car would be parked. She was thinking what to do with Jude once they had got rid of her father.

'Tell yus what,' William said. 'I'll take yus for dinner. Like that?'

So the three of them went to dinner.

Halfway through the meal, Alice felt a piece of bacon from her burger slip uncertainly towards the back of her throat. (She had a special fear of choking. William and Oonagh used to tell her about a niece who had choked and died at the dinner table, right in front of her horrified and ineffectual parents. Ever since then Alice held a practice choking fit with her food at least once a week.) She began faking a cough. She gasped in air. William slapped her hard on the back.

'Yer all right, child.'

Alice was not so sure. It was hard to control a highly greased item. Particularly when it had a piece of mozzarella soldered to it.

William was talking about Oonagh. The extraordinariness of his success with women was in fact matched only by the extraordinariness of his failure with Oonagh. Even though there was, he said, 'history' weighing in his favour. By history William meant his great-grandparents had once been happily married. The husband was an entrepreneur and a romantic.

'Yer know what he used to say? He used to say, "Just give me my health, Lord, and that's my wealth!"'

'Must have pulled women left, right and centre with a line like that,' Jude replied.

'Sure what would you fuckan know?' William replied good-humouredly. 'But I know what she thinks. She thinks she'd be happy with one of them Saints. Never been happy with me, anyway. And if we lose the house –'

'Is that likely?' Alice interrupted.

'Could be. Might have to move out for a while. I could rent it, yer see, to cover the mortgage. But Christ knows what she'll think of me, then. I'd have to start a big fire up the yard if that happens.'

'Whatever for?' she asked.

'It gives me great peace of mind. It's one of me two main hobbies . . .' The other was watching the clothes go round in the drum of the washing machine ('therapeutic'). 'Molly understands,' he said finally, as if that explained everything.

'Molly's the cat.' Alice turned to Jude.

'She be's bringing me her mice in, right,' William continued, 'when she thinks I'm depressed. She lays one or two out in the office, like, early of a mornan, for summat to cheer me up. They're not always the best. Sometimes they're half chewed, right. She wants to be generous, then she gets a bit peckish hessef, I spose. But she means well. We do have these great talks between ussefs sometimes, me and Molly. Anyway, I'll tell yer summat for nothan.'

He waited to be asked. 'What's that, then?' Alice volunteered.

'Yer mother'd soon know all about it,' he opined, with gloomy satisfaction, 'if she didn't have me any more and she had one of them Saints instead.' Then he asked, 'Who's William Langland?'

William was eyeing the spine of the paperback that poked out of Alice's bag. 'Oh, him.' She told him that he didn't need to know. Langland was a medieval poet and very grim about things. The flesh, in particular.

'But you'd have liked Chaucer,' she suggested, as though they might all have met for beers if the bard had only managed to hang on that bit longer. 'Geoffrey Chaucer,' she explained, 'is very rude.'

William asked what did she write about them. Alice had a sense this was a question her father had been wanting to ask for some time.

'Oh . . . I try to prove the opposite of what everyone normally says about them.'

'Is it difficult?' Jude asked with interest.

'Not really. More like – devious.'

William looked pleased. He pursed his lips and kissed approval. Alice continued. In her essays she tried to invent theories and see if she could make them work.

'And do people believe yer?'

Generally people did believe Alice. She didn't need to believe her own theories. She needed them to. So it was all rubbish, really, was it? William asked. It wasn't always rubbish, and sometimes Alice found her own accounts of literature quite persuasive, but she wanted to please. Yes it was all rubbish, she agreed, and William concluded that things were, as ever, much as he had suspected. She was just like her father. She was just like him. Devious. Carbon copy.

'Paper,' he stated confidently, 'doesn't resist ink.' By which he meant you could write anything. The paper could not object. It could not say, 'Hey – get off me! I don't WANT YOU to touch me.'

'Paper,' he clarified, with resolution, 'is not like yer mother.'

'*Lady Chatterley's Lover*,' Alice added. Jude seemed puzzled. Alice did not explain what she meant: Mellors, writing to Connie at the end of the book, said that if he had been with her, then the ink could have stayed in the bottle. Because the ink was semen, Alice's tutor said.

'Yah, yah, we read all that in the sixties,' William replied shortly and stood up. 'We passed that book round the buildan site like a whore.' He paid the bill and the waitress offered him a regular member's dining card. There were 10 per cent discounts on Tuesday afternoons between three and four.

See that?' William nudged Alice. 'She wants me back.'

'And your name, sir?' the waitress asked routinely.

'John West, my love,' William replied firmly and winked. Alice marvelled at the confidence. Her father had taken his first and favourite alias from the salmon tin. His second, Mr Raj Singh, generally worked only on the telephone.

They walked back to college, William telling them about a young female assistant in Next who had buttoned his shirt in the changing rooms with her own hands, thus provoking further managerial jealousy. Alice speculated about where she might take Jude if she managed to get him on her own at last. To the bar? It didn't seem the thing. Back to his car at the gate? She didn't want to. To her room? Surely not. Or if the room – not, she put it to herself, not the room *exactly*. The staircase? The picture gallery below? Yes, the gallery. Which she knew very well would be closed. But it mightn't be, might it?

Then, as they approached William's car, she heard her father asking Jude, 'Want a lift to your car? Save you the walk?'

'Um, OK, I will. Thanks.'

William kissed Alice goodbye. Angling his cheek, Jude pretended he wanted one too.

'Not kissan you, lad. I'm not like that. I remember in 1961,

I'd a landlady said to me I could have my room for a pound instead of a pound fifty if I shared with a guy. Jer think I was going to be in bed with some guy, all dirty and smelly? Did she think I was some kind of a pervert? I asked her. Told her I'd share with any lady lodgers she had, though – and I'd pay the full price too.' William turned to Alice. 'Jer reckon it's even *safe* gettan in a car with him?'

Suddenly they were both waving at her. Then they were gone.

Chapter Fourteen

Alice ambled defeatedly through the college quadrangles, head down. Consolations were few. Flowerless beds of mud and sections of lawn were laid out like the shapes of a toddler's puzzle. The position of her knickers had shifted when she left the restaurant. She could feel the skin grooves made by the knicker elastic during the course of the evening filling out again. Probably the mirror would report no extraordinary tyre marks in the verges of her hips by the time she was back. There was still her bra, however. The underwire of the left cup had begun to poke out lately, leaving practice stigmata. There might even be a bicycle-track mark under one or both breasts.

'Alice!'

She turned round and there, running towards her, was Jude, who had told himself, with Grecian pride, that 'where there's a willy, there's a way'.

'I thought you got a lift to your car,' she said.

'I did. I followed him for a couple of streets, then dropped behind and came back. He'll never know.'

'Did you park in the same spot?'

'Of course not.'

Alice smiled. Entering the hallway, she pointed to the

descending set of stairs. Unusually, there were lights on. A warning sign from above? She wasn't vain enough to believe it. The world wasn't full of signs sent specially for her decryption. It had to be a coincidence.

'There's a picture gallery down there,' she explained. 'They must be having a preview of the new exhibition.'

Jude was intrigued. 'You live above a gallery?'

She nodded. He looked mischievous. 'Let's go,' he suggested. There was a pause. 'Why not?'

'But we're not –'

'Invited? Just hold on.'

She half expected him to produce an entrance card from the pocket of his stripy jacket – the divine miracle that would save her from the crime of inviting him to her room. Instead he turned his back and began running to the gate. 'You'll need the key,' she shouted, scrabbling in her hand for it.

'Won't!' he replied, without turning back. She saw he was right. There were two boys in black tie ahead of him. If he ran quickly enough, he'd catch the gate before it closed. He made it, and held the gate ajar for his return by removing his left shoe and employing it as a wedge. Thirty seconds later he was back at the gate, replacing the shoe without tying the lace, and running towards her again. He had something under his arm, inside the jacket. He showed it to her at the doorway.

'You can go anywhere,' he swaggered ironically. 'With a camera.'

It was a professional's SLR and, under its envoy, they descended.

The entranceway was dim, low-ceilinged and concrete-floored. About as welcoming as a gas chamber. The foyer was deserted. Everyone was in the gallery. To the left was a table with a few unused, and many more used, champagne glasses.

To the right was the desk where, in the daytime, admittance tickets could be purchased, or, in the case of members of the college, a visiting book signed. There was no one on duty tonight.

'Shame,' Jude said, when it was apparent all the champagne bottles were empty. He deposited a glass in his pocket all the same. Its head peeped out like a Joey.

'You have champagne too, I suppose, in the car?'

'As a matter of fact – I *did*. But now it's in the fridge in your corridor, where it's getting infinitely better to drink. Didn't you see me, earlier?'

'No.' She replied uncertainly, not knowing if he was joking. 'You should have put it in my fridge. It might get stolen.'

'Didn't know you had one. Take a glass. They'll probably be serving refills.'

In the gallery, Jude became increasingly purposeful, as though he was no longer concerned with her.

'Go and look at the pictures,' he instructed, when a waiter came up and filled both their glasses.

Instead she selected a salmon canapé from the silver platter proffered by another smiling butler, and sat with her back to a Byzantine crucifixion panel at which it seemed best not to look – arguing its paganism, really its celebration of pain disturbed her. She watched Jude making his way around the main gallery space. Mostly he photographed people. Mostly they looked pleased to be so important. Just as he predicted, no one questioned his presence.

Twenty minutes later, he said, 'We're done here. The champagne will be cold.'

Leaving the gallery, she followed him up. It seemed necessary to secure the safety of the champagne by taking it out of the public arena, and that was how Jude got into her room at last. Once there, he admired the high ceiling and the sash windows and the cushioned window seats, matched by pale green curtains with delicate peach Japanese flowers. Jude loved beautiful things. As a boy he wanted to be a Methodist rather than a Worldwider, because the route to their church was tree-lined and the building itself had large stained-glass cathedral windows. On the Sabbath in those days he kept his head down as he was made to walk to church, past neighbours and schoolmates in jeans, while he was wearing grey flannels and a bow tie on an elastic string. Later he worked in a men's dress shop that specialised in large sizes. When he arrived, thirty-five suits were stuffed into each bay, padded shoulders rubbing against each other. He discovered that fifty suits could be arranged into the same space if the shoulders were alternately dipped and raised. It was a graceful arrangement, each bay presenting the final pose of a Busby Berkeley dance routine.

'I worked in a health food shop once. I liked the price gun,' Alice said simply. 'And the till.'

Jude put bottle and glass down on a pale olive silk rug, with Japanese calligraphy, in front of the electric fire. The fire was fitted inside an elegant white wooden mantelpiece that they both agreed deserved better things.

'What happened to yours?' he asked.

'The glass? I put it back on the table.'

'Then we'll have to share.'

Clearly he was less alarmed by this prospect than her mother would have been.

'So,' he continued. 'What did you think of the exhibition?'

'I don't know. I didn't look.'

'You didn't *look*?'

He was looking – now at her hair, now at her hand. He reached out and began to stroke the hand, but with a commentary on the wonders of touch that made the feat seem less terrifying to her and more in the nature of a scientific enquiry. Alice saw her hand as though it was no longer her own. It was half a spider and Jude's was the other.

A few minutes later he began to stand up, glass in one hand, Alice in the other. She fluttered momentarily about where they were going. He could not see. She found they were sitting together on the right side of the mantelpiece. She was leaning her back against him while he leant his against the wall. Her legs went out to the left, his to the right. He folded his arms around her. Then he asked – politeness was the way – if he might kiss her.

Alice paused to consider.

She had been kissed before. When she was five, by a boy called Harjinder whose lips were decorated with tiny pieces of Wotsits crisps.

When she was six, by a boy called Gareth who bizarrely blew air into her mouth.

When she was nineteen, by a milkman who lapped her closed lips like a cat.

But after this beginner's luck, she'd had to wait till now. And now, she knew better. Kissing was crossing the moral line. It was all quite clearly stated in her thickly annotated copy of the book, *All About Dating and Courtship Leading to Christian Marriage*. Displays of physical affection should not precede engagement with a firm commitment to marry in the very near future. By displays of physical affection, the book meant holding hands and kissing chastely while in the company of others. (The dangers of privacy were well known.) But kissing *chastely*? Alice had pondered that one. There was, the book said, a way of kissing that aroused desire for sexual intercourse and a way of kissing that did not.

Never had there been so many openings for bad kissers.

What a very good Christian a very bad kisser might make.

The book said only bad kissing was allowed, not merely to

avoid putting yourself in the path of temptation, but also because: *why would you want to arouse powerful emotions for which there is no clean outlet?*

'Clean outlet' sounded like a sewage system. Only married Saints had one. They were allowed to kiss and even to have sex. They could flush it hygienically down the toilet afterwards. Wash their hands and dry them. Close the door with a neat click. Pretend they'd never been there.

But people like Alice were not to have sexual thoughts. They were only to kiss unerotically and to hold hands with their betrotheds – a category Jude did not enter.

Alice now recalled another phrase from the book. *Set limits to your displays of physical affection.* Decide it all in advance, how far exactly you'll go. But what kind of limits could you set, she wondered, under these conditions? If you were holding hands, how much of your palm should eclipse your fiancé's? How long should they be stuck together? How *very* uninspiring should your kisses be? Suddenly she remembered the third possibility she'd forgotten. The book mentioned chaste public kissing, chaste public hand-holding and, *possibly*, embracing.

So there was the grey area. Don't get reckless about cuddling.

'Do you think anyone's ever done this before?' she asked.

'What, cuddling? Absolutely not,' Jude mocked. 'We're the first ever.'

'Good idea, though, isn't it? Who'd you think invented it, really?'

'Um . . .' Jude paused. 'Got to be the serpent. Definitely the serpent. Obvious, isn't it?' he said, lifting his arms and snaking them tightly around her again. 'Or its sexier cousin, the anaconda.'

'What's – ?' Alice hesitated.

'What's sexier about the anaconda?' Jude said for her. 'It's bigger. The serpent in a state of excitement.'

'Oh, right.'

So that was cuddling.

And kissing? All the Worldwide couples Alice knew kissed each other, wedding breakfast fixed up or not. This was not risking her immortality, she felt sure. So she turned her head and pointed her lips in the general direction of Jude's, and let him do the kissing. She wondered how she was ever going to learn it, this swimming of your tongue in foreign waters. She could only make up for her feeling of inadequacy by saying, as though he were the novice, while this kind of thing happened to her all the time, 'You don't have to *ask*, you know.'

'Great,' Jude said flippantly, as he began to kiss her again. She knew it was a good thing in about five seconds.

She turned her head forwards again, and then, as though she were a Sindy doll, twisted her body around to match. Now it didn't feel as comfortable as it had before. Suddenly she felt irritated, disappointed.

'It doesn't feel as comfortable,' she complained.

'So – adjust,' he said lightly. He sounded wise and knowing. She tried to do as he suggested. Still it wasn't the same. What did that mean? Anything? Nothing? He began stroking her hair and talking, but she wasn't listening.

'You'll have to speak to my father,' she said suddenly.

'Will I?'

'Yes.'

'I thought you said I didn't have to ask.'

'Ask *me*.'

Then there was more kissing for which no hygienic outlets could be readily found, and Jude folded her into his legs. In the small of her back she felt movement, a presence hardening, the anaconda thickening, flexing its muscle. Chastely, *politely*, Alice decided to look the other way, as it were, to think the movement most probably caused by a mouse. A *mouse* – she silently screamed the appropriate response. This was even less perfect than before.

'Look, I'm going to have to go,' Jude said.

'Where?'

'Home. Well, actually, the vicarage first. The pastor wants to see me. Maybe I'll get my jobs back, you know.'

'But I told you – I don't care about that.'

'I know, I know, but I'd like your mother to think I'm respectable, at least.'

They kissed their last kiss. It was more difficult than pleasurable. A starving body clings on to any morsel of food and refuses evacuation. It does not know when it will get any more, and is not taking any chances. Alice and Jude were starving. They clung on to their last kiss as if it were resuscitation – desperate, prolonged, ineffectual. The spittle shone in Jude's stubble. Her lips hurt.

Jude gone, Alice sat on the bed trying to decide *what did it mean* when it no longer felt so perfect. She listened, for clues, to the two promised 'masterpieces' Jude had brought with him. The first was Michael Nyman's orchestral score to *The Piano*. There seemed to be only one melody, like a luggage carousel with one unclaimed Antler suitcase. She began to feel depressed. Oddly disappointed again. Her habitual terror was upbeat, at least. The second 'masterpiece' was Madonna's *Something To Remember*. Unusually, Madonna seemed just as bleak. Pop music invited emotional identification. Madonna must want everyone to be very unhappy. Alice attended to the lyrics, anticipating a message from Jude. But it was like reading the message on a greetings card and she found she couldn't do it.

Chapter Fifteen

This kissing changed things. There now seemed a clear obligation to tell her parents what was happening. They were coming up the next weekend, but Alice couldn't wait. When she telephoned home, her mother answered and Alice told her to put William on the extension.

'I've something to tell you,' she said quickly. Her lips were pink with gloss and guilt.

'Is this about Jude?' her father replied straight away. 'I've been watching that lad for years,' he continued, without waiting for her. 'He's always been trying to talk to yer. But Alice. Yer don't have time for this. *Finish yer degree first.*'

'Not now. *Wait,*' her mother added, in case there should have been any ambiguity about it. There was a pause. Alice sighed. William stifled a snort.

'What?' Oonagh said defensively into the silence.

'You may be right, Dad.'

'Of course I'm – we're – right. We're always right. We've never been wrong. Between us – we've more than a hundred years of experience. Anything yer want to know, yer just ask yer mum and dad.'

'Right.'

'That's what yer've got to understand, Alice. Coming from us – yer've got *stability*. Not everyone's had the kind of normal upbringing yus have had. Listen, yer've never had boyfriends. As I've always told yer, *anyone* can be a baby-making machine. So don't start now. Yer'll go to loss.'

'A baby?' Alice laughed. 'I don't think that's the idea.'

'There's many said that,' William replied.

'He says he wants to see you. He asked specifically if he could.'

'So he should,' Oonagh agreed.

'And he's trying to get his jobs back.'

William advised Oonagh to take Alice to the church, confident the idea would wear off that way. He said he would even go himself that weekend. They all said goodbye, and Alice put the telephone down. Straight away it rang again. It was William, calling from his mobile.

'Something I wanted to ask yer, love.'

'What?'

'Come out with me, Friday night. If yer get the coach down, I'll drop yer back messef.'

'But you're all coming up Saturday?'

'No bother to me, love. I'll do anything for me daughter, yer know that.'

'Will Jill be there? Is that what this is about?'

'Would *I* do that?' he asked humorously. 'Now you know I wouldn't do that . . . Oh, yes, Jill'll be there,' he bragged.

'If you've fallen in love with Jill,' Alice attempted to bargain, 'then surely you ought to understand why I –'

'*Love*! I haven't fallen in *love*,' William objected. He said the word as though it meant *shit*. 'I love yer mother. Trouble is, she doesn't fuckan love me. So you just make sure you don't tell her. Yer got it?'

The telephone rang again three times in the next hour.

'I said I would come, didn't I?' Alice replied, exasperated. 'I'm trying to *read*, you know.'

'I'm just checkan. I don't want to be embarrassed by saying yer'll be there and then yer don't show up. And Jill will be there. Yer like Jill. And Jill likes yer back. Because yer just like me. Everyone says it. Trev, Bill, Tom. Even Henry. It's in the way he barks, when yer come up the yard. Except – they all say how nice you are.'

'Yes. I'm polite to them.'

'Don't be like that. Yer mustn't be like that about people.'

'Like what?'

'There's nothing wrong with them.'

'I didn't say there was. I said I was polite to them.'

'Of course you are.'

Two days later, William picked Alice up at the stop.

Chapter Sixteen

The pastor said he was not willing to reinstate Jude to his former shelf-stacking and accountancy duties. Nothing grandiose like that. Instead he handed Jude a small rectangular slip of recycled paper. It assigned him one of the short Friday-night speeches. All members of the church were encouraged to take a turn. The title of Jude's assignment was 'Masturbation – A Sin That Leads To Sin'.

'I gave my first talk, you know, on this very subject,' the pastor said. 'It wasn't easy, masturbation. Of course I was far younger than you.'

It was unclear whether this was a commiseration or a boast. Jude felt it did not make anything better. First time, last time, any time – it was still him who had to do it this time. He turned the paper upside down, folded it, and attempted to manage his dismay origamically.

'It's only a five-minute speech, anyhow,' the pastor added. Five minutes was plenty of time for masturbation.

Someone had committed masturbation. (Not 'practised', the *mot juste*, because masturbation was considered as grave as murder. Once was enough.) So much was clear to Jude when the pastor told him it was 'a particular item of concern' in the

Church locally. Whenever sins were confessed, it was necessary to give a Special Speech denouncing the vice in question. So, Jude thought, there was some poor bugger his speech would be attacking. At least only the pastor knew who it was. There had been no official Disciplinings – expulsions from the Church – lately. Whenever one *was* announced, the nature of the offence was never disclosed. Instead everyone had to wait for the Special Speech. Curiosity was satisfied. Vice was not usually suppressed. It was too crude a mechanism for that. The Special Speech assumed that whatever one person had done, the next sinner would want to do as well – as though a judge, having dealt with one case of Grievous Bodily Harm, would find the defendant in the next case guilty of this crime also. The Special Speech did not recognise that the hormones had bolted.

When the night arrived, the church was a syllabub of excitement.

So, however, was Jude's inner tubing. He felt seized, molten, seismic, infernal – speechless. *Not* the church lavatory, he said to himself. A speech on masturbation, even – he'd give it readily enough instead. He certainly couldn't give it now. For a minute or more, he was in remission – able to smile (a little wanly) and exchange laconic greetings with members of the . . .Then the tectonic plates began to shift again. For a minute or more, he was unable to walk – without consequence. He was very still.

It begins benignly enough. Someone – in Jude's case, his parents – asks you to suppose, just for a second, that there is a Creator. Well then, if there is a Creator, then that Creator must have a Plan for Man. That Plan must be written in the Bible. It's only fair: no other book is available to 98 per cent of the world's population and if God has a message and a Plan for Man, then surely it's available to all (writing off the 2 per cent as the allowable margin of error). It is God's Plan that you should tell your neighbour about that Plan, and that you should remind your fellow Saints about it as well. And before you know it, you find yourself instructing them all about masturbation: why it is no part of God's Plan for Man. And you are so nervous about this that you are feeling your way, like blind Pugh, towards toilets at the bottom of a stone staircase.

The two cubicles were directly opposite. The urinals were tucked around the left corner, in case masculine appendages should be spied, by users of periscopes, from the top of the staircase. The sinks were around to the right, in case hands should expose themselves in a similar fashion.

Jude felt vulnerable for two reasons. Both irrelevant in this emergency.

First, the doors of the cubicles were absurdly tiny. They stopped at least a foot from the floor. His ankles were on parade in crinkled, apparently outsize trousers. There was also a two-inch gap between the door and its frame on both sides. He was nervous about what could be seen through those gaps. He had never tested the possibilities when other users occupied the toilets (on account of what the Bible called 'fellow feeling' for your brother's plight). A tea-cloth would quite possibly have offered him greater dignity.

Second, the top of his bowed head was clearly visible to anyone descending the stairs.

Fortunately, his ordeal was solved with one long amplified wet fart – boil-in-the-bag chicken marsala. Fortunately, too, Jude was one of those extraordinary creatures who, defecating (diarrhoea notwithstanding), wipe, leaving no trace whatever on the paper. Jude knew he did not need to wipe. But he did it for the sheer joy of knowing that he did not need to.

'You cunning bastard,' he whispered to himself, making brief eye contact with Peter who had begun to descend the stairs.

Back in the church, Jude noticed another extraordinary thing. People seemed excited by the prospect of his speech. They pricked up as the title was announced and tensed as he took to the stage. It had not been easy to write. Writer's block? Jude had shopping-list block. Thank-you-card block. However, speeches were not an opportunity for showing creative flair. They were like copying someone else's To-Do list, with a couple of minor changes. *Book hairdresser Wednesday*, instead of Thursday, maybe. Jude stuck closely to the words of William P. Pope.

'This talk will answer three questions. First,' Jude raised an index finger. He carefully avoided all male eyes. Then he thought the offender could easily be a woman. He began to avoid all eyes. He looked instead at his finger. 'First,' he repeated, 'why is masturbation a sin? Second, how can this sin lead to other sins? Third, what practical steps can we take to avoid this sin in the first place?

'People of The World,' Jude pronounced, 'do not generally regard masturbation as a sin. Experts say it is "a common hobby" among young people. But Pope has a powerful counter-argument. He says that the common flea is also "common". Does that make it desirable? No. Does anyone want fleas? No. Likewise with masturbation. Just because it is common, it doesn't mean that it's a good idea.

'Experts also say – and I quote – that "*occasional* mastur-bation will not seriously damage your health or others around you". But how reliable are these experts? At one time, they said masturbation would make you go blind. It would make you barren. It would make you depressed and introverted. They called it "self-abuse". Now they have changed their minds. They may change their minds again. By contrast, what *never, ever* changes? The word of God. The Bible never changes. It always says the same thing. So we can rely on what the Bible says.

'What, then, does the Bible say about masturbation?'

Jude paused.

'The Bible does not say anything about the practice of masturbation. You will not even find the word "masturbation" in the index. Does that mean, then, that it has nothing to say on the subject? On the contrary, I would like everyone to turn to Exodus chapter 20 verse 15.'

Bibles were opened and pages were duly turned.

Jude read, 'Thou shalt not perjure thyself.'

He began his exposition. 'This verse throws a great deal of light on God's feelings about masturbation. William P. Pope explains that the masturbator is, in effect, a perjurer. Pretending piety and truth before the court of mankind, he sins in secret. He denies his deeds. He disguises his deeds. That is wrong. Note how the verse says – perjure *thyself*. Moses is referring to something one does to oneself. Perjury was a stoning offence in the Old Testament. Today, in countries like Sri Lanka, perjurers have their tongues cut out. That shows how serious the offence of masturbation really is.'

Jude paused again. He noticed that some of his listeners appeared to be enjoying this arousal of communal shame. It was spanking for Christians. They looked at each other slyly for reactions and blushed.

'Some,' Jude continued, 'have deceived themselves with contrary reasonings. They have thought that masturbation is a way to avoid worse sins, like fornication. We now turn to our second question. How does the sin of masturbation lead to these other sins?'

Masturbation led to sin, Jude explained, by making you think about sex. (Jude felt privately that William P. Pope was under-representing the short-term benefits of the sin. When you had masturbated recently, you did not think about sex in the least. This was why people did it before they went on first dates. It put sex clean out of their mind. Then they were all conversational and virtuous.)

'Why does the masturbator think about sex?' Jude asked. 'William P. Pope explains it is because he – or she – is lonely. The masturbator engages in "forlorn sex acts". Whereas sex requires two people. It is less forlorn. The loneliness of masturbation may lead, however, to other sins, like suicide. The masturbator may feel so forlorn, so depressed, that he kills himself. And that is a grave sin. Again the Bible does not say anything about the practice of suicide. Again the word does not appear in the 1962 index. But, if you still have your Bibles open at Exodus, you will see that in verse 13 God also forbids murder. Murdering yourself is a form of murder. This is how serious masturbation really is.

'In fact masturbation leads only to frustration and misery. "It is an appetiser for a banquet that will never appear, a hunger that can be sated only by wedlock." Hence William P. Pope asks us, "Do we really want the happiness of our lives to be continually unsettled by sexual yearnings? None of us wants to be so unhappy, do we? Sexual feelings make unmarried people unhappy. So would it not be better to learn to suppress those feelings . . . *altogether*?"

'And yet,' Jude continued, 'masturbation also causes grave unhappiness in marriage. The unhappiness comes because pre-marital masturbators have learned only how to satisfy themselves. They do not think about how to please their spouses. They have forgotten the manifold responsibilities of marriage.'

(Which were?

Wearing a wedding band, eating breakfast in bed for two, remembering your anniversary with a card.)

'Unhappiness in marriage is not a sin in itself, but it could easily lead to sin. Like adultery. Like suicide. Like homosexuality. In fact, Pope entitles his chapter on this subject, "Masturbation and the Homosexual". The yoking of these words tells us a great deal. A lonely boy will seek out other lonely boys. A lonely girl will seek out other lonely girls.

'How, then, can we avoid this trap?

'William P. Pope has many suggestions of a practical nature. Do the shopping, he says. Hang out the laundry. In the day, try not to be on your own too much. At night, ask a mature Christian friend or relative to share your bedroom.'

The idea, Jude explained, was that the masturbator would feel too embarrassed to sin around Ma, or Deacon Pete. Rigorous genital hygiene was also recommended. Grot rot could get you thinking about touching yourself.

'I will quote William P. Pope directly on this point,' Jude said. 'He says, "Some may reason that washing their genitals is a provocation to sin. Yet as long as one's intentions are honourable – washing to prevent the itching that can lead to arousal and sin – then one need not feel guilty or anxious about taking these necessary hygiene measures."'

Jude bolted his closing lines. He was thinking of soap – the glib harlot of the bathroom.

'The effort is all worth it. It is a misery to be enslaved to your body. It is a joy to please God.'

He got down from the stage and looked at the carpet as though following the emergency lighting on an aeroplane.

His speech was followed by a dialogue between Maria and her friend, his ex, the Italian. As the pastor called them to the stage, Jude watched Maria's pert skirted bottom appear over the top of her seat rest. Isabella converged from the right, and four legs went pleasantly down the aisle. The women took seats at a table. Female Saints could not stand up and address the church directly from the podium because they were female. So they scripted an awkward conversation, a friendly biblical chat, around their given theme. These themes could be uninvolving.

'A friend of mine thinks he might be predestined. How can I explain to him that he isn't?'

Or.

'Listen, I'm awfully worried about polygamy. What should I do?'

Or, in this case, the sin of Ancestor Worship.

The Italian started the conversation. Nervousness made her breathless. She spoke rapidly and, Jude recognised, with a more lilting Italian sound that she would normally allow herself.

'O Maria, I must a-speak-a with you. I have been a-feeling like a-worshipping my dead ancestors lately. Any advice?'

'Oh, jes, sure. We look in the Bible together for three scriptures and then joo will see why God He is so unhappy if joo worship joor ancestors. H'okay?'

Halfway through the dialogue, the Italian forgot one of her cues. Maria started laughing.

'I think joo want to ask me something,' Maria extemporised. 'I know it is the very bad sin to read the other people's minds, jes, but I think what joo want to ask me is this – "Can the dead people get angry with us, or no?" And I tell joo, no. No, they cannot. Because – they are dead. It make sense, jes? So we don't have to give them the worship. H'okay?'

Two minutes later the two women descended. Jude kept his eyes on his feet, in case Isabella should think he was looking at her. People always thought he was looking at her. They didn't get it. Isabella bowed her head anyway, and her smooth bob fell about her face. Maria, chin up, walked past her row, past Jude, and straight out the back. Jude felt the air move. He heard the door close behind her. He realised he was waiting for her return. He heard nothing of the next speech. Then – there she was.

For the next forty-five minutes he studied her. He saw each tiny shift of her weight. The way her right arm moved slightly forward as she draped a scarf, for modesty's sake, over knees that were exposed by her short skirt. How her bra showed through her blouse, at the back, and how the blouse tightened around her body when she leant forward to get a book from her bag. The pedalling of her foot as she rocked on a heel. She turned, smiling, to Isabella, and he enjoyed her profile. He thought he would like to photograph her. She held Peter's hand during the last prayer. First tightly. Then it lapsed. Then tightly again. The service ended. Jude considered trying to speak to her. But she was inaccessible between his ex and her husband. He left promptly.

Fifteen minutes later, he lay on his bed and opened his fly. He had been definitively circumcised. Not a shred of foreskin remained. He teased a wrist over the head. The skin of his inner arm was soft, like a woman's. Then he turned over. He pushed into the mattress and pretended he was making love. Jude had never made love, fornication being one of the Church's top bans, and could only imagine that it would be like wearing rather tighter underpants than usual – and that somewhere, in that sartorial novelty, lay bliss unimagined. Raising himself on to his knees, he did not feel in the least lonely or suicidal or homosexual or doomed to failure as a husband. All the good advice of William P. Pope served only one purpose now. Jude knew he should not be doing this, and knowing that made him want to do it more. Ah.

Chapter Seventeen

William's car approached the kerb.

'Get in the back, will yer love?' he instructed Alice. 'It'll give her the confidence, if she's in the front.'

Alice demoted herself obediently. Jill walked briskly down the path in a black flared trouser suit. She kissed William as she got into the car and turned round, beaming nervously at Alice. Alice realised the only thing she really liked about Jill was that Jill was more obviously nervous than she was. This made her feel better.

Jill grasped William by the arm as they walked to the restaurant. She was tiny and round. Alice assumed short people could conceal their weaknesses more easily. They had less body to hide. They needn't stoop in embarrassment. They needn't drag their feet on the ground in the hope of getting that bit shorter.

The restaurateur, Ahmed Mahfooz, showed them to 'Mr West's' usual table, where he intoned his compliments with a mouthful of gold teeth. '*Hello, my two loverly ladies, loverly ladies . . . oh ye-es, ye-es, my two loverly ladies you are.*' Mahfooz's plain song, its uncertain melody, embarrassed them but not him. Sometimes Alice saw him buying twenty little gem lettuces in Waitrose, and feared he might start up a musical compliment there. To bulk-buy in Waitrose seemed to her the beginnings of a mental decline. Didn't he have a cash and carry facility?

Mahfooz stopped singing abruptly. 'And now, what can I get for you?'

William took charge of the ordering.

'She'd like some wine,' he told Mahfooz, indicating Jill. 'Some Chardonnay. This one.' He pointed to an entry on the drinks menu. 'Let's have a glass. If she likes it, we'll have the bottle.'

Mahfooz came back promptly with the wine. Jill took a sip. William took the glass from her and sipped.

'She likes it,' he said. 'Don't you?'

Jill reddened, nodded quickly. Alice watched.

'So what do yus fancy?' he asked. 'I thought we'd do what we did last time. Share the Mahfooz Special – it's a bit of everything, yer know, but it's too much for one.'

Jill swallowed. She seemed to be preparing herself for some very bold proposition. 'I was thinking,' she said quietly, 'of the vegetable korma. With plain rice.'

'Were yer? The *vegitibble* kurma? With the plain rice?' William repeated it loudly and incredulously. Jill shrank. 'Well, if it's what yer fancy . . .' he continued, doubtfully. 'But what yer want to be havan is the Mahfooz Special.'

Alice intervened. Her father seemed unaware of Jill's discomfort and pleased by the brilliance of his plan. Alice liked her power to alter the course of events. 'How about *we* share the Mahfooz Special,' she suggested, looking at her father, 'and Jill has the korma? Then everyone's happy.'

'Right, then,' William agreed.

The food arrived twenty minutes later. Jill made two trips to the toilet. Alice made one. This was what Alice liked about Jill. Alice's bladder was weaker than most people's – nervously uncertain of itself, like Alice. But Jill's bladder was weaker still. Statistically, Jill's trips made Alice's look negligible, normal even. Frequent toilet trips made people suspect you had a period. Alice covered for this by leaving her handbag very deliberately on the tabletop. This said, 'I'm not putting a tampon in, you know.' Sometimes she would even hand her purse to someone for safekeeping. This said, 'I won't be using one of those twenty-pence tampon/towel dispensing machines in the toilet, you know.' But now she did not need a handbag or a purse to hand across. She had a Jill.

Alice and William halved a banquet: four curries set like jewels in 'silver-service' oval dishes, a clutch of onion bhaji, a concertina of poppadom, and a granary of vegetable fried rice. Jill was just back from her second visit.

'How's yours, love?' William could not resist asking. He turned to Alice and confided, 'Vegitibble kurma: puke on a bed a rice.' And this rice was waterlogged. 'Fuckan rice field, that.' He turned to Jill. 'Shall we send it back?'

'It's fine,' Jill insisted.

When they left the restaurant, William tipped Mahfooz a furled tenner, and winked melodramatically. There were harnessed, tasselled, burly morris dancers in the street. William hooked each of the women with an arm, and began to mimic the men. He kicked up his legs and hopped about. Everyone laughed, even the dancers. Jill seemed much happier. They watched the dancers for a while, then went for a cider in the pub next door.

'Time is moving on.' William hauled a gold pocket watch on a chain out of his trousers like a convict.

They dropped Jill back. Jill kissed Alice goodbye, said she hoped to see her again very soon, and walked to the gate with William. William told Jill that Alice would love to be invited in for coffee.

'Doesn't think yer'd invite her, see. She'd be thrilled to bits if yer did.'

'Oh, well then,' Jill replied, hesitantly, 'I'd love to.'

Alice saw them looking back at the car. She waved to Jill as her father approached. He opened the back door and whispered to Alice that Jill would love to invite her in for coffee.

'Doesn't think yer'd come into her house, see. She'd be thrilled to bits if yer did.'

'Well . . .'

'Go on. It'd be a kindness.'

'Coffee?' Jill asked Alice, indoors.

'Actually I can't drink coffee,' Alice replied. 'Have you got any herbal tea? Or water? Water would be fine.'

'I'll have a look.'

In Jill's living room, Alice glanced around. It made a statement. Its micro-mood was classic vanilla elegance.

She settled back on a furry cushion.

She leaned forward to inspect the shelves. With a shock, she saw her father in every photograph. William and Jill, faces squashed together like two tomatoes. William and Jill and what seemed to be Jill's teenage daughter, in a silver frame. An oval terracotta mould bearing the names, WILLY AND JILLY, on the mantelpiece.

'Well,' her father said, coming back into the room, 'whaddyer think?'

'Very nice,' Alice managed.

Her father began to whisper. 'Rebecca – she's Jill's daughter, right – she's upstairs. But she's too shy to come down. Will yer go and talk to her? She's only a young one. Yer the older one. It's you who's got to do it.'

'No thanks.'

'Al-ice,' her father said warningly. 'Go on now. It's only right. I told Jill you would.'

So now Jill was expecting it. Alice sighed loudly. This was where politeness got you.

'And how old is she?'

'Twelve.'

'She looked older in the picture.'

'She might be thirteen.'

Alice stood up.

'Second door on the right,' William called after her.

Alice tapped on the fifteen-year-old's door. There was no reply. Maybe she hadn't heard. Maybe she didn't want to answer. She decided to knock again and go in.

'Hi. I'm Alice.'

'Hi. I'm Rebecca,' the girl parroted sarcastically and went back to applying her mascara, Pink Glamour lips parted with concentration.

'Oh, right. Er . . .' Alice looked about her desperately. Her eye caught the cover of a U2 album. *Achtung Baby*.

'Brilliant album,' she said.

'That's what my boyfriend said,' the girl replied, 'before I dumped him.' Alice noticed how *dumped* took on a special onomatopoeic quality in Rebecca's mouth.

'I see.'

'He was useless in bed.' She paused and studied the effect of the mascara. 'Bit like your father. My mum says he hadn't a clue till he met her. My mum says your mum should be shot. You got a boyfriend?' she asked abruptly. 'I know,' she pronounced, 'all about it. Not allowed one, are you? My mum said your dad said you don't have boyfriends. He said you're one of those weirdos that knock on people's doors instead, selling them Bibles.'

'We don't sell them. We give them away.'

'That's a bit stupid, innit?'

'People can give contributions if they like.'

'And do they?'

'Not very often.'

'There you go then,' Rebecca replied triumphantly. 'As I said: *stupid.*'

Alice decided to go back downstairs. Rebecca followed. William began to extol the virtues of virginity to Rebecca, using Alice as an example. He'd done this sort of thing before. Jill giggled with embarrassment. Rebecca was apparently trying to hypnotise the cornice. Alice nursed a huge mug of boiling peppermint tea, which would take time to cool. It would take more time to drink it. There was no quick exit. Jill, whom Alice had rescued over dinner, recognised no obligation to reciprocate. Alice found, however, that she was neither embarrassed nor panicky. She felt detached. Her situation was now so bad she was interested only in how much worse it could get. She blew on the tea. She relaxed into the sofa as she heard that she was so entirely devoted to her studies and to God there was no room for boys 'or any of that nonsense'.

Chapter Eighteen

At 9 a.m. on Saturday morning, Alice breakfasted with her parents and then William drove them promptly to the Oxford branch of the Worldwide Saints of God. A deacon with more broken veins than a blood orange, flustered by his own importance, greeted them. They were ushered through the first set of double doors, with reinforced glass panels like graph paper. Alice and Oonagh turned immediately right into the ladies' room. Oonagh smiled admiringly at herself in the mirror, smoothing her stomach, while Alice felt her heart gain pounds.

'Don't you ever,' Alice suggested, 'want to start again? With Dad, I mean. You know, just put the past behind you and make the marriage happy? You could be nicer to him. He could be nicer to you.'

'You've no idea what you're talking about, Alice.'

'But surely, *surely*, it's quite simple? It's just a case of deciding –'

'Alice, you don't know what your father's really like. Your father,' she declared, 'hasn't got the capacity to care about anyone except himself.' Oonagh was fond of talking about 'the capacity'. In her mind it had assumed the status of a technical term in a divorce handbook. 'Take it from me. This man, do you know what he did to me?'

Alice shook her head.

'He brought people into my living room and right as I was standing there, he told them they could rent it as of next month. *My* house.'

'I know, he told me he might have to. But that doesn't mean he doesn't care. I know he cares about me.'

'You think he does.'

Alice was irritated. 'I'm not having that. Of course he does.'

'Well,' Oonagh smiled patronisingly, 'you can believe what you like.'

'Like you do?' Wounded, Alice wanted to wound. All her resolutions of discretion on the subject of Jill were briefly forgotten. 'Where do you suppose he is when he's not at home? Where'd he say he was last night?'

'With you. Like – the Friday before.'

Oonagh sounded less sure of herself. She hunted Alice's eyes. Alice retreated. It wasn't right to tell her, certainly not like this. 'Things improved between you and Peter yet?' Alice volunteered instead.

'No. Why should *they* win? Oh, no.' Oonagh turned back to the mirror, practising imaginary confrontations. 'They've got another thing coming if they think I'm going to give in. I'm going to give as good as I get, so I am. Oh, yes, they'd better watch it.'

'Don't you think this is all – a bit – destructive? Dad, and now them too?'

Oonagh's voice turned bitter. 'Youse are all the same. Youse blame me. Youse are just like your father.'

Alice braced herself. 'Youse', for the second-person plural, was a very bad sign indeed. Sounding hints of 'useless' and 'louse', it was Oonagh's launch pad for ultimatums.

'I'm telling youse now, I'm not going to try and please *any* of youse any more.'

Alice sighed. 'Fine.'

She waited for her mother in the hallway. The Oxford branch of the Worldwide Saints was another office suite, though pink instead of brown like the one at home. The air conditioning was supposed to maintain a permanent spring. This spring was early, more March than June, mighty frosty. Prepared, Alice wore a long black coat with a thick brown fur collar and cuffs. Buttoned down the bodice, it swirled outward like a pastor's cassock as she walked. She had on a pair of long black suede boots as well. Her father was equally formal, in a navy three-piece suit and dark cashmere coat. He stood about like a funeral director – it was the gloves – and reiterated his belief in the superiority of the boyfriendless girl. If the kissing with Jude had not happened, Alice considered, then she might have conceded her father's point. But it had. So what was she to do?

Tucking each of her hands into the opposite coat sleeve, she was reminded of bisexual mating worms.

'Spring again!' She turned, with mock-incredulity, to her father. 'How lovely.'

'Lord God Almighty! But it puts the spring in yer step: too fuckan cold to stand still,' her father replied.

They giggled and, as Oonagh joined them, went through the second set of double doors, taking seats in the back row against an internal wall with a large window. The library was inside. Like the mirror window of a police interview cell, you could not be sure who was in the library, watching. Seconds later, the door twitched open again. It was the deacon.

'Can't sit there,' he said, although they had done so on every other occasion. 'New arrangements. That's for the Penitent Disciplined.'

'The disabled?' queried William, who'd heard right the first time. 'Oh, well, if it's for *the disabled* I've no objection to moving.'

'The Disciplined, I say.'

About a hundred Saints in Britain were Disciplined every year. Mostly they made their way out of the Church through the perils of sexual intercourse. This case, though, was different. The deacon explained, in a proud whisper, the ins and outs of the decision the pastor had reached about the Disciplined parishioner. She had left in 1989, when a major split in the Church occurred.

'Yes, we know all about that,' Oonagh interrupted briskly.

Oonagh did not want the deacon telling her husband, a non-believer, what had happened in 1989, when William P. Pope's son proved not so apostolic as his father. Pope Junior was found in bed with a masseuse. Expelled from the Church, he promptly set up his own. Disillusioned with Pope Junior's Church, however, the parishioner had now decided to return. But the pastor was taking a hard line. Any prodigals would be treated as penitent fornicators and adulterers: they would have to *sit in the back row*, apart from the rest of the flock, without speaking to or being spoken to by anyone. They would have to show they were really sorry about things till the next Festival at least. Then he'd see.

They moved to the last row of the main flank of seats. The deacon waited until they had settled themselves. 'Can't sit there either,' he said, placing his hand on William's shoulder as though he might arrest him.

'Why not?' William replied. 'You can't have *that* many

Disciplined people, can you? What sort of a church is this I'm sending my daughter to?'

Alice stood up, angry too, but because the deacon made her panic. She pulled him aside. She worried that she was not going to manage to say what she needed to. There was nothing for it but to try.

'Look, with all due respect, you know my father isn't a believer. He brings me sometimes because –'

William brought her, not because he had the remotest idea of living forever or dominating the universe, but because he believed the church was the safest place for his daughter to be. Not much premarital sex in the church, he had heard.

'Because,' she continued, 'I think he may convert, given time. We need to encourage him. So can you just – just – you know, cut us a bit of slack here?'

'Sorry, but that row's for latecomers now. So we don't have to disturb people when the service's started. You'll have to move.'

Alice fumed. She went back reluctantly with the news. 'He says it's for latecomers.'

'Well, they shouldn't be late, then.' William winked. 'That's not very spiritual, being late for the Lord, is it? *Bloody latecomers.* Sorry, dear Lord.' He swooped his eyes briefly to the ceiling. 'For the French!'

'I'm so sorry about him,' Oonagh whispered to the deacon. 'People of The World, they just don't know how to behave.'

They cast about for other unobtrusive seats. People were arriving fast. They all sat waiting for the first hymn and the Disciplined sinner. The opening chords struck on the piano and the deacon swept past, spanking and wiggling his tambourine. People were still coming in. Far more were late than penitent, that was sure. The new seating arrangement was statistically unjust. Even the Penitent Disciplined woman was late. She sidled in at the close of the first prayer. Alice caught her eye and smiled.

'You talked to her?' Alice asked her father approvingly, afterwards. 'You're the only person who can, you know. What did you say?'

'Just the usual. I told her she was a really lovely lady and that her husband, if she had a husband, was a fuckan lucky man.'

'That was nice of you.'

'Well, the women expect it from me, don't they? And *you* smiled at her. I saw yer.'

'Oh,' Alice laughed, 'I suspect that's only because the deacon would prefer me not to.'

Chapter Nineteen

Five hours later, William stood with his back to the tilting cloakroom mirror. He held another small, vanity mirror with a purple handle to his right temple and squinted at the reflection of his bald patch. Taking a metal comb from his pocket, he began to tidy up.

'Vurility,' he said to himself. 'That's what it is. I'd never have credited it, but it's a man without hair that the young women be wanting. Specially a wee fat one like messef. Sure it's a by-logical fact,' he added confidently. 'The Darwin fella. The young ones know he can look after them if he's always been able to stuff his own face.'

William put mirror and comb down on the tiled window-sill with a clatter, and snapped off the light.

'And where do you think you're going this time?' Oonagh trapped him in the hallway in a narrow strait of brown cardboard boxes, which read *This Way Up* ↑ and *Moving House? Better Do It With Us.*

'Out.'

'Out with who?'

William exhaled impatiently. 'Peter and Maria, right.'

'I don't believe you.'

William lifted up his mobile telephone. 'Well, fuckan phone them, right, and find out. Go on.'

'You think I wouldn't phone them? You think,' Oonagh was getting hysterical, 'you can use this as a cover? You think I'm that *stupid*?'

She twisted the telephone out of William's hand. It might as well have been a powder compact she was dialling because William had locked the keypad. She thought she didn't know how to use it. With a shriek of annoyance, she threw it to the floor. William was now enraged himself.

'You silly little bitch. Could've broken on the parquet.'

Oonagh ran to the telephone in the living room. William tried to wrest the handset from her. 'No, no,' she shouted. 'I'm going to do this.'

'I'm just trying to save yer,' he cried, 'from yussef.'

'Peter,' she said when he picked up. 'It's your mother. I want to know. Are you going out with your father this evening?'

Peter hesitated. 'I don't know what this is about. I'm not getting involved. Goodbye.'

'No, no.' She sounded alarmed. Peter relented.

'It's a simple enough question. Are you, or aren't you?'

'We are.'

'That was all you had to say, then,' she said stiffly.

'Knows about Jill, does she?' Peter asked William when they met later that evening. William waved the question off irritably.

'I told yer. There isn't anything *to* know about Jill. Anyway.' William wanted to know if Peter had 'sorted' Maria out yet with a pregnancy.

'Well, it's not that easy.'

'Course it's that fuckan easy. Yer just –'

Peter peered ironically over his glasses.

'I think he *know* what to do,' Maria interjected. 'I think that is not rilly the problem here.'

'So yer know what to do – good. It's a good beginning. But I was never too sure about yer, lad. Yer were always a late developer. Yer didn't read till yer was nine years of age and still didn't wipe yer arse properly when yer was all of sixteen. I remember Mother showing me the pants –'

'We need – money. Quite a lot,' Maria interrupted again.

Peter scowled. 'Maria . . . we discussed this.'

'No, joo tell me what joo think. Joo always do. Now, I tell him what I think.'

'Money? Is that all?' William replied with a lightness he did not feel. 'No bother, love. I'll get yer money. How much jer need?' He slid slowly down the pub pew as if it were a Stanner stair-lift. 'I'll give yus money,' he repeated. Getting married was the first adult thing his son had ever done, and he would do everything he could to support it.

'Thanks, Dad. But – we couldn't take it anyway,' Peter objected.

'Why ever not? I don't remember yer saying that when I paid off the Barclaycard. And that was near on a grand.'

'It's not the money. It's what she wants it for.'

William waited. Peter gestured his eyes upward. William asked if there was something wrong with them. Peter stood and the two of them walked to the bar.

'You know how, in the Plain Truth, we've never accepted medical treatment?'

'Sure that's a lot of fuckan nonsense. Sure I've spent years telling yer mother –'

'Well, now we can.'

'Oh.' William stopped short. 'They're improvan up that church, then. And not before time.'

'Anyway, what matters is . . .' He plunged his voice down like a brimming bucket. 'Maria thinks I might be *a Jaffa*.'

'A what? What's a jaffer? Excuse me, young man,' William addressed the bartender, 'you got any idea what a jaffer is?'

'Innit – seedless?'

Peter's head bobbed agreement. 'Firing blanks. Can't get the lads to swim.'

'Are yer, son?' William softened at this admission of infertility.

'Well, that's the thing. Personally, I don't think I've got much of a problem, right? I think it'll just take a bit of time. But you know what Maria's like – wants everything yesterday. And even if we did have a problem, we wouldn't have the treatment. There's something about this particular procedure that isn't right.'

Peter had taken the pastor's advice on fertility treatment. Now that medical treatment was permissible, Maria rejoiced and bought Anusol and Canesten in quantities. A difficulty still remained – the prohibition on masturbation. A married Saint could not spill his seed into anything but his wife directly. William P. Pope, the pastor reminded Peter, had ruled there could be no exceptions. Not even spilling your sperm into a plastic cup in a hospital room for the purposes of fertilisation. One should not forget how often in scripture barrenness was a sign of God's disfavour. Fertility was a blessing, and if the Lord had not chosen to bless Peter and Maria in this way, then sin was not the way to achieve it.

'We've got to try to do what's right, you see,' Peter continued, 'even if we don't always understand the reasons why.'

'*Right*? Are you some kind of a fuckan halfwit? Did I bring yer up to talk about what's right? I'll tell yer what's right.'

William, after two hours of sermonising earlier in the day, felt impatient and angry.

'Don't tell me, for Christ's sake, yer still on that one. Don't talk to me about what's right and what can't happen when yer not even willing to take what's available. When the Lord God put us on His earth, what did He tell Adam? He told him: *Be fruitful and make do.*'

'Please don't turn this,' Peter replied with gentle disgust, 'into another attack on the Plain Truth.'

William took advice slowly. 'You know the real reason why this religion is so half-witted? It's so half-witted because it's American. There's this new technology coming out, right. DVD. It's like a disease, right. You hear about it?'

'No.'

'Well, it's going to do to videos what CDs did to cassettes. Yer man was telling me about it in the caff, then I read it in the paper. You know how many frames per second they're gonta have on the American DVDs?'

'No.'

'Twenty-four.'

'You know how many they're gonta have on the British ones?'

'No. Twenty?'

'Not very bleedan patriotic, are yer? How would it be *less* than the Americans? It's twenty-five. Now what does that tell yer? Americans, they're slower. They believe all this type a nonsense. They can't read between the lines. But you ought to know better. Cop yussef on, lad. I'm warning yer now. Don't be a fool. Yer could lose yer wife over this, and where would you be then? Look at it this way, lad.' Again William searched out a biblical parallel. 'Where would Adam have been without Eve?'

'Far further forward,' Peter replied shortly.

'Lad, I'm telling yer. Be warned.' As he saw Maria approaching the bar, William paused emphatically and turned the conversation. 'Anyway . . . there was something I wanted to ask. Yer man Jude, with the mad dad. Whaddyer know about him? Turns out I was right. As I've always suspected, the dirty wee bugger's in love with Alice.'

'Oh? Well . . . he's not very spiritual. But he's not bad.'

'Why not very spiritual?' William asked with alarm. 'Not very spiritual' meant, so far as he could gather, very sexual.

'He just isn't. First there was all that stuff with him and Maria's friend.'

'What stuff?'

'Well, I can't go into details . . . He gave quite a good speech, though, last Friday.'

'Speech? What could *he* give a speech about?'

Peter repeated the title. William blinked.

'*Wanking?* Speech in the church? What goes *on* in these services? Yer know, when I was a boy, and they had one of those readings in our church from Leviticus, one of them rude porny bits like – *if a man hath an emission of fluid from his member* – I used to make *money* on it,' he exaggerated. 'I could take paying Cathlick guests in. But I have to hand it to yer. Yer *filthy*, you lot.'

'And ever notice what he does when he sits down?' Peter was beginning to enjoy himself.

When Jude sat down, the zip in his trousers created a suspicious rise. Sometimes eyes would fall on the rise. Jude would hold the eye of the enquirer, smack his hand down on the zip, and say, 'Nothing doing.'

'Yer've a point there,' William agreed.

'Joo canno condemn a man,' Maria objected, 'for bad taste in the trousers. I think – he try very hard lately. I think – leave him alone.'

'So anyways,' she coaxed Peter in the car on the way home, 'joo didn't tell me who is the Special Speech for? Who has been playing with his chorizo do joo think?'

'I don't know. The pastor didn't tell me. You know I couldn't tell you anyway. But I think . . . it was sort of meant for you, *chiquito*.'

'For *me*?' Maria replied indignantly. 'I have never bin doing this disgusting seen. Who say I have? *Joo*?'

'No, but you wanted me to. And you know I can't.'

It was the sin that led to sin.

'Led how, eh?' Maria sneered amiably. 'Joo make the sperm in the plastic cup and then what? It lead how? Joo want to make love with the cups instead of joor wife? Joo get so lonely with the cups in the hospital joo want to kill joorself? I think – *no*.' She could not help laughing.

'I think no too, in a way, but we've still got to do what's right. Yeah?'

'Eh – no.'

Peter fed a Sting CD to the car player. Sting sang that he was a passenger on Noah's ark. His girlfriend was getting fed up. They'd been on the boat, mucking in with the pigs and the elephants, for far, far too long. Surely they could get off by now? Surely the waters had receded enough by now? Sting reminded her they were sailing with the Lord. And you couldn't do better than that.

'*Cos we're sailing*,' Peter strummed the steering wheel happily, '*With the Lord!*'

Chapter Twenty

When Jude next arrived in Oxford, Alice decided to implement what her father had said about boyfriends. She put a plan of friendship to him – even though it meant (sadly) there would be no more kissing for a long time. The rule was you didn't kiss people without formal declarations of courtship leading to honourable Christian marriage. And Alice wasn't in a position to accept such an offer. All this was implied as Alice sat on the thin peach carpet explaining. But Jude did not think along these lines. He was willing to kiss and take his chances. Not that he actually said so. He said nothing.

He held out his hand. A sky-blue MGM postcard of Roadrunner lay on the floor. Stupidly, she imagined this was what he wanted and tried to pass it. He refused to take it.

And continued to look at her steadily.

Alice pinked. She gave him her hand. He drew her towards him. She hid her face on his shoulder and discovered his silk shirt was very nice to put her cheek against.

It was Sunday afternoon and they went for a walk. Along the river they paced themselves by a swan with the wind caught in his feathers, who sailed the small vessel of himself. In the college meadow they lay on the grass and held hands, gradually surrounded by cows with tagged ears and glazed muzzles. Jude gazed up, Alice at him. Jude the Cyclops in his baseball cap.

After the eye, the incised lips. Alice's major preoccupation was whether any kissing was ever going to happen again. Could friends kiss, perhaps, after all? Not being the kisser herself, it was all rather dependent on Jude.

She was farting like popcorn. Another preoccupation was her period. It had started that morning. She feared a leak through the back of her knickers on to her jeans, leaving a stain that would be visible as they walked back. The makers of sanitary towels couldn't cope with gravity. Even a super-towel could only cater for things if you were strictly upright. Lying there, her body was in the night-time position without night-time sanitary protection. How could she know she was going to lie down? She could feel something moist in the crack of her buttocks. It might be sweat – sanitary towels were made of special sweat-inducing fibres. Or it might not be. Advertisements for nappies and sanitary towels showed a small glass of water poured on to 'a lockable core'. But the challenge wasn't the absorption of the liquid. It was making sure the liquid was poured somewhere near the lockable core in the first place. She decided to take an optimistic view of gravity and looked up at the sky with Jude.

She said, 'We're not going to heaven.'

'No.'

'You know what John Donne says about getting to heaven?'

'The DJ?'

'The poet.'

'No.'

'Even the angels, who have wings, use a ladder. So it can't be easy.'

She began telling him about Jeremy Adams. At the age of twelve – the age Jesus was when he back-chatted the rabbis in the temple – Adams predicted The End of the World for November 1902. He would be sixty-two then. However, he did not expect, personally, to die. Adams was convinced that one November day, he would rise slowly heavenward in his black crêpe frock coat, while the flames of Armageddon warmed his cold, white, aspiring feet.

Alice wondered how people really felt about ascension. Imagine thinking that you might be caught up to heaven at any moment. Every time Adams stood up that November – especially during the first week – were his ankles tingling? What about his disciples, who also woke expecting to levitate? Perhaps it would happen as they sat on the edge of the bed, feet feeling for their worn slippers. Or while they were brushing their teeth with salt. Still in pyjamas and nightgowns. As they pulled a nightgown over their head. Sewing a button on a shirt, snapping the thread with their teeth. Were there believers who secretly feared heights? Believers who bought heftier boots, so that they would not rise too fast? Were others confident of ascension at the communal breakfast, brother linking hand with sister and floating (in defiance of the ceiling) in a great circle to God? A slow, stately ascent, holding your skirts down, as your hair spread in a wide nimbus around your head.

Then it didn't happen.

Because it isn't easy, getting to heaven. Especially when you're still alive.

'No,' Jude agreed. 'Gods and goddesses of the earth, that's us.'

He was being ironic, Alice assumed. Obviously. And that was entirely compatible with faith. In social situations, sometimes members of the Church made light of what they really believed. She didn't dare ask what he really thought. She didn't dare say what she really thought herself. Doubts could not be voiced. She might discuss things with her mother, but she could not question fundamentals like the existence of God or the absolute truth of the Bible. Everyone's beliefs had to be identical, as though the brain was an identical packed lunch box – filled with regulation items.

'Did you ever read *Women in Love*?' she asked, as they lay there. She was thinking of Birkin naked on the heath.

'No – but I saw the film. I remember two men wrestling naked by a fire.'

They started to laugh and turned their heads towards each other. Then the kissing did happen, and all things returned to the happy state of the week before.

They went back to Alice's room after dinner. There was more admiration of the ceiling and the windows and the seats and the mantelpiece. Alice was glad about this, because her shyness made it hard to look Jude in the face for very long. He got around this problem intuitively, by standing behind her. He began stroking her back. His hand skied cautiously down, in long diagonals that were practically horizontal. Eventually he made it to the edge of her jeans, then took a sudden dip inside them. The propriety of this worried Alice. She reassured herself that it was hard to say where a back ended and a buttock began.

It could be said that Jude was stroking her back.

That did not seem excessively fornicatory.

Then he murmured, 'You are so beautiful.' Which immediately raised suspicions. Her father had always told her to watch out for obvious lies like that. Next Jude felt something plastic in the back of her knickers. He tugged it playfully.

'Is that what I think it is?'

'Yes.'

Alice was surprised not to feel embarrassed. But Jude's straightforwardness liberated her. Discussing sanitary towels was in the nature of a lusty conversation for him.

'So what's the difference – I mean, how do you decide whether to wear Tampax or, what are these things called again?'

'I used to use tampons. But then – I stopped.'

'Why?'

'Oh, I don't know. I just – did.'

Alice's menstrual career had been a bleeding disaster. The stories were legend. Aged ten, she stood on a wooden stool to reach a book on a high shelf. She slipped and landed in the splits. The stool broke and some of the splinters cut into her labia. She began to bleed. Her mother gave her a sanitary towel to wear. It felt like nappies – a regression rather than maturity. It was apparent that menstruation was not to be her strong point. She had not *the talent* for it.

What had she done only a few weeks later? That was right: stabbed her thigh accidentally with a pair of scissors during sewing class. She ran home to her mother, blood coursing down her leg. Two boys in long trousers pointed at her in the grey street and laughed. Why? Alice asked. Because they thought it was a period, Oonagh explained without explaining what a period was.

Later, there were explanations – but, like plot summaries of operas, impossible to absorb in advance.

So there was another mistake.

Having produced a little pale brownish liquid, Alice showed Oonagh her powder-pink cotton gusset and asked, 'Is that a period?'

Alice herself was doubtful that it was really menstruation. As she understood it, menstruation was like weeing. You gushed a stream of blood continually for several days and it troubled her to think that if it started while you were on the loo in school, you might not get home for a week. But she figured her mother would know for certain. Surely she had had a period or two, in her time? Oonagh took three days to reach a verdict. It was a yes.

Her parents couldn't think themselves into the situation of the ten-year-old child. They were full of their own concerns. So there was much talk about pregnancy. There was much talk about William's anxieties on this score. And there was much advice about the biblical ban on copulation during menstruation. And there was much talk about Oonagh's anxieties on this score.

However, when Alice produced only white liquids of various consistencies in her knickers, her mother never mentioned the matter again. Alice concluded that she was indeed having periods, almost every day in fact. What else was she to think? Everyone tells little girls about periods. No one tells them about vaginal fluids. This is inconsistent with the facts. There is much more vaginal fluid in the world than menstrual blood.

Why were these 'periods' white? On her limited information, Alice arrived at a brilliant but mistaken solution.

She concluded it was *because her periods were anaemic.*

From the *Encyclopaedia Britannica* she learned that loss of blood during periods was a contributory factor to the anaemic condition. She realised swiftly that she was in a vicious circle. She began to eat liver and broccoli. Yet the situation became worse. She noticed distinctions in the liquids. Some were not white. Some were actually clear. This must – mustn't it? – be a sign that she was now *so* anaemic that she could not even produce the white menstrual blood, but only this translucent glue. What might she produce next? If she wore her mother's sanitary towels, might that encourage her womb to do the job properly? Like carrying an umbrella in the hope of rain. When her mother discovered a pair of Alice's knickers containing one unbloodied sanitary towel, Scottish fury about the cost was vented.

Alice was bleeding translucently to death with no one and nothing to help her.

But the last disaster was by far the worst. She brushed with the potentially fatal Toxic Shock Syndrome, caused by over-long use of a tampon.

Alice – nineteen and now an entirely satisfied Lil-lets customer who had managed menstruation for the past six years – was in love.

For three years Alice had been silently devoted to a Saint of the Church seventeen years older. Not so silently, however, that her best friend Sophie did not know all about it. Sophie smiled sympathetically. The Saint was Derek Jolley. Derek had the palest skin. He never ventured abroad because, he said, the sun made him feel sick. 'Pathetic, isn't it?' he would admit endearingly. Alice imagined a honeymoon in Iceland. The beds would be reindeer skins and polar bear fur. They would dissolve marshmallow hearts in mugs of hot chocolate all day long.

What about his acerbity? Sophie would ask. His cynicism? More to the point, his hair? Which was manifestly dyed and straightened. Alice explained in detail why none of this mattered. It was actually a bonus. She maintained that Derek was 'non-traditionally good-looking'.

'You mean he's ugly,' Peter said. Sophie, in her usual empathic way, poached each one of Alice's reasons for loving him. When the wedding finally happened, she was shocked by the resentful way Sophie said, 'Well, you always get what you want and now I have what you want.' Miserable, distracted, she thought she had inserted a tampon without removing its predecessor. This predecessor was now lost up the blind alley of the fornix – whether anterior or posterior, she could not establish, even with the continuing aid of the *Encyclopaedia Britannica* and the small square mirror of her eyeshadow palette.

She set about it in the bathroom. Leaning volume nineteen (TO–VA) up against the mahogany panel of the bathtub – so she could consult the illustration and refer to the text – she grasped the mirror with one hand while she hunted her innards with the bitten fingers of the other. She could feel nothing, she could see nothing, but still she could not be sure.

Days passed. The worry became a self-fulfilling prophecy. She felt unwell. When she preached the word, she was unable to concentrate on explaining why God permitted cancer or why He was not a Trinity. She thought she should seek professional advice if she ever hoped to preach the gospel effectively again. Oonagh managed to negotiate a special dispensation from the pastor. A visit to Dr Sulakahn was arranged – on the grounds that this did not count as medical treatment. It was merely the removal of a physical object from a place where it no longer belonged. It was like moving house.

'Young lady,' Dr Sulakahn said, frowning below an aquamarine turban and twisting in his swivel chair, 'why did you not come straight away? Have you any idea how *dangerous* such an infection would be?'

He sent her to the couch in the nurse's room. A sheet of thick green paper lay along it. Alice parted her legs as bidden.

The nurse said, 'Ah yes, there it is. I can see the white string.' But then she proved unable to extricate anything. She fetched the doctor.

Dr Sulakahn said, 'Nurse, that is not a piece of string. That is a thread of mucus.'

The effects of this experience on Alice might not have been so far-reaching if Dr Sulakahn and the nurse had managed to agree. When Dr Sulakahn finally unscrewed and removed the stainless-steel speculum, Alice snapped her legs shut like a new spectacle case.

The nurse said, 'Shall I give her a shot of antibiotics, then?'

And the doctor replied, 'Whatever for? She has no infection. There isn't anything *there*.'

Did you need antibiotics for an infection you didn't have? It sounded like a paradox. She couldn't have accepted the medicine anyway. But the issue wasn't that. Was there something there, or was there not? Was she all right, or was she not?

She was all right. She cried with relief as she walked home from the surgery. But found that she couldn't stop crying. Big tears. Tears *comme un citron pressé*. With so much mucus the wings of her nostrils soon looked varnished with blood.

For the next six weeks Alice experienced the world's first nervous breakdown over the presumed internal presence of two tampons simultaneously.

Eating was difficult. She could not make it over the mountain that was mashed potato on her dinner plate. She could not stop crying despite consuming large quantities of vegetables containing vitamin B, said to be sustaining for the nerves. She could not open a Bible. Or any other book – until Peter sat down quietly on her bed and read George Eliot and Henry James aloud. Long stories about why she, Alice (Dorothea Brooke, Isabel Archer, Catherine Sloper), was so much better off without Derek Jolley (Mr Casaubon, Gilbert Osmond, Morris Townsend) anyway. One day Peter finished off with Webster. He assigned Alice the part of the heroine so she should have to say, 'I am Duchess of Malfi still.' And she managed at last to get out of bed.

She never had a best friend again. Or even a friend. But still she could not help thinking that maybe, somewhere inside her, black as a blood sausage, was the dead tampon, a fraying grey string for its tail. By day she remembered a wine-dark tampon stuck for months to the ceiling of the fourth-year girls' toilet. The memory made her feel seasick. By night she dreamed she was spitted like a chicken – on a narrower, more piercing speculum.

Now she sighed and, in reply to Jude's question about Tampax versus sanitary towels, said nothing. He suggested, at a loss, 'Just felt like a change, was it?'

'Mmm,' she agreed vaguely. 'I suppose it was.'

She felt more unable than ever to face him. So Jude shadowed her body with his, kissed the back of her neck. He began to move his hands over her shirt: there seemed to be some sort of a general movement towards its removal. Alice felt a surge of expertise and she assisted by lifting up her arms like a child being undressed for bed. The snow of her deodorant began to fall. Applying it, she never knew when to stop. Each extra stroke might be the one that saved her from social disgrace – or, in this case, won her love. Oral hygiene was no different. Each further brushstroke, or *dkkk* of the flossing tape, offered her the chance of getting it right. Each decision to stop at last – held the possibility of getting it wrong.

Then the shirt was on the floor, Jude was stroking her skin, and suddenly, he was no longer stroking. He was actually *pinching*, through their satin casing, Alice's nipples. She winced. What was he saying now? Something about 'liking it' when 'they' – the nipples – 'went hard'. These phrases were still more shocking to Alice. So he had done this before. Had a general opinion on the subject, even. Knew how to set about it again. Clearly.

Immediately Alice resented the assumed homogeneity of the human body: it had to be that Italian woman seven years his senior who was responsible. She told him she didn't like it. So he went back to the stroking and Alice found she did not give a shit either about the common sink of the flesh or her spiritual conscience any more. Then he began to negotiate the clasp of her bra.

'But . . .' Alice protested.

'You're right,' he said, giving up. Her discarded shirt was suddenly off the floor and in his hands. He put Alice's arms through it. But instead of rebuttoning it, he held the edges of the shirt together down the middle and held Alice all at the same time.

'I just don't know . . . what's *allowed*, exactly,' she said. 'They don't spell it out, exactly, about breasts, do they?'

Alice remembered something biblical about rejoicing in the wife of your youth and that the wife's breasts featured prominently. That limited it to married couples – didn't it? She scanned her shelves for *All About Dating and Courtship*. She didn't have enough books to fill them. She had bread, tins, a toaster, Alka-Seltzer, packet soups, Daz, Andrex, PG Tips, Kleenex, Tate & Lyle, Rose's Lime Marmalade and other items that would have done well in the corner shop of a Peak District village. She had everything, in fact, except a copy of *All About Dating*. It must be at home. She'd have to get another copy at the Friday-night service.

'I don't want to do something,' she continued, 'and then find out afterwards that it was wrong.'

'Is that what would make it wrong?'

She stood inspecting her shelves, trying to decide. Jude expanded for her.

'S'pose you'd murdered someone without ever having been

told murder was wrong. Wouldn't you *know*, instinctively, that murder wasn't on? Or would the murder be OK if you read in a book somewhere it was OK?'

'What about murder in self-defence? Anyway, instinct isn't a good moral guide, is it? That's what we need the Plain Truth for. Plus I remember saying something to Peter once about courting couples kissing and holding hands, et cetera. And he said to me, "What do you mean by the *et cetera*? There is no *et cetera*." – Is there?'

'Well, Bartholomew Smith boasted to me once, *in church*, about having felt some girl's breasts. I believe they were Sally Jelly's.'

But Bartholomew Smith and Sally Jelly were not good Saints of God. Their consciences – instinctively, separately, both together, in all feasible modes of operation – weren't any kind of guide. Alice had gone to school with them.

'They were hopeless Saints, reeds in the wind, those two,' she explained.

'I'm not sure I was such a shining light at school either,' Jude said. 'Didn't you find it difficult?'

'Not really. I knew I was right. You can do anything when you know you're right.'

However, her breasts disagreed. She got back on the floor and found Jude's mouth. They began to kiss again and her tiny shirt fell open.

Difficult as it was to stop a second time, she had to roll away from Jude. 'Definitely not,' she said, as though his body had been mouthing a question to hers. She couldn't behave like Bartholomew and Sally. She was too morally snobbish. She needed a better reason. She would look some things up.

'OK. Get back to me when you've finished your research,' Jude muttered.

He left. She watched sequentially from her windows as he crossed the cobbles towards the gate. She undressed, got into bed but could not sleep very well. She drifted in and out of a dream about opening *All About Dating and Courtship*. It was full of mathematical equations she could not understand.

Chapter Twenty-One

The first time Alice met Sally, she began to suspect that breasts and being a Christian were incompatible. Sally had shiny straight ginger hair. Her demeanour persuaded Alice it was really blonde. Let that be her character note.

Two dark pink combs, one on either side of her head, held in place parts that had been tonged into sprouting broccoli of wild abandon. The effect was Selective Electrocution. Sally's mother left them to 'make friends'.

Sally said immediately, 'I notice you don't wear a brassiere.'

'What's a brassiere?' the eleven-year-old Alice asked.

'Oh, you probably call it a bra. But you don't wear one. Sophie wears one.'

Sophie, future bride of Derek, smiled sympathetically at Alice. She knew how determined Sally could be. It went without saying that Sally wore one.

'So *is* that a vest?' Sally asked, peering at the top half of Alice. 'Or attached to an underskirt?'

'It's attached,' Alice admitted. She knew that would be more infantile. Attached things always were. It began with the ready-made feet in sleeping suits. The strings sewn into coats cut into your shoulder blades – so gloves would not be forgotten – and took the prize for discomfort. In any case, she was a realist. She had only one slightly puffy nipple to offer the inside of a bra. Its irregular bulge resembled a frozen milk bottle top. The other was still the size of a press-stud. It didn't seem enough. It wasn't enough. Who knew what Sally had. Her mother was vast – a corseted ocean of oily swell.

'And do you *always* wear dresses?' Sally pursued.

Sally's neat pink suit was from the petite section in Principles. Her matching gloves gave her the air of a bride in a going-away suit. She wore pearls and white high heels. A pink leather bucket bag, with a gold clasp, was demure on her wrist.

'And you have a son as well?' Sally's mother, alert to the nuptial implications, asked Oonagh.

Then Alice saw the pastor approaching.

Then Alice prayed Sally would not speak of bras.

Instead Sally tapped his arm. She pouted. She leaned into his personal space to introduce Alice. Her pink padded shoulder grazed – just fractionally – his elbow. It was all a great relief. It had nothing to do with bras. Apart from the moment when Sally fingered the right strap through her thin pale pink blouse and held the pastor's eye as she chatted. Finally she flicked her should-have-been-blonde hair and turned knowingly on her four-inch white heel.

Yet at school, as Alice discovered in the weeks following, the bra-wearer was less composed than in the church foyer. Sally began to waver, and school was not the place for a Worldwide Saint of God to do this. Stands had to be taken, trials endured. From infancy Alice had been a very saintly sort of Saint. She wasn't merely averse to sin. She was actually in love with goodness. In the playground, in the rain, *against* the rain, she had taught the Bible to heathen girls and boys. She had preached with assurance before the Powers That Be: she was a good bit past nine when she proved to her head-master, from three scripture texts, the immortality of her mother's soul.

However, the trouble with thinking you've got it all figured, as she began to say to herself, is secondary school. Everyone is a genius in their middle school. If they had only stayed in their middle school, everyone would have been Shakespeare, Einstein or, at the very least, Nigella Lawson. By the standards of Worldwide Sainthood, Alice might have been a Christian missionary in Outer Mongolia – or Space – if only she'd had the strength of character to remain forever among the Field School Juniors.

It was true that middle school had many who sinned by celebrating Christmas. But among the Field School Juniors, things could be explained with great satisfaction on all sides. Kids quizzed her: 'What's wrong with you, then?' And she replied: 'Well, Christmas is a birthday celebration for Jesus, and the only two birthdays in the Bible were celebrated by pagans and at one of them John the Baptist even got his head cut off.' They were definitely impressed, quite quietly respectful. They deferred to her in many matters of religious education.

In secondary school, however, no one was having any of it.

'So you're telling me you don't believe in Christmas, or birthdays, or *anything*, because you're afraid of DEE – CAPEE – TAY – SHERN? How bloody stupid is that!'

And everyone laughed.

The worst of it was, Sally Jelly laughed too. Pretended to know nothing about it. Not her. That was the other Sally Jelly who went to the church and turned it on for the pastor.

When you looked to Jelly for solidarity, it was liable to turn into one quivering mass that preferred to stick to itself.

Still, Sally Jelly was not the worst. Bartholomew Smith was another fine young rising hypocrite. During registration one day, 1C was asked who wanted to help with the Harvest Festival preparations. Bartholomew's flabby hand shot up. Alice watched it with dismay. Their form tutor, Mr Dudd, asked Alice to join him – operating on the premise that the nutters were best kept together.

Bartholomew said, 'Certainly, sir, it would be an honour, sir.'

Alice said, 'No, sorry, I can't.'

'Can't? Or won't?' Mr Dudd never had this sort of trouble when Bartholomew's elder sister was in his class.

'Can't. It's against my religion. Sir!'

'Well, it's not against *mine*,' Bartholomew clarified helpfully.

In that awful moment the truth was all too plain. Sally Jelly's sins were sins of omission, but the Smith kids were actually sinners. *Imagine*, shocked Alice said to herself, they *brought in* tins for Harvest Festival. They *wrapped* birthday presents. Finally Alice saw Bartholomew's sister Megan *selling* the school's charity Christmas cards – in the lobby beside the great Christmas tree with the evil twitching fairy lights.

These were not accidental actions, moments of weakness in the midst of the worldly crowd. These took *planning*.

'They sign birthday cards,' Alice informed Peter dolefully.

'They don't!'

'They do.'

'But birthdays are an abomination!'

(Birthdays were too much worldly glorification for one person alone.)

(For some reason, though, which Alice had never been able to discover, twins did not get away with them either.)

'I know they are. And . . .'

'And what?'

'Lots of other abominations too. All sorts of them. You wouldn't believe.'

It put Alice in a very awkward position. It is one thing to tell a teacher you cannot do something because you are a Worldwide Saint of God. It is quite different when *other* Worldwide Saints of God in the school will do what you won't. The teachers start to suspect a Worldwide Saint *fundamentalist* – one of the 'orthodox ones'. Whereas the whole point of being a Worldwide Saint is that you *are* a fundamentalist. There is *nothing but orthodoxy* in the Plain Truth.

Unless, that is, you happen to be a Smith.

'I don't mind a conscience,' Mr Dudd began, tense with indignation in the staff room. Hands clasped behind his back, he rose on his toes. He frowned at an assembly of orthodox identical smoky brown plastic mugs and a plate of hard core scones. 'A conscience – that's respectable, that's noble. That's Christian. Bartholomew Smith has a conscience. Anyone can see that. But these girls like Alice . . . these, what I would call . . . *histrionic fundamentalists*,' (Mr Dudd was Head of English), 'now *that's* what I really don't like.'

And it wasn't prejudice. For hadn't he praised, God damn it, Indira and Ananya, the two Indian girls in the fourth form, for their 'milk chocolate' skin?

Alice felt disturbed and miserable. Sooner or later, she would have to confront Bartholomew. They had too far to go together. Harvest Festival was merely the first hurdle. The pagan celebrations of Hallowe'en and Bonfire Night loomed with calendrical certainty. As for Christmas . . . The school curriculum was constructed principally around making cards and decorations for heathenish events. Why? Briefly she wondered if it might be theologically acceptable to make a card with a simple snow scene – so long as there were no incriminating reindeers. Surely winter was winter and a season couldn't be denied simply because it happened to have Christmas in it?

No, it was not acceptable. In her heart, Alice knew it was Satan who was rationalising. 'You just can't write off a quarter of the year like that.'

The plain truth of it was, no season was really safe.

A few weeks later, after music class, Alice had her chance. She listened with disgust to every false semiquaver in every false semibreve the young Bartholomew emitted. Oh, the *treachery*. He was prepared to play 'Silent Night' on his French horn. She was not. Her violin was not so degraded. It was ninety-four years old with a seamless sycamore back. Alice sat tightening and loosening the horsehair bow, fingering the mother-of-pearl inlay. She peered through the sound holes and read, for the umpteenth time, a tiny cream notice that said the maker was Heinrich Schwartz. Then she waited. Instruments were interred like dead babies into velveteen-lined cases. The music master collected the triangles and the recorders of the less gifted and stored them in two former raspberry ripple ice cream tubs. Bartholomew stood up. Palpitating with righteous indignation, Alice revealed to him the essence of being a Worldwide Saint.

'You just can't *do* things like that!'

And Bartholomew revealed to Alice the politics of compromise.

'Well, the thing is, if you make a great fuss about being a Worldwider' – and it was clear enough to whom this speculative clause applied – 'then it brings a lot more reproach on the Lord and His Plain Truth if you do something wrong. Whereas if you just sort of lie low, you know *integrate*, then no one sort of notices too much what you do. Look at Sally – she's got the right idea. You protect the Plain Truth that way.'

Of course he was absolutely right.

Of course he was absolutely wrong.

Chapter Twenty-Two

On Friday night, Alice wore her boots to the service in the Oxford church. She stood queuing at the counter where they dispensed the complimentary literature of William P. Pope. She had a great sense of height – the boots were the objective correlative of her inner moral state. She had, too, a sense of mischief that felt more acute for having halted sin five nights before. The red deacon was behind her in the line. She thought about what she would say to the literature Saint.

'Copy of *All About Dating and Courtship*, you say?' he repeated.

'Yes. There are quite a number of undergraduates in my college who are very interested in the Plain Truth. But they lead lives of moral depravity and would be greatly helped by this book.'

'Spiritually dangerous place to be, the university, isn't it?'

'Not if you don't get involved with them socially. I stick to reading books and answering questions about the Plain Truth.'

'Maybe you'd be wanting more than one copy, then?'

'I'll see how it goes. Students are used to sharing things.'

She turned round and the deacon, instead of asking for his

order, stopped her. Alice began to panic. She tried to calm herself by concentrating on the brown discoloration of his right canine tooth.

'So,' he said, as if it were a statement of fact, and the fact was Alice's guilt. 'How are you getting on?'

'Very well – I was just saying, I've got lots of interest going in the college.'

This was less than true. Alice wanted to be taken seriously and therefore left lay preaching to the Born-Again Christians. But people knew she was a Worldwider and she was willing to answer any enquiries.

'I hear,' said the deacon, 'the students like to share more than the books. Rooms and things. Boys and girls, I mean. How can you live in a place like that?'

'Actually, that's not true,' Alice said, suddenly glad of the antique regulations of the college and that she had, one lonely night, read them. 'There are very strict rules about things like that. It's not like The World in general, where anything goes. It's an institution. Boys and girls can't just *live* together. The college knows it would be wrong. There are lots of other rules too. Eight people in a room counts as a party, and you have to apply in advance. *Not*, of course, that I go to parties. But I read it in the rule book.'

'I see,' said the deacon, looking frustrated that he hadn't caught her out this time. 'Well, if it's as you say . . .'

'It is.'

Throughout the service, Alice longed to open the royal blue covers of the book. She did not dare. People might think she was troubled. She thought of taking it in her bag to read in the toilet. But then people might think she was constipated. She'd have to wait.

She listened to the usual condemnations of money, sex,

other religions, entertainment, work, careerism, ambition, anything intellectual. It was a succession of negatives, writ in bright grey. The Ten Disparagements. She sighed and turned to her fingernails as the Lord was praised for not giving the Plain Truth to the educated and rich people of this world. It was too unsophisticated for them, and they resented it for that reason. Plain and simple people really appreciated it.

Alice bristled. Restlessly, she crossed and uncrossed her legs, took a tissue out from her pocket and returned it, picked her bag up from the floor and put it down again.

Then she realised she was *enjoying* bristling. She wanted to get annoyed. There was a guilty pleasure in this.

When she got *too* guilty, however, she thought she ought to pray. Though she tried, she had the sensation she was merely talking to herself. She tried to stop this becoming a thought – but by thinking it, it was already too late.

She'd told her mind before there was no point in thinking this thought. If she *was* talking to herself, then she was only embarrassing herself in the privacy of her own mind. OK, she could live with that. So why not assume she *wasn't* talking to herself, just in case she might not be?

'In spirit and in truth, amen,' she finished, in a formulaic spurt.

She had little hope of believing anything. But if it was hopeless, how was she to give herself a fighting chance of living forever?

Everyone stood for the second hymn. It was about miracles. Alice believed she might have believed perfectly well if only lots of miracles were still happening. It must have been so much easier to work up some conviction in the days when you saw Jesus changing water into Chardonnay, or Lazarus back from the dead, tangled in his grave bandages like the

Andrex puppy. But the Church said there was *no need* for miracles nowadays. You could read about the miracles in the Bible and be impressed by those. Which was much like saying you could stuff your mouth on a roast dinner photographed in a recipe book. Nor would the argument work if you wanted children. Read all about them. Instead of kids, the word – polyphiloprogenitive.

And what about the warrior Gideon? The hymn lyrics said Gideon wanted to be sure God was on his side before he started hammering the life out of the pagan Midianites. So he asked for a miracle. He left a dry fleece out at night and asked God to soak it by morning. God could easily have said, 'Listen, mate – haven't you heard of the Exodus? I can part seas. I can drown whole Egyptian armies, me. And you want me to wet *a sponge*?' Instead, God agreed. But Gideon was still not sure. So he asked God to reverse the miracle the next morning – a dry fleece on dew-soaked ground. And God agreed. No doubt God would have agreed to do it again and again, indefinitely. It was just as well Gideon had got up some courage at last. Otherwise, the entire Bible after Judges chapter six would be the endless tale of Gideon getting his sponge wet. Or dry.

Gideon was finally persuaded by a man who told him a dream about 'a cake of bread' rolling down the hill to the camp of Midian and 'smiting a tent' so that the tent toppled over. It was a vision of bread-and-butter pudding murdering a man in a sleeping bag – no wonder Gideon had so much faith.

No wonder Alice had so little.

Surely, though, God would not hold a little doubt and cynicism against her. No, indeed, *surely*, He would be even more pleased with the best efforts of one who laboured with such doubts.

Maybe Alice couldn't solve the problem of belief. Maybe she

could never know what was true, and what was not. But she could manage good behaviour. Just look at the way she'd hauled up archives of conscience at Jude's request for a kiss, and then again at the assault on the hooks of her bra. She would escape the sentence of mortality on the grounds of Good Behaviour. This was the way to survive, should The End of the World be coming, after all.

Striding out of the church on her booted legs, Alice even managed a sense of moral superiority. *Imagine.* Out of her own self-willing virtue, she was adhering to the Church's strict moral discipline, while not entirely relishing either the company or the theology. It was all very well for a believer to pride herself on behaving properly. But a doubter? A closet reader of Richard Dawkins?

That took real self-determination.

'You know what you were saying about the college?' the deacon called after her.

She swung round. 'Yes?'

'Well, there's something else.'

'Yes?'

'Well, your own work. I gather you study literature. But how can you read all those worldly books, with all their worldly philosophies, and not let it affect your thinking? Or your behaviour, come to that?'

'Not a problem,' Alice replied with new confidence. 'Shakespeare is very edifying. Langland, perhaps even more so. Langland knew The End of the World was coming. But we do a lot of Shakespeare. Two whole terms of it, in fact.'

Shakespeare was considered safe, wholesome recreation. There had been a picture of his Complete Works in a recent issue of *The Plain Truth*. At the time, Alice had thought it humorous. Shakespeare was full of cross-dressing, fairies, murder, politics, war, rude jokes, fine language – and other things disapproved of by the Saints. But she was glad of the picture now.

Back in her room at last, Alice read that hands should not go roving under clothes.

The book didn't mention breasts specifically, but clearly you couldn't get to them by another route. All the same, she thought it might be all right to rove Jude's chest, because it hadn't any breasts. So, kiss, handhold, maybe cuddle, maybe rove the non-erogenous zones. But keep a discreet distance till your wedding night. Then what? How would the instantaneous mutation into a sexual being happen?

Alice had a strong suspicion that, in many cases, it was going to be a disaster. Married Saints emphasised the value of a sense of humour – which didn't sound promising. Her mother had told her all people were completely compatible anyway, so there was no need to test things out beforehand. But then, it was also clear Oonagh had no interest in sex. William said you had to give six months' notice to have any hope. This was supported by various images. Her mother flinching when her father tried to kiss her. Her mother's stern stare as she told him to *back away slowly*. Her father's nakedness around the house, her mother's pudeur.

'I wish you wouldn't. It isn't right.'

William replied, offended, 'I'm not some bloody pervert. If I were some bloody pervert, then I *wouldn't* walk naked around the house, would I? I'd be being some bloody pervert. Besides, think of the advantages . . .'

Oonagh looked grim.

'No – not you, my love. I meant *her*. Won't be a shock to this wee girl, I can tell yer, when she gets murried.'

This was William's idea of sex education. Whereas Alice

only remembered having seen her mother's cunt once – by accident, when she opened the toilet door in their first house. She was perhaps three years old. It looked like a huge ham, crawling with insects. It had terrified her – the glinting wetness of painfully red skin. But her father had a speckled back and wore his nakedness lightly. He winked at his growing daughter and boasted larger tits than hers.

Two days later, he telephoned her again.

Chapter Twenty-Three

William was a great fan of the black Bakelite tele-phone. Gazing at the rotary dial, he was puzzled that anyone wanted the push-button kind. He liked the continuous clicking every nimble, horseshoe movement of his index finger accomplished. All this pleasure was suppressed, however, when he spoke to Alice on Sunday after-noon. Something terrible had happened. But he couldn't say what it was over the phone.

'Just come quickly, will yer? I'll pick yer up at the stop.'

'No, it's OK. I can get Jude to do that.'

'Jude?' Antennae tensed in William's voice. 'Why – the lad's never there with yer now, is he?'

'No, of course not.'

Jude stood three feet away. Her heart reverberated to her father's words. Next to the telephone, though, her upturned glasses lay with folded arms, brave as a nightclub bouncer. She explained that she meant to telephone Jude, and ask him to pick her up at the coach stop.

'All right then,' William agreed impatiently. 'Whaddever. Yer remember the way to the house?'

Her parents had already moved out of their home and

returned to their previous residence, which William still owned. 'Yes.'

'Right, well, I'll love yer and leave yer. Just be quick.'

On the journey, Alice's endless, alarmed speculations about the nature of the 'terrible' tragedy irritated Jude. Then a tiny pissing could just be made out from the hind wheel of a coach in the middle lane. A coach with cystitis. Jude's left hand made overtures to her right knee, but she crossed it out of his reach.

Alice's objections were starting to get him down. He was Moses on Pisgah. He'd been given a sight of the Promised Land. He'd seen the size of the grapes. And now he was being shut out. His cock sank.

Their old house had been built after all the others in the street. It was set back further from the road. The walls were stoned with pebble-dash, the roof was spattered with lichen-like bird shit.

Alice had not been here since she was eleven. When William bought the bigger house in Westwood, he had let this one. With his financial difficulties, the arrangement was reversed. Half the living room was now taken up with his office. None of this was going down well with Oonagh.

The garage door was tilted half open. There was a large red van parked in the driveway, and numerous cars in the street. William emerged carrying two small blue rectangular packets from the freezer cabinet. He spotted Jude's car and waved. Alice and Jude followed him indoors.

'What happened to the Bentley?' Alice asked her father.

'It's parked up the yard,' he replied. 'Can't afford to run it. Whaddyer think of the van? I'm like a postman now.'

William began to sing *Postman Pat* lyrics, but his joviality seemed forced. Alice could see why her father had chosen the van. It was not an old Mercedes or a BMW or anything approximating to the grandness of the Bentley Mulsanne. It was so absurd there could be no comparison. The house, by contrast, solicited comparison because it was strained with the contents of their former residence. The hallways were narrow arteries, capillaries clogged with spare table nests, jardinières and Chinese rugs trussed like joints. Nothing belonged. Paintings that needed light and distance went without. Stacked pastel portraits of the family faced the walls. An onyx umbrella stand, like a pillar of cloud, stood elegant and inscrutable – in a bewildered wilderness of possessions.

There were a bewildering number of people as well. Almost the whole church. They seemed to have emerged from a 1980s clothes catalogue. The women wore fuchsia silk blouses with modest necklines, high heels and jeans. The men grandad T-shirts, basketball boots, the odd paisley tie. William kept asking, 'How are we doing?' – without ever pausing to have the matter cleared up with a reply.

Alice could overhear Bartholomew Smith saying the house wasn't as large as it appeared, not when you'd been there once or twice, and the light fittings weren't gold-plated.

She put her head around the sitting-room door. On the wall above him there was a painting by Manuel Blasco, a cousin of Picasso. Bartholomew hadn't noticed it yet. Blasco put a one-legged man in every painting. This one struggled across the bottom right-hand corner of a Spanish Easter celebration. There was also a tiny cross on a pink pageant wagon. Easter and crosses conflicted with the plain truth of things, if one-legged men did not.

It looked like an auction.

'Oh, yer mother's having a BBQ,' William explained. 'Wants to show she hasn't lost face.'

'You got me here for *a barbecue*? I've been worried out of my mind!'

'Yer did right, child,' her father said, drawing her towards him and speaking in a whisper. 'It's terrible, what's happened. We've been burgled.'

Two paper plates passed Alice's ears. She caught sight of her mother in the corridor – her hair was dyed darker and in a girlish ponytail. She looked younger, less majestic than usual. There were plaited gold hoops in her ears and she was wearing a stretchy white T-shirt. She was saying hello to Jude.

'*Burgled*?' Alice was confused: the blue packets in her father's hands were burgers from Netto. 'When? How can you be burgled when you're having a barbecue?'

'Before they arrived. Almost all the jewellery's gone – not yer mother's, but the bits in the second safe. Can yer credit it?'

Alice could not credit it. Her father had told her often enough, when she was little, that she was not to be frightened if men came with guns wanting the safe opened. He would have stage-managed the whole thing, in order to claim the insurance.

He could see she was remembering this now.

It was a pity, she felt also, that the 'burglars' did not have more of a line in rugs and paintings.

'Oh, Alice, Alice,' he wheedled, 'I'm devastated. I lost my gold pocket watch, yer know. I'd not have lost that wee watch for the world. And there I was, hoping . . .' He sighed. He paused. He put his hand tritely on his heart. 'Hoping one fine day to be wearing that watch to yer wedding.' He sighed again. 'Come up, will yer?' He passed the burger packets to Oonagh. Alice followed him up the narrow flight of red stairs to his bedroom. 'Would I lie to you?' he asked.

Unable to reply to this truthfully, she said nothing.

He seemed really grieved. Alice did not wish to disbelieve a sincere man. Neither did she wish to be made a fool of. It wasn't pride. It was love. A lie would show he didn't love her, didn't trust her. It was true she had lied to him, only an hour before, about being with Jude. But that was different. She had a good reason. What was his? She did not understand why he should be lying. She tried gentleness.

'You can tell me the truth. It's all right. I won't mind.'

'I *am* tellan yer the truth.' William was indignant. 'I'm tellan yer the God's honest truth. With no word of a lie,' he added, as though this clarified the first two sentences.

'Well, I'm sorry for your trouble, then,' Alice replied, an Irish turn of phrase that sounded as though they had only met once or twice before, briefly, on a railway platform. 'But there is, I suppose, the insurance?'

'Ah Lord God Almighty!' he declared, as if suddenly struck by a revelation. 'The *insurance*. I'd not have thought of that, messef. And if, *if*, I'd anything to do with it,' he speculated, 'd'yer think I'd pick a night when yer mother had got her big thing going on?'

'I suppose not.'

'That's what I can say to the insurance people,' William suggested excitably. 'I'm just gettan to thinkan about it now. What I'll say. I know it looks bad – but that's why they'll believe me, yer see, when I tell them the truth. I've nothing to hide. I've money troubles – everyone knows that. So I'd hardly burgle my own safe now, would I? It'd look too obvious. They'll know no one would be so stupid as that.'

Alice wondered what the insurance people's official policy was on the double bluff.

'You do *believe* me?' He looked at her intently and gripped her arm.

'Of course I believe you.'

'Good girl. I knew you'd understand. And thank God yer do. Because that fuckan witch of a mother of yours doesn't. She thinks . . .' William brought his face closer and raised a confiding eyebrow. 'She thinks – *I* did it.' He was affronted. '*Me!* D'yer think yer could have a word with her?'

Alice did not reply. They stared at each other. 'And Paddy died, yer know,' he said, out of the silence.

'Paddy?'

'Ah fa fuck's sake, don't tell me yer don't remember Paddy, now.'

'Oh, *Paddy*. Yes.' Alice floundered. '*Paddy* Paddy, you mean. Not – the other Paddy.'

Embarrassed, she took the firm decision to sip her drink again – then noticed her hand was not holding one.

'Absolutely,' she affirmed instead. 'Sorry to hear it.'

'Yer'll come with me, to the funeral?'

'All right.'

'And you'll speak to yer mother?'

'All right.'

Again Alice had the uncomfortable sense that her father might be lying – inventing the funeral to gain sympathy and agreement. But she was equally uncomfortable to be so suspicious.

'Don't forget what I said about yer mother, now.'

The decorous swish of Oonagh could be heard on the stairs. William murmured in her ear, 'Dearest petal of the softest silk, yer a woman of the greatest beauty.' Oonagh smiled when he added, 'The vicar man told me he fancied yer, anyway. And Jude. That dirty wee bugger.'

'Don't be silly,' she beamed.

'Oh, woman,' he muttered to himself on the way down, 'have an ounce of wit.'

Before her mother could join her, Alice had a few solitary seconds in the old nursery at the end of the hallway. She flicked the light switch. Her eyes noted various irritations: pink walls competing with orange curtains, a wallpaper border of posies, the painted porridge of the woodchip ceiling. She stood in front of her old empty bookcase. Term was over in two weeks. Then all the books could party.

'Alice!' Oonagh hissed, closing the door behind them. 'I can't believe what he's done to me now, of all times. Even if I did get a lot of refusals.'

'Did you?'

'Well, there's a lot of jealousy. It isn't just any kind of BBQ, is it, when it's in our house? It's – an event.'

'Peter and Maria here?'

'Maria. But the point is, I've got people coming up to me, offering me sympathy, and I feel revolted. It's all a lie, it's so disgusting. Why can he never be *straight*?'

William would not have conceded straightness in a ruler.

'But he says we've been burgled.'

Oonagh stiffened. 'I should have known you'd take his side. You always do.'

'No, it's not that.'

'And I see Jude brought you.'

'Yes.'

Jude was in the kitchen, talking to the pastor over a field hospital of bandaged sausage rolls. 'Fine speech, young man.'

'Thanks.'

'This has been a time of requests for you.'

'It has?'

'Yes, I gather you were asked to bring Alice home from the coach stop this evening.'

'Yes.'

160

'I gather also,' the pastor continued, 'that you have been spending quite a bit of time with Alice, is that right? Some have said you may even be courting. May I be the first to congratulate?'

'Alice hasn't finished her degree yet.'

'But, let us say, if Alice *had* finished her degree, and you were the young man driving her home, where exactly would she be sitting?'

At this unexpected turn in the conversation, Jude said, 'I don't get what you're driving at.'

'No. *You* are the driver, young man. You have responsibility for the lives of all of your passengers. Life is a sacred thing. We all know this.'

'Well, in the passenger seat, I suppose.'

'The *front* passenger seat?'

'Yeah, the front.'

The pastor paused. He cleared his nose decisively.

'Recent directives from William P. Pope have suggested it is inadvisable for single unmarried persons to occupy the front seats of cars simultaneously, even if they are in motion.'

Jude wondered if William P. Pope could possibly have seen the film *Crash* by David Cronenberg. Taking a gamble, he asserted boldly, 'I don't believe that directive has appeared in any issue of *The Plain Truth*.'

'You are right, young man. I am giving you advance warning. It is a New Idea. Shortly to be announced at the Festival of Booths. I take it that you will be going to the Festival? And driving Alice to it also, *ne c'est pas?*'

The pastor meant this deviation into French to indicate familiarity with the romantic.

Jude nodded weakly. There had to be someone else to talk to.

In the kitchen each Saint held his plate high. There was a mown lawn of carrot still untouched on the top of the salad. He concentrated his eye carefully on a bowl of ready-scalped strawberries.

Then Maria entered the kitchen from the back garden. She'd had an idea.

Chapter Twenty-Four

'Come, come, I show joo,' she said to Jude, as though continuing a conversation. Jude looked up and frowned so as not to seem too pleased. Maria purled their elbows and took Jude down the hallway and out of the house.

'And how are joo, Jude?' she asked, pronouncing his name with difficulty.

'In need of a drink,' he replied. 'That's the trouble with these Worldwider parties. Never anything to drink.'

'Es so *boring*, I know.' She steered them right, and right again, into a tiny keyhole close. Then single file down a steep high-sided breeze-block alleyway. Their steps echoed. As the path turned left, they emerged on to the side of the canal. There was no one about. Maria took them under a weeping willow.

'So,' she said.

'No Peter tonight?'

'Oh, this man,' Maria sighed, with an uninhibited backhand smash. 'He is completely *empossible* to me. If he have the idea, joo cannado nothing with him. *Nada*. One day I think I will go in Espain again.'

'What sort of idea?'

'Any idea,' she declared. 'Like tonight. I am ready, jes? I am standing in front of the mirror. I am holding the tongs. And then he say, no, I am not coming. I am coming somewhere else. So. I burn my ear. Joo see?' Maria tilted a small perfectly unbranded lobe in front of Jude's lips. 'And then I come on my own. Oh, jes,' she insisted. 'Es true.'

She paused.

'And now joo are with Alice, jes? I warn joo, these are not the easy people.'

'But Alice is nice.'

'So joo are telling me that she never make the difficulty? That she never have the crazy idea? That she never say, *The Plain Truth* of Willyum Pop is more important than *joo* and *joor* idea? Sorry, but I don't believe this. I think she is the same.'

Maria paused again.

'Sorry, I offend. I don't mean this. Joo will be very happy together and make many, many babies I am sure. We go back now, h'okay?'

'OK,' he replied, disappointed not to hear more open scepticism about the teachings of William P. Pope. Maria parted the bead curtain of the willow and he followed.

'Jude.' Maria turned and stopped halfway down the alley. She put her hand on his arm. 'I have the better idea. Joo take me home in joor car?'

'Um . . . I'd have to tell Alice.'

'Why jes, of course.'

Maria waited in the car while Jude returned to the barbecue.

'Where's Alice?' he asked William.

'In her room with her mother.'

'Well, tell her I said I'd give Maria a lift back. And I can give Alice a lift back to the stop tomorrow if she needs it.'

'I hope they're fuckan payan yer for all this,' William said drily. 'These women – whadda they think? Yer a fuckan taxi service?' He nodded. 'All right, lad, I can see yer tryan hard.'

Jude drove past small, detached houses with diamond panes and shiny Austrian blinds. In the park there was a charred circle where the scout hut had once been. Over the bridge of the canal, a death zone of boarded-up bungalows and failed retail attempts.

'Es so ugly, no?'

'Let me take you for a drink?'

'Somewhere nice?'

'Oh, not here.'

He drove her to a wine bar in the next town. The frontage was like a greeting card: gold lettering on white panelling, reading *Champers! Champers! Champers!* Maria said champagne was her favourite drink.

'I know,' Jude replied. 'I remember you said that once.'

'Did joo?' She smiled delightedly. Jude watched a parenthesis appear at one side of her mouth. Magic. 'I like the Don Pérignom. He is always my special friend.'

'Everyone,' Jude laughed, 'likes Dom Pérignon, young lady.'

'What do we celebrate?'

'Escape from the Church barbecue.' He clinked glasses. 'It was tough. But we made it.'

'No, no, the barbecue, this is the easy bit. But I tell joo, this morning . . .'

With an air of scandal, Maria leaned forward to explain. Jude could see a grain of mascara lodged in her thick lashes. 'I go in the preaching, jes? With Mrs Saint Jelly. And, because she is scared of speaking to the people, she *pretend* – jes, jes, believe me – she *pretend* to press the doorbell. She just strokèd it, like this.'

Maria demonstrated.

'But there is no ringing or tinging. *Nada.* So I know she is pretending. And we are standing on the doorstep of one very big, very posh, very nice house, jes? After she *pretend* to press the bell, a man he comes and says, "Is there any particular reason why joo are gossiping on my doorstep?" And he is looking at me, like, a why joo bring this big fat *wobble* person to my house? And then, because he is a black man, jes?, she start to say to him, "It's h'okay, sir. We don't mind what country joo come from. God isn't prejudiced. *The man in every nation who works righteousness is accepted by him.* My friend Maria – she is a Spanish. And God doesn't mind." And I am looking at her, like, I *rilly cannot beliff* she is saying this so stupid thing. In Espain we call it *tontadas.* Stupidities. She show him the leaflet we are giving: *Planets At Peace: How Will It Be?* And then he says, "Do joo know who I am? I am an Admiral of the Navy. So beat it."'

Jude laughed. 'You meet all sorts. Well, when they open the door, you do.'

'Oh, these things that are happening to us.' Maria sighed. A second later she perked up and put her hand over Jude's. Her eyes were lit with collusion. 'Don't joo ever think, how no one knows what we know in the Plain Truth?'

'Like what – the demons and stuff?'

'No, like when the person comes to the door and they have that thing with a chain?'

'A latch?'

'A latch. And joo say to the person, "Hello," and then they close the door. And for a minute joo don't know if the door is closed because they are finished with joo, or if they are closing it so they can take off the chain from the latch and talk to joo for a long time. There is this moment when joo are waiting. And joo don't know . . . what will happen.'

'I think you're really on to something there.' Jude steepled his hands earnestly. 'I've always found it thrilling, myself, that moment.'

'Now joo tease me.'

They synchronised slow smiles.

'Tell you what else,' Jude said. 'Flats are much worse.'

'Why?'

'You know when you press the buzzer, right? And there's no reply. So you wait a bit before you press the next buzzer. And then suddenly, the person from the first flat is there, opening the door wanting to know what the hell you want, while the person from the second flat is *also* trying to talk to you, over the intercom.'

'This is never happening to me.'

'Trust me, it's a tough call when you're on your own.'

'Oh, jes? And I tell joo something else as well. Me, I *hate* the introductions.'

'Yeah. Why can't we say something straightforward like, "Hello, I'm a member of the Worldwide Saints of God"? Why's it got to be something cryptic like, "Hello, who do you think was the most important man who ever lived?" '

'Jesus Christ.'

'But *they don't know* it's meant to be him, do they? So you get "My husband" or "Tony Blair" or something. Or if you say, "Hello, what do you think is the greatest problem in the world today?" they say their dishwasher's just broken down.'

Jude found the enterprise of preaching futile.

'What kind of a way is this to deliver a message to the world? Might as well send a message in a bottle. Attach it to a pooh-stick. Anything'd be better. *And* it takes up so much time.'

Maria nodded knowingly.

'Don't you hate it,' Jude continued, 'when people say,

"Haven't you got anything better to do with your time?" I want to wring their necks and say, "Listen, *you*. You haven't a clue. You don't know the half of it." They think it's just the time we spend on their doors. What about all the services and practice sessions we've got to go to? It's *three nights a week*. It's a joke when we're warned against idolatry. When would we find the time for that?'

Maria poured them both more champagne.

'Well, es because joo work full-time, no? Joo must remember, most of the peoples in the Church, they don't work.'

'Yeah. And they're always the ones who give the speeches about how we should spend less time working and more time preaching. When we all *know* they're on the dole. Three days a week knocking on doors, and four days in bed, and then the pastor gives them some title like Special Minister. I'm surprised the *Daily Mail* hasn't rumbled social security is subsidising the Worldwide Saints.'

'Es disgusting, jes.'

'Anyway . . .' Jude trailed off and began to sip his champagne. The second glass was wonderful. New rules applied. It felt safe to admire Maria openly. He tapped her lightly on the arm as he spoke.

'You're very beautiful, you know.'

'Oh, jes?'

'I would like to photograph you.'

'H'okay.'

She went to the lavatory and returned with redder lips.

'Snow White,' Jude said.

'What?'

'Red lips, white skin, black hair. Beautiful.'

'Oh, jes, we have her in Espain too.'

'Why did you ever leave?'

'Oh, because all the men they are so short. They are so selfish.'

They finished their glasses. Jude said he couldn't drink any more and still drive. Grandly he got up to leave, with a third of the champagne still in the bottle. Maria picked it up.

When they reached her house, Jude left the engine running. 'Aren't joo coming in?' she asked. 'Come, I drink the champagne with joo.'

'Don't you want to drink it with Peter?'

'Oh, he stay with his friend in the Birmingham. He said to me, if my mother ask joo where am I, then joo can tell her this, and it won't be any difficulty for joo.'

'Well, in that case,' Jude said lightly, 'maybe I'll watch you drink it.'

In the living room Maria turned on bright spotlights.

'The road to Damascus,' laughed Jude.

'H'okay, joo are right, I dim them.'

She twisted the switch and took a champagne flute from a low teak sideboard. Jude was on the sofa. She sat herself beside him.

'Close your eyes, jes?'

Jude closed his eyes. He felt the hard lip of a glass.

'See if it taste different.' She poured a little into his mouth. He opened his eyes, snatched the glass from her, gulped a quarter, and smiled mischievously.

'Joo want to kiss me,' she said. 'I know this.'

Jude hesitated. He was afraid.

He was conscious that his limited erotic experiences had taught him little in the way of transferable sofa skills. He had kissed Isabella's pubic hair but gone no further. He had felt her inner thighs but, again, gone no further. But he could do this. He could do kissing. He found Maria's mouth. And he could do unbuttoning as well. She gleamed in her underwear, a rose-pink satin bra with an overlay of black lace. She moved her fingers to the front clasp he had not seen.

He heard himself breathing.

Then his hand found the weight of one breast while he kissed the other. She pulled his face up to her mouth. This time he kissed her slowly, subtly. He kept kissing as he thought about what came next – if he didn't come next. How difficult could it be? His penis was cabined, cribbed, confined. Harry Houdini in a straitjacket. He heard her telling him to stand up. She unbuttoned his jeans. Then, ah. She let him out. This relief was greater tension. She took his penis in both hands like an Oscar and kissed it. Then she ran its tip all over her eyelids and cheeks. They heard a noise. Jude flinched. Maria laughed reassuringly. It was only the television next door.

'Risk is sexy, jes?' she whispered. 'It make you come?'

Jude felt there would be no difficulty there.

She lifted her skirt like a cancan dancer, dropped it, and demurely swivelled the waistband so she could get at the zip. As she stepped out of her skirt, she said, 'I sorry for my under-knickers.' They were old white lace. 'But my mother always tell me, the men, they don't care . . .'

'We don't care,' Jude agreed, as he unbuckled his belt and lowered his jeans. His shoes were still on, so he was shackled by the ankles. 'I mean, we *do* care. Of course we care. *I* care.'

(Jude had views on lingerie but this was not the time. What was the point of abrasive lace? Who wanted to graze his cock against *that*? Jude wanted the Special K breakfast cereal girl, with her simple soft cotton knickers. Or Alice in a pair of Calvin Klein boy shorts. But it would be better not to think of Alice.)

'Maria, you're . . .'

'H'okay. Enough. So joo care. But, there is one thing, eh? No fancy tricks, hey? It go *in here*' – Maria pointed to the parting of her legs – 'thank joo very much.' Her cunt was shaved.

Jude lowered himself to his knees and felt her with his finger. It slid past the entrance. She guided him back. He looked down at her body and remembered Helen Best. Seven years old, in the changing room, getting ready for mixed PE, Helen put an arm across breastless nipples. But her belly stuck out child-ishly. And the front slit of her tiny smooth hairless mound, like two cheese triangles, was visible. He had never seen anything more beautiful. It was too much. As he struggled on to the sofa, Maria took his penis in her hand again. He came in three spurts and two after-tremors. Alice!

'I thought I tell you, *no fancy trick*!'

'It wasn't – a trick.'

'H'okay,' Maria sighed and brightened. 'Es h'okay. Now. Joo touch me like a this . . .'

Jude obeyed all further instructions and she came too. On the long and sticky journey home, he felt awful. In his mind, he promised Alice it would never happen again. He began the process of mitigation, special pleading, back-lighting, air-brushing, rearrangement. (Perhaps 'air-brushing' wasn't the right word.) He had not touched himself. The ejaculation was entirely involuntary. It was not really his fault. There had been a moment of noble hesitation. (When?) He had too much to drink. (But not enough to stop him driving.) While it happened, he was thinking of Alice. (Or Helen Best.) After it happened, he thought of her more.

Chapter Twenty-Five

The ash tree in William and Oonagh's garden was leafless. Instead it fostered a colony of stag beetles and flamenco flounces of brilliant orange velvet fungi. Every so often, a flounce fell.

William cradled a hunk of fallen fungus in his hand as he sat now, straining the possibilities of a green plastic chair. Lethargic lightning flashes of white appeared and disappeared, at intervals, in the plastic. The family's Pet Rock, a triangular corner of slate, sat on his knee. It did not bark at strangers (like Henry G.). Nor did it walk like a fashion model along an invisible tightrope, feet in a perfect straight line (hence the name, 'catwalk'). Behaviour which pleased him. On the other hand, it did not shit or moult or fart, behaviour which pleased him less. It was.

He sipped Tuborg out of the tin. All the guests had gone, no one hopscotched now on the coloured paving stones of the patio. (Not that there had been very much of that.) 'See yus all at Armageddan, then!' he mouthed to their departing backs. 'Should turn out to be a decent gatheran too.'

In the kitchen, Oonagh dealt with the latest stag beetle. With patient mechanised clumsiness, it slowly pawed, slowly clambered, slowly slid against the glass of a rinsed honey jar, tightly screwed. Oonagh posted it into the newspaper-lined bin. The jar fell a good distance but did not break. No bin men would cut their hands or lose a finger to the beetle's mandibles – not that Oonagh cared either way. But she was anxious not to be sued.

Alice saw William from the kitchen window. He was talking to himself. Two lemon candle flames sashayed on the small table where she joined him. 'Who are you talking to?'

'Me father.'

'Your *father*?'

'Don't yer see him?'

William's father had been dead for three years. Alice stared about for a ghost.

'Over there.'

William stopped stroking Pet Rock and pointed to the herbaceous border. Hydrangea and azalea. No ghosts.

'Wait. The wind will flick the security light on. Then yer'll see.'

Alice waited. The light came on and she could see the privet hedge.

'He's there.'

'Where?'

'In the bush. Don't yer see him?'

Alice looked for an old man in pyjamas. And trainers, too, on account of the mud. He was a very prepared old man. He had built two coffins and lined them with purple satin, one for himself and one for his wife, half a century in advance of their possible use. There were cloth bags, variously sized, for the children and the dogs.

'I don't see.'

The light flicked off, then, with another gust, snapped back on.

'There's his nose – ah Christ!' her father shouted, as though he were witnessing its dismemberment. 'The wind's catchan hold of it again.'

Alice searched for a floating nose, then realised her father was seeing imaginary shapes in the privet and its shadows. She concentrated, singled out a leaf which curled a tongue. She could not imagine her grandfather sticking out his tongue.

'Yer see it now?' her father asked, eager for confirmation.

'Yes.'

Suddenly William stopped.

He stared hard at the two candles – at the stooped wicks. Bent, burning, martyred. He said he was not alone in his suffering. The ash tree had been lopped, simplified to a tuning fork and a trident. It was plagued with growths. And although Alice herself felt only a touch chilly in the English evening air, she was burning bravely as well.

'I see things. We're not like other people. We see what other people wouldn't. We see,' he whispered ominously, '*things.*'

He said the word as though it were sacred. He nodded. Alice nodded back.

'Yes, I see things,' he repeated. But now his voice was no longer pitched between reverence and laryngitis. It was sprightly, matter-of-fact boastful. 'Not everyone would. They don't have the eye for it. We've the eye for it.'

William, like God and the Queen, used the first-person plural with confidence.

'Uh-huh.'

'We'll have another drink,' he suggested, again deploying the royal 'we'. The two of them finished off – courtesy of William's mouth – another can of lager.

It was a kind of trinity, she thought, the situation between them. Officially, Alice was contemptuous of the Trinity. She did not believe in it. What could this shared mind of God possibly be like – poor man's schizophrenia? Not one person with two minds, but three persons and only one personality?

At the same time, Alice could see it was nice to be included in the plural – *we* can do this, that and the other, we can.

'Us lot,' William said, 'we're not like them. They're not tough like us.'

'No.'

He continued swigging. They sat staring at the privet.

Paddy's funeral was the next day. William explained the complexity of the situation. Paddy was his first business partner. He had taught William everything he knew – arson, cunning, privet-gazing. These William considered particular distinctions. He also admired Paddy's indefatigable sexuality. Women offered the deceased hand-jobs in deserted car parks 'well into his seventy-eighth year'. From then till his death, William paid for his house to be painted, his garden trimmed and his wife's hair shampooed at home. He did this without expectation of return. But Paddy's family had been leery of William's kindnesses. The reading of his unaltered will – which contained no reference whatever to William – had not allayed their suspicions.

It was a vast modern Catholic church, a walk-in industrial refrigerator. Alice and William sat at the back. Windows, shaped and stained bright as the notes of a child's xylophone, let in the gloom of the summer. The priest presided far, far away, saying Mass first, as usual – as though the deceased's funeral were quite ancillary to the proceedings. But then he addressed, with assurance, Paddy's recent passage to heaven. It was a happy time, he said, to heads shaking their agreement.

You couldn't live forever, after all.

Paddy had left behind him four Catholic daughters, ten

Catholic grandchildren of assorted sexes, and one baptised great-grandson. And there were three sisters too, for whom his loins now assumed an implicit responsibility. His wife, to whom he had been devoted, had died in his eightieth year. (Nothing was said of his seventy-eighth.)

At the crematorium, the velvet curtain lifted up a corner like a dog taking a piss, and Paddy was gone.

'Sure he had the right idea,' William muttered admiringly. 'Get me an urn.'

'What?'

'Stands to reason, doesn't it?' He cheerfully clarified the idea. 'An urn is the way. Why would I want to stop in Pinner cemetery when I could just sit on me own mantelpiece? And get yer mother an urn too. Yus can put us on the same shelf, just on the special occasions, like.'

As for the urn, he had no preference. Chinese blue vase or modernist pot – let the survivors decide. Then there was a good chance they wouldn't mind having it permanently on display.

'I thought you wanted to be buried in the back garden,' Alice objected. 'There was so much room, you said.'

'There's two rabbits there now.'

Before driving to the reception, mourners gathered on the raked steps outside. William shook hands and patted arms and introduced Alice. Each time he said, 'And this is my daughter,' Alice waited for their reaction, like the fall of a coin. Heads they looked up to William and regarded him with fondness, tails they thought him an odious little man. And whatever they thought of him, they thought of her. The first-person plural refused to let her go.

As people descended carefully sideways to their cars, William remained on the steps.

Finally they were all in order. The lead car carried wreaths back to the family home, the second and third had the chief mourners. Paddy's sisters wore extravagant black chocolate-box hats. As they waited for the lead car to move, there was nothing to do but look out the window. William, still on the steps, with only Alice now beside him, nodded back to them.

And it was then, without warning, that he wept.

He fell on Alice's shoulder, then, raising his face, wept thick tears. The release of emotion was brilliantly timed. Alice regarded her father's performance on the concrete fan of steps with sick admiration. Her foisted role was Supporting Actress.

She'd had practice. Pretending to believe what she didn't, what in fact she couldn't, putting on a performance for the love of her mother.

Then suddenly, she saw what it really was. It was the lie that was the truth. The performance did not mean he was not also grieving. He had loved Paddy. But it was the stress he was under that allowed him to cry. The loss of the house in Westwood and the loss of the Bentley were destroying him. He felt a particular failure because he had once prom-ised Oonagh she would never have to leave Westwood. Even his voice failed as he tried to tell Alice that people in the café laughed at him for not having the Bentley any more. Not so rich, now, are we? they taunted.

'It'll be fine,' Alice said, stroking his hair. 'You'll see. Shall we go for a drink?'

'Would yer?' he replied, sniffing. 'Would yer come with us this evening?'

'Well, I meant now . . .'

'Too busy, are yer, for yer old dad?'

'I've got to get back to Oxford.'

'Well, come with me first. Then I'll drop yer at the stop.'

'Meeting Jill?' Alice enquired as they drove to the pub that evening in the red van.

'Jill? . . . Oh, I've got a new one now.'

'But I thought you said she was an adopted child who needed support?'

'Well . . .' William shrugged callously.

Sarah, the new one, turned up in an emerald-green satin blouse. She was another blonde, but younger, with long hair and a pixie nose. She looked as if she was about to burst out laughing because her lips barely closed over her prominent teeth.

'I thought you'd be wearing green, too,' she added.

Alice was mystified.

'St Patrick's Day,' Sarah said, pointing to a poster which displayed a large pint of green beer with curly white locks. Alice looked about her more closely. There were people in green paper hats and T-shirts with shamrock designs. William suggested that they go to another pub, in Kilburn, where there would be Irish dancing too.

'I love dancing,' Sarah said.

'Kilburn?' Alice objected. 'That's a long way.'

'Time for yus to get to know each other, then,' William said.

The second pub was full. William shouldered his way with difficulty to the bar. There were no Irish dancers, but the music was loud. Alice tried to talk to Sarah. Just to the left of Sarah's head Alice thought she could make out a familiar face. Jill. Looking nervy. She was talking to a man with a ginger crew cut. Alice was suddenly furious. Her father must have intended this. Jill lived nearby. William knew she came here on the big pub nights. He wanted to show off his new woman. How embarrassing and unpleasant.

'What is it?' Sarah asked.

'I thought I – saw someone I knew.'

Sarah turned round.

'I think it's Jill,' Alice said.

Sarah swung her head back. 'So it is.'

'You *know* her, then?'

'No.'

'So how do you recognise her?'

'Oh,' Sarah replied improbably, 'I saw her in some photographs once.'

This was too much. Sarah must be enjoying herself at Jill's expense too. Alice drew a breath.

'What is it?' Sarah repeated.

Alice looked at her hard, and decided to say experimentally what she really felt.

'One day,' she said, 'you will be Jill. And will we talk to each other, then?'

'Ooh, I hope so,' Sarah replied lightly.

'No, you don't understand. What I mean is: you will be humiliated like this. I will be standing here, with my father, and you will be over there. And how will you feel then?'

'Alice, I don't think you –'

'Dad!' Alice tugged his arm. 'Jill's behind you. Don't you think we should talk to her? This isn't on.'

William turned round briefly. His face darkened. He wouldn't look up.

'Is he –' he asked Alice, staring at the floor, 'much younger? The guy with her.'

'What's he got to do with it?'

'She dumped me for him. I got this text one day: *dont call dont visit its over.*'

'I don't believe you. It's always another sob story with you.'

In the ladies', Alice leaned over a sink with a Molton Brown

Cream dispenser which promised to smooth her hands. Her face looked righteous as she leaned in to the speckled mirror.

She returned to find Sarah chatting to the ginger man. Jill was at the bar. Her father was alone.

'Yer should never have done that,' he said in a low tense voice. 'Told me Jill was there. Made me look round. I wasn't thinking. I was so embarrassed.'

'OK – I'm sorry.'

William's bravado was gone. There was scurf on his lips. He was a little drunk and weepy again. 'I spose you think I'm terrible, don't yer?'

Alice sighed. 'No.'

'I love yer mum, right,' he explained. 'All I've ever wanted is for yer mum to love me. But she doesn't. And she doesn't understand anythan I'm trying a do. She just doesn't get it. She's on my case on a continual basis. I get no support at home. I'm just tryan to have a decent standard of living. That's what she doesn't seem to understand. It isn't *easy*. It's – whaddycallit? – difficult.' He lapsed further into the lager. 'There's someone else for her. There always was. The One That Got Away. There always is. And they love him. Sure there's always one. They lie t'yer about it.'

He merely nodded when Alice said she'd telephone Jude for a lift. An hour and a half later, Alice and Jude sat together on the edge of her college bed.

Chapter Twenty-Six

'Nothing's the matter.' Guilty, mendacious Jude moulded the brim of his baseball cap. 'If something was the matter, I would say something was the matter. Can't a man be quiet?'

'I was only asking.'

Coldly, without a word, he stripped her to her underwear. She, just as promptly, put on a bathrobe – the better to be undressed again. It was Egyptian cotton, with a Japanese letter on the left breast, and originally William's. Jude was lying on his back, and asked Alice to lie supine on top of him, too. She assented readily. They would not see each other's faces. His left arm gripped her firmly around the waist. His right tugged the girdle of the robe undone. She was wearing a pair of grey silk knickers – a cast-off from her mother, for whom they had been too small. With remarkably little friction and jiggling of the grey silk, Alice came. Lightly, quickly, helplessly, the way she did in her dreams – which, so the *Encyclopaedia Britannica* said, ought to happen about three times a year but in Alice's case occurred about three times a week. This time, it was a success short-lived.

Alice got up abruptly, still wearing the knickers, the open bathrobe buoyed behind. She retied the girdle tightly, deliberately, and sat on the window seat, her back to Jude, chin on her chest.

'Alice?' Jude was sure he had gone too far. He got up from the floor – a loin-cloth Christ in his underpants – and tried to put his arm around her. She twisted away. He sat on the carpet beside the seat. 'I'm sorry, I just wanted it to feel nice for you, that's all. I didn't mean to upset you.'

There was silence. Alice was inventing appropriate punishments – a scouring pad, dragged across her clitoris; a slow genital stoning, with shards of flint and broken seashell. She tried to banish these images. She couldn't. What had been done could not be undone. It could only be avoided or repressed.

Or repeated.

'It will be all right,' Jude said quietly.

'How?' she demanded. 'How will it be all right?'

Well. Jude's fingers had not come directly in contact with Alice's body – only via the inert medium of grey silk. Perhaps technically they had committed no sin.

(He did not see why technicalities should not count *for* him this time. Technical specification had counted against him before, when he had confessed to the pastor his activities with Isabella. The pastor declared it oral sex: the fact that her teeth had barred his penis further access and he remembered stubbing himself on a canine was immaterial. She found it revolting. Jude did not explain any of this to Alice. Obviously.)

'Don't torture yourself,' he said.

'So now it's my fault.'

'It's not anyone's fault. It's not about fault.' Jude, ostensibly advising Alice, was addressing his own situation with Maria. 'We don't have to do it again. That's what the pastor always said about me and Isabella. It was worse because – we kept doing what we were doing.'

'Doing?'

Alice was impatient for details.

Julie sighed. 'All I can say is they seemed to be most concerned about acts that were penetrative. And less concerned about acts that were not.'

'*Acts*? Meaning what?'

Jude stuck to generalities. 'Forms of penetration. Which we haven't done.'

This phrase offensively implied another *we* which had. Alice had the sense of labyrinthine experience on his side and nothing on her own.

She remembered how Bartholomew Smith had said, self-righteously, that he'd never touch that woman after what Jude had done. So Bartholomew knew what 'what' was. Alice didn't.

Suddenly, though, she wasn't sure she wanted to know. There was authority in the little he had disclosed. Instead she became hysterical – speculating about what her mother, her brother, her father, the pastor would say.

'But Alice,' Jude intervened, puzzled, 'it's not as if *they* know . . . And they won't ever know, unless you tell them. So I don't understand why you're putting yourself through this. It's like you're living your emotions in advance.'

This comment only raised new anxiety in Alice. 'Do you think we should, then? Do you think we should tell?'

'I can't tell you what to do,' Jude sighed again. 'You might feel you have to.'

So it was not a *we* for him, Alice thought. It was a *you*.

'Like you did?'

Jude looked back at her wearily. 'Yeah, like I did. Listen, I've felt what you're feeling and I just can't feel it again. I can't say I got a whole lot out of it, going to the pastor. Well, not in the end anyway. At the time – it was a way of regaining some little bit of control. I was like this little puppy and she'd treated me like crap, you know – two-timing me with that lump of lard she married. And she'd got away with it. There was nothing I could do. And confessing was a way of doing something. I couldn't see what else to do.'

'So it was *revenge*?'

Alice was shocked. What a betrayal of intimacy – nastier, perhaps, than the Italian woman's betrayal of him with the lump of lard. Suddenly Alice felt she was in a trap. Would it happen to them? People had warned her that Jude's heart would not stand a second breaking. Look at what had happened last time, they said. The scandal, going away to St John's Wood, coming back to the church, not sitting down for months. Alice felt afraid. Now he had evidence to pin *on her*. And who could tell when it might come out?

'Not revenge, exactly. But I wanted people to know what she'd done to me. It didn't seem fair that she should get away with it.'

Oh shit, Alice thought. *Not revenge, exactly*.

'Alice, my whole life had imploded. I lost her, then I failed my accountancy exams, then someone crashed into my car. Pretty much all I had left was my portable CD player.'

Jude moved on to the window seat. She let him put his arm around her this time, and he kissed her on the head.

'Shall we go and get something to eat?'

'How can we eat at a time like this?'

'I don't see that it helps to keep brooding on it. It really doesn't have to be this bad. We can just try to be better behaved in future.'

Oh great, thought Alice. *So that's it – now you've got your evidence, you decide to be good.* She didn't know what she was to do.

'You're right,' she lied. 'It isn't so bad.'

And she kissed him on the cheek.

The next morning she woke up with the desire to be tiny. So tiny she might slip out of sight altogether. She imagined herself curled up naked on a comma, blotting out its blackness.

She had dreamed she was on the swing in the garden at home. Instead of swinging backwards and forwards, she twisted round and round, and tangled up like a marionette. Until her neck was roundly wrung.

Something made her mother, at the critical moment, look out of the kitchen window. Oonagh ran out, rescued her and told her she would never die. Alice coughed and believed.

Alice turned in bed, trying to get comfortable. She and the bed did not get on. On the mattress ticking was a dried splash of somebody else's blood: the day she arrived she'd seen an old brown stain, the shape of a Viking long ship. She reversed it. She was still doing her best to forget about it.

Then she saw Jude sleeping on the floor. For much of the night, while Alice was asleep, he had wandered the room with his penis between his legs – trying to imagine how anything could ever be right again. He had betrayed Alice with Maria. Now he had pushed Alice too far and passed on his guilt like an infection.

He was also burdened by the Church's accusation that if he wanted premarital sex with Alice, then he couldn't possibly *love* her. Jude spent the hours meditating how he would make amends. In the Church, love and lust were supposedly incompatible feelings, but he reckoned he could manage them. Acts of lust would from now on be balanced by scenes of love. He was naturally courteous and kind but present circumstances were releasing his genius. Then, at last comforted by these thoughts, he fell asleep.

When he woke he rang work and said his girlfriend was sick. Alice was taken by the word 'girlfriend'. It had never been used in relation to her before. Then he rang his parents and said he was staying with a friend in London. He stayed with Alice for two days. He could not leave her like this.

They walked around the quadrangles. Her changing shadow – long, then squat as a wheelchair – seemed emblematic of her younger self, spiritually precocious and now reproachful. In the old days, things were simple. Alice was righteous. Almost everyone else was wicked. But now she was becoming wicked herself. Of course she'd tried sin before – but experimentally. She had once pissed in a sink instead of the toilet. She'd substituted the occasional antonym when singing hymns ('wicked' for 'righteous', 'Satan' for 'Jesus'). In church she had written the letters backwards in covert notes to Peter – whose resistance to corruption was such that he did not even give them a glance.

But Alice, if you looked into her very deeply, had no ambitions to be a devil or raise hell. She was just testing she could do it.

They went shopping for things to eat – salad, quiches – but she watched them wilt and shrivel on her plate in front of the electric fire. When Jude went away she was able to think.

Repeatedly she opened the tabernacle half-doors of her sink parlour – as if to take herself by surprise, like a sculptor seeing his work reversed in the mirror. She waited as the automatic light tottered on. Who was she? How had she arrived in this situation?

The light gave a faint ping and steadied. Now she could see. She was surprised, when she thought about it, that this *was* her face. Unremarkable, nothing sinful about it. For once, she studied it attentively, the way other people did.

Dark brown eyebrows. Eyebrows her mother had offered to pluck and shape. It would open out her eyes wonderfully, Oonagh said. Alice couldn't see it. Her eyebrows did not seem unduly profuse. There were a few superfluous scattered hairs. Not the classic commas, the two tapering dolphins, then – more like a wing beat and its force field. Her mother's eyebrows were so 'shaped' they were invisible without a thick black pencil. Unpersuaded Alice raised her left eyebrow.

Two to three inches above this approximate circumflex were two facial indents – created by the continual unconscious raising of her left eyebrow when she was concentrating or anxious or quizzical. They were more herself than anything else on her face. Still, she did not exactly recognise them either. She knew only what her face felt like when it made those marks. Not what those marks made her face look like.

Alice stared. In the mirror her face began to refigure itself. So she could see the beautiful sallow bronzes of her eyelids. Their taut folds of tarnished twilight. Darker avenues of eyelash. Her otherwise pale skin. Everyone said she was her father's daughter. Certainly her narrow Modigliani face and long cranium looked like her father. But there were suggestions of her mother in the fine hair and the prow lips a quarter-inch in advance of the rest of her features.

The three of them – joined inseparably in her face.

What would her mother think?

What would her father?

Quick, quick, something else. What else did the mirror show? Eyes like an El Greco saint – large and glassy and doll-like. The tiniest tag on her left eyelid like the pull on an invisible zip. The recession of her chin because she'd sucked her thumb. To tell the truth: *still* sucked her thumb when things got bad; still slept with her little comfort blanket.

With the thought of the blanket, immediately she wanted the blanket.

Leaving the half-doors ajar, she walked to the bed. In the large square room, her bed was tucked the other side of the sink unit, in the least obtrusive position. That way it disturbed the grandeur of the old college room less. Her ancient blanket was under the pillow, fibres falling off its frail materials. It was quilted: milky nylon squares, stuffed with greying felt, softened by washing and by long years of friction from her cheeks and fondling fingers. Much of the covering was gone, only the stuffing was left. There were gaping holes even in this.

She held the blanket in the crook of her right arm, and buried her face. Held it to her chest, inhaled its human smell. It was alive, familiar. It lived in her bed, after all. There were times when she banished it to a drawer, trying to rid herself of it, and it began to smell inanimate. Merely like the wood of the drawer, or the laundered clothing it lay beside. It felt cold then. It fell limp. She would yearn for its company, take it back into her bed, and, if she was patient, after a night or two, it came back to life.

Her fingers began to play with the crannies and oubliettes of the blanket. Things were getting calmer.

Afraid of being accused and punished and disgraced for impropriety, paradoxically Alice felt she ought to confess. But first she had to get her facts straight. She needed to know the Church's technical definition of what they had done, and *All About Dating* was not advanced enough for this. There was only one place to look: her mother's extensive library of William P. Pope. She would have to go home again. Leave the city of the dictionary, where the meaning of everything was decided, and discover the true definition of her misdemeanour.

Saturday morning, her father arrived. 'Yer all right, are you?' he asked, without stopping for an answer. 'Well, I'm not. That fuckan woman. I don't know what her big fuckan problem is. I'll tell you what her big fuckan problem is. She's Scottish. They can be seriously fuckan nasty.'

'Yes. Look – I'm not well.'

'Are yer not?' William asked, suddenly anxious.

'Let's not go to church today. I want to go home. Maybe I'll go with Mum this afternoon.'

'Yer all right, child,' William said soothingly. 'I'll take yer home.'

On the journey, he continued to remonstrate with his wife.

'She should try livan with some other man, then she'd know all about it. She isn't *real*, yer know. I don't think she realises I'm human too.' He paused. 'Did I tell yer Fox Plant went as well?'

'No.'

'Caught me for fifteen thousand. That's forty-two grand in the last quarter. But. You know me. It's a long road but there's always a turning. Police came yesterday about the burglary.' He glanced in the rear-view mirror. 'I'm putting in a claim for two hundred and eighty. I was clever about it. I was very clever, even if I do say it messef.'

Discreet research was not easy. Oonagh's library was two bookcases in a radial hallway. At any moment a door might open. Alice pulled out the indexes – first the index 1900–1990; then, in case sexual intercourse should have changed forever at some point thereafter, 1991–present. It was apparent that the 1970s were boom years for sex among the Worldwide Saints. There was also a hardback copy of *The Joy of Sex*, another seventies production Alice had once dipped into – and soon discarded. It recommended avoiding the use of deodorant because lovers would want to nuzzle the natural scent of her armpits. Alice was not really 110 per cent sure a lover would not want to do this. Her impatience was partly a way of banishing her fear that they might, after all.

The Joy of Sex was one thing. It was the filth of The World. It was not the facts of the Plain Truth.

And these were far worse than Alice had suspected.

How do you define a sexual caress? According to William P. Pope, you call it fornication. You might have done only the tiniest thing but it counts for the whole lot. You are hung for a lamb chop. What fornication *is* in William P. Pope is less exclusive than what is *not* fornication.

Fornication and pornography, Alice read in the fifty-seventh volume, *are sometimes thought to be things different. But etymologically, and for all practical purposes, they are the same.*

In ancient Babylon, a temple was consecrated to the Great Fornicatrix and the temple prostitutes went about their business . . .

Alice heard her father breathing heavily up the stairs and clapped the volume shut.

'They know I wouldn't have done it messef,' he reassured himself. 'It's the sofa, yer see.'

'What?'

'They interviewed me – two policemen – on the sofa. Yer know why I bought it?'

'Because we needed a new sofa?'

'No. Purity, isn't it? The colour of it. We look *pure*.'

'The sofa's mushroom.'

'Cream. White. It's all the same thing. It looks pure.'

'If you say so.'

'Like it?'

William indicated the mismatch of his shoes. One was a brown pockmarked brogue, the other a blue trainer. He liked people to think he was an idiot. It was this under-estimation, he explained, that had disarmed the police.

William went to the bathroom. He sat on the toilet, pulled two strips of toilet paper off the roll and folded one neatly onto each thigh. He prided himself on always being prepared.

Alice continued reading. Not surprisingly, what she and Jude had done was also fornication – intervening layer of grey silk notwithstanding. The fifty-seventh volume called it *the grossly indecent handling of another's genital organs*. Alice steadied her nerves by asking what purpose 'grossly' served in the definition – except as an intensifier to spice things up. It was like 'radically' in an exam question on Shakespearean comedy. She began to feel some relief. This was all ridiculous. What was the plain truth of things coming to, if everything was to be considered the same? If there were no distinctions, no degrees, if foreplay was fornication, then smiling was laughing, pouting was kissing, and the palest pink was really the deepest shade of plum.

Chaos.

Alice returned the books, oddly elated. Her father emerged, less pleased, from the bathroom.

'Sure Christ, I'm shitting air.'

Alice frowned impatiently. 'Isn't that – just – farting?'

'No, it's shitting air.'

'You know you do talk a lot of rubbish sometimes.'

'I'm not talking rubbish. I *know* when I'm talking rubbish. I look in the mirror and I say to messef, "Hark ye, friend, have yer got a padlock on yer arse, that ye shite thus through yer teeth?" Don't you?'

'No.'

'Course yer do. And I bet yer smell yer own farts under the covers in bed, of a night.'

'Oh, piss off,' she replied agreeably.

William stopped, surprised. 'I never heard yer swear before.'

'Oh, well.'

'Yer feeling better, then?'

'Yes.'

'Good. Yer like yer old dad. Nothing gets us for long. I'm doing all right, yer know.'

'Are you?'

'Got Sarah now, haven't I? She's terrible fond of me, yer know. It's all innocent a course. She wouldn't *sleep* with me, or nothan like that.'

'Wouldn't she? Why not?'

'She's not like that. She's nice.'

'Can't you be nice and sleep with people?'

Alice was pleased to be liberal and tolerant. William seemed frustrated he couldn't persuade her that nothing was going on.

'It's only *bodies*, isn't it?' Alice suggested into the pause. 'Is it that big a deal?'

'It's not *like that*, Alice, I'm telling yer.'

'But you're happy?'

'Well . . .' He smiled and churned the air with his hands. He was happy.

Alice's new liberalism did not solve the problem of Jude,

however. The Church's definition of fornication might be nonsensical – just as its old definition of adultery as something you could do with your own spouse was nonsensical. Yet she could be taken to task for it nevertheless.

Jude came in by the front entrance of church that afternoon. He took the opposite aisle and Alice looked up, hoping he would cross and sit next to her. But he wanted to reduce gossip. He hadn't liked the enquiries of the pastor at the barbecue. She thought he might talk to her, at least. But it seemed he wouldn't do that either. He sat down in a middle row, a few seats along from Peter and Maria, talking to no one.

'Look at that,' Oonagh observed tartly, as she placed her hand on the back of Alice's chair. 'Doesn't want to know you.'

Alice sat her bag in her lap as though it might protect her. Each hand held tightly on to one of the leather handles. The service began.

The opening words of the pastor's sermon were, 'A fine young cock was one day strolling around the farmyard . . .'

Alice stared crossly at the pastor. All things were pure to the pure. But *cock*? Surely he realised how that sounded. Surely he had given some thought to his opening words. So why not *cockerel*, for God's sake? She heard the rest distractedly. Standing for the hymn and hearing her mother sing enthusiastically, Alice thought she might cry.

After the service, Jude came to the house and took her for a long drive, ending in a golf house car park. Alice had noted down a series of extracts from the irremovable *Plain Truth* series. In reply, Jude said that he would not go to the pastor again, no matter what *The Plain Truth* of any decade said. But he would not try to stop Alice from going if she so wished. And he was willing to pray for them both.

Rain was spotting the windscreen as he closed his eyes and prayed that they might have forgiveness for crimes of passion past, and the strength not to commit crimes future. 'They' included him and Maria as much as him and Alice. He ended with the formula 'through the great and holy and most magnificent name of Our Lord Jesus Christ, amen'. Jesus's name had to be mentioned in every prayer, in acknowledgement of his role as mediator between God and man. So, not only was Jesus disallowed his own personality, he was forced to eavesdrop on everyone's prayers as well. There was no way around him. Alice had long felt the praying arrangements created unnecessary embarrassment on all sides.

After the *amen* her eyes opened and she began the long wait for sinlessness. Jude switched on the ignition and put the car into gear.

Chapter Twenty-Seven

Five days before the end of the summer term, Alice was in the lingerie fitting room of Marks & Spencer's. She stood in front of the mirror and inspected herself with care. *Set limits*, the wise book of William P. Pope said. That was what she had to do. She was trying on a pretty cream nightdress. Thigh-length, it comprised two thin layers of gossamer material, the under-piece longer than the other. There were pink bows on the straps and tiny whipped cream flounces on the hems. The gossamer was gathered across the bust. Alice would say to Jude, 'See how long that is?' Jude would look. She would draw an imaginary line across her thighs and say softly, 'Your hands can go no further.'

He would long for her thighs.

He would see how much fuller her breasts looked in the gossamer.

It was hopeless.

This purchase was incompatible with a real commitment to chastity.

Alice bought the nightdress. It was £14. Sometimes she thought that, had it not been for M&S, she would not have been debauched.

During the Long Vacation, she would be home for three months. Jude came up at the weekend. William was expected at lunchtime to help move Alice's things. There was a shared sense that since the sin was already entered in the red column of their account and that since opportunities would be rarer for the next three months . . .

They lay down on the silk rug. Jude's chest felt like sunned alabaster. There was a harder bit in the middle, like the end of a metal pipe. Jude said, 'It's called the sternum.' Then, 'This floor is killing my back.'

They looked across at the bed. There was nothing about the use of beds in the complimentary Church literature. Soon they were tucked up inside the pink cotton duvet of Alice's childhood. A Claes Oldenberg igloo.

'Can't you *do* anything about this?' Jude asked, indicating the duvet.

Alice was wounded. She saw nothing wrong in the imperfect white stars and four-tone rainbows that chased each other across the pale pink cotton sky.

Still, she said, 'When I grow up, I'd like pure white sheets. Like a hotel.'

'A worthy ambition,' Jude agreed, as he slipped an arm around her midriff. 'Look at that,' he said. 'The curve. It's so beautiful.'

Alice looked down and considered. It was *all right*, but Jude's wonder did seem disproportionate. She turned her body to Jude's. Their thick cotton shirts met. Under Jude's he was virtually hairless. Like a child.

Like his head.

She wanted to touch that too, but was afraid it might hurt him. His traumatised head flaked. It flared in patches. It was a love wound, scalped by Isabella, the Italian Delilah. Leaving

196

a surface of Samsonite. The remaining hairs were shaved down to splinters. For once Jude wasn't wearing his cap. Alice put out her hand and touched.

'Does that hurt?'

'No. Why would it?' he replied touchily.

She wondered and returned to the shirt region. Her hand found his nipples. She lifted up the shirt and peered across the low hills of his body. Then she pronounced it 'ironic' that so much attention could be given to his chest and not to hers.

'There will be a time,' Jude said dreamily. 'Think of a day in Italy.'

Italy was real pistachio ice cream and all other vital ingredients for romance. So Alice did think of Italy, briefly. But Italy seemed too far away. Her breasts wanted touching *prontissimo*. Alice had a brilliant thought.

She said, 'What about the Song of Solomon?'

He said, 'What about it?'

Jude could never remember the Bible very well, so Alice summarised. A young maiden, engaged to a shepherd boy, was courted by the great King Solomon. She stayed faithful to her betrothed. The story had always been an embarrassment to the Church. It was gorgeously erotic. It was full of squishy fruit. The Catholic Church got around this problem by redescribing it as An Allegory. Since the lovers were 'really' Christ and his Church, it was all right for them to sound frisky. The way the Worldwide Saints got around this problem was by a simple act of misreading.

It turned out that everything was really a declaration of physical chastity *per se* – everything the girl said about remaining faithful to her shepherd boy and resisting Solomon's advances. She wasn't doing anything with anyone. The shepherd boy's intimate knowledge of her breasts was a detail not taken into consideration. In fact, didn't her elder brothers say she had no breasts?

'Bastard perverts,' Jude interjected. 'What've their sister's tits got to do with them?'

'Well, they're kind of like fathers, those brothers. She's an innocent little girl to them. Not "an open door", you know, sexually.' Alice hesitated, started to laugh and decided it would be better to speak plainly. 'Actually, anyone who's read a couple of chapters before, knows that she was pretty willing when the shepherd boy knocked her up one night.'

'*Was* she?'

Jude relished anything that smacked of corruption in the biblical great and good. Obvious examples, like David and Bathsheba, were too obvious, though. The writer of the Book of Kings was already scandalised himself. Jude wanted to hear bits of hidden scandal, furtive scandal – as though the true meaning of biblical texts had been swept under the straw matting for many centuries and he and Alice were the ones to find it out at last.

'Have a listen to this bit.' Alice fetched her Bible and read aloud. '*My beloved put in his hand by the hole of the door, and my bowels were moved for him . . . I opened to my beloved; but my beloved had withdrawn himself and was gone.*'

To Jude this sounded like a description of disappointed anal desire, but he was willing to interpret it the way Alice preferred.

'So what do you reckon?' Alice asked.

Jude smiled. He sat up in the bed.

'I reckon you should write *The Plain Truth.*'

Alice's breasts were allowed. She became a simple shepherd girl loved by her simple shepherd boy. Jude unbuttoned Alice's shirt. Smiling, she rebuttoned it.

'Oh, come on,' he begged. 'What happened to Solomon? I thought you said it was all right.'

'It is. I just, well, I just wanted you to unbutton it again, that's all.'

Jude obliged. They stood up and he began to move his chest up and down against hers. It felt comic, as though he were ironing her while forbidden the use of his hands.

'You like it?' he asked.

'Very exciting,' she enthused.

Then they went through her whole wardrobe. She put on every top, every bra, she possessed and Jude took them off.

'Again, again,' she said, laughing, like a small child learning through repetition.

Jude was envious. There she was: Alice of the Breasts. She had her pleasure. She even had scripture to prove its permissibility. She was getting all this – with theological impunity – whereas his nipples did nothing for him.

Momentarily he regretted venturing down this line with Alice in the first place. He cursed the blazon: why were there not fuller, focused, specific descriptions of the masculine body in the Song of Solomon? The bent bow of his desire. That kind of thing. The gathered sack of heavy seed. That kind of thing. (English literature was no more helpful, Alice could have told him. Sir Philip Sidney was every bit as gender-biased in this line as the Bible.) He began to turn over his mind other possibilities. He had had moments of inspiration about the female body before.

Chief among them remained his riposte, as a boy of thirteen, on the subject of breast size. He and two other boys had been leading a cross-country race when one had made the panting pronouncement that small breasts were to be preferred. They were 'well cute'. Jude was for a moment deferentially silent.

But then he said, 'Not *too* small, though.'

'Oh, the smaller the better,' the boy declared cheerily. 'Anyway, what would you know?'

'Yeah,' chipped in the third. 'What would you know?'

Jude was as on the spot as a runner through the muddy woods can be. He had contradicted the boy for the sake of it. Now he was obliged to supply a reason. Various beach scenes came to his aid.

'Well, if they're too small, then when the girl lies down, they just disappear. And you still want to be able to see something, right, when you're in bed with her, don't you?'

The first boy weighed this, and Jude could tell he was impressed. It was a victory he never forgot: who won the race became immaterial after that. Now, it was clear, he needed an insight of this magnitude if he was ever going to advance things with Alice.

He turned the conversation to Michelangelo. Here, at last, was somebody who was all about the male body. Even female figures, like Eve in the *Last Judgment*, were fundamentally transsexuals, with breasts but also bloody big hands. Jude suggested that they might one day go to the Sistine Chapel. Alice replied perfunctorily that she should like it very much. Then Jude asked her – the connection was tenuous, he knew – if she liked the idea of testicles also.

Alice thought anxiously. Which were those again on the diagram? She squeezed her brain for a clearer recollection of her GCSE Biology Revision Guide. Then she felt cross that she should be subjected to this kind of examination in the aftermath of her exegetical triumph over the Song of Songs. No answer forthcoming from Alice, Jude put the case for testicles being like breasts.

The implication was clear.

The equation – that is to say, the exchange of favours –

ought not to be her nipples and his nipples. If breasts were allowed, if Solomon had said it ('Not Solomon, but the persona of the shepherd boy,' Alice corrected sharply), then testicles should be also.

Alice struggled to imagine where, on his slim figure, Jude could have secreted anything approximating to a pair of breasts.

'Come here,' he instructed.

They lay down on the bed again. This time he began to take off all her clothes and she did not try to stop him. She had forgotten all about the nightdress from M&S. There was no time for nightdresses or clever demarcations of her body now. Without warning, the heart was beating in her cunt. Then Jude grasped her right hand.

Alice was propped on one elbow and keen to kiss. He lay curiously still, like a man in a frieze. One of the damned. Clearly in pain. He guided her hand into his white jeans. Alice felt coarse hair and a hot pillar with a suede tip. Alice had already rehearsed how – while quietly rejoicing over her luck – she might win love by declaring that she did not mind in the least, that small penises might be preferred, like small breasts. She would have to think again.

She kept her right hand still, where Jude had placed it, while the marble moved. Then he conducted her hand further down. She felt warm dough, the infinitely stretchy softness of a sac in which two small jellies sheltered. How beautiful it was.

'Testicles,' Jude announced. 'Like them?'

Alice lifted the sac and the jellies slipped around. 'I love them.'

Buoyed by this success, Jude told her the tip of his penis was the most sensitive part. For some inexplicable reason, Alice found this statement deeply implausible. Instinctively, she suspected Jude of inventing it simply to bring her fingers up his stalk again. Short-sighted, she said to herself. What can he say to get my fingers to go down again?

Still, she did as she was bidden. Now the suede tip was a window cleaner's chamois, with a little wet ooze on her finger-tips. Jude's eyes were shut and he was breathing like a steam engine.

'Jude,' she asked. 'Was that an orgasm?' A question to which she believed she knew the answer already.

'No.'

Alice, knowing nothing of pre-ejaculate, wondered why Jude was lying.

'Are you sure?'

'Of course I'm sure.'

'But – how do you know?' she persisted.

'I know.'

It seemed better to change the subject. She thought of Iago, suggesting that two people might lie naked abed, an hour or more, and not mean any harm. He meant to sound implausible. It was impossible.

She stopped a kiss to ask, 'You know *Othello*?'

'Not personally. Look, can we talk about this another time?'

Alice had not another bookish thought for three minutes. The desire to have him take her knickers off proved enough to occupy her. Then she started to say, 'Did you notice how my mother . . . ?'

'I don't want to talk about that right now.'

Jude's irritation gave Alice a sense that she was intruding on a private experience. She was partly curious but mostly adoring him. Jude, though, seemed lost in some little world to which her hand was the critical accessory – not herself or her self. She picked the penis up and the heavy mass of it surprised her.

There was rapping on the windowpane. *Shit*. Her father, *already*. The curtains were not even drawn. He'd be at the door soon. Alice yanked her hand out of Jude's jeans and hustled him into the stairwell. 'Hide in the toilet till I let him in. Then *go*. You can come back a bit later.'

She realised she was naked. William was used to her being in bed when he arrived. Generally he sat in the uncomfortable pink institutional hair-cloth armchair, while she got herself ready. In her alarm Alice forgot all this. There was time only to put her jeans on, top button done up, and a jumper, no bra. A minute later she was pulling back the door with one hand, while she held up the other, as though swearing on oath that she would speak the truth, the whole truth, and nothing but the truth. It seemed an incriminating gesture. She pitch-forked her hair instead, catching the smell of Jude's genitals as she did so, and panicked that her father had noticed too. But William was jovial and efficient.

'The police,' he opined, 'are sariously fuckan stupid. *Sarious*, now.'

'Oh, yes? How's that?'

'Well. Here's the thing. They came back, right, for a second interview, right, and now they want to know why I've got the *two* safes, both in the same house, and not just the one. I mean, it should be pretty obvious that if I was going to steal me own bits, then I'd only have the one. Because then everything would be gone. Whereas, the way it's happened, Mother's big diamond ring and the amethyst choker and all that, were untouched. But they're suspicious all the same. They just don't seem to get it. Can yer credit the stupidity of it?'

'It does seem . . . remarkable.'

'Where's Jude?'

'Not arrived yet.'

'I saw his car outside. I thought he was in the toilet. Must be buying yer flowers, then, love.'

'Must be.'

'And I said to them, the police and the insurance man, hmmm, I wonder how it could be done if I were doing it messef. Now, if I were doing it messef, then I'd do it like this . . . because obviously I wouldn't be talkan like that if I had done it, right?'

'Right. Although –'

'What?' William asked keenly. He was caught between two categorical imperatives. He needed his daughter to believe his official story, so she would corroborate it if necessary. And he wanted to show her how tremendously clever he'd been. He wanted her to see what he was up to.

'They may think you are boasting. You know, sort of winding them up subtly.'

William's eyes shone. 'Would I do that?' he asked. They both knew that was exactly what he was doing.

'Where are those fuckan flowers, then?' he challenged Jude, ten minutes later, as he answered the door to him. He held Jude up in the doorway and turned to Alice. 'Jer want to let him in?'

'Yes.'

'All right, then, we'll let yer in. But it was close, lad, very close, I can tell yer, that time. You want to watch it.'

There was a pause.

'Business going well, then?' was Jude's lightly intended opening gambit.

'I'm up against it,' William moaned. 'On a continual basis. Then there's the mother of this one. Women,' he continued authoritatively, 'they never appreciate a good man. And it's not as though I make trouble. I don't eat much in the house. I don't sit in the chairs. Christ, I don't even use the towels.'

'*Towels?*' Jude repeated.

'Towels. Summat wrong with yer ears, lad?' William paused, then proceeded to explain. 'If I use any type of a towel when I've had me bath, right, it's always the wrong fuckan one. I tried using the small ones, like, to show I'm not worthy and that, but then she went fuckan crazy sayan they were for hands or faces or some fuckan thing peculiar.'

'So what do you do instead?'

'Nah, I don't touch the woman's towels. I flick the drops off messef in the bath. Like this –' William mimed a horse on its hind legs, pawing the air. Shockingly magnificent. 'And then, if there's anything left, right, I use this.'

William took out a neat white ironed handkerchief. He was a hero who managed to dry his fourteen stone on its tiny cotton surface. The handkerchief was, in turn, a hero of absorption. He shook it open and blew nothing into it noisily.

'But you know me.' William turned to Alice. 'I've a plan.'

'Still,' Jude interjected, 'have you heard what happens in the William Pope Seminary?' The others stared in surprise. He ought to know that conversation was concluded. This was bad manners.

No, they said, they hadn't.

'In the William Pope Seminary,' Jude pronounced, on the authority of several friends, 'you only get a new towel once a fortnight. The reason for this, they say, is that you're already clean by the time you get out of the shower. No dirt should be rubbed off on to the towel, only clean water. That way, the towels don't get dirty and they don't need washing.'

'And they *believe* this?' William asked. 'I like that!' He slapped Jude on the back. 'Just wait till I tell that to the mother of this one. By the way, did I tell yus she was ill?'

Chapter Twenty-Eight

Everything matched. The curtains matched the paper border that ran around the tops of the walls. This, in turn, matched the pieces of the paper border that had been super-glued inside the beaded segments of two white plastic wardrobes. These wardrobes matched the headboard. The repeated throb of interior decoration.

Oonagh was in bed with a cold. She lay under a bridal-oyster duvet scalloped like an Austrian blind. The headboard was wood composite coated like a tablet with white plastic. Two chests of drawers hung from it like the padded shoulders of a quarterback.

'Why don't you get rid of it?' asked Alice, who found it ugly.

'I need it to put things on. Besides, I like it.'

'What things?'

There were several empty cassette cases, an opaque neon green tower to hold them, a couple of William Pope's heftier volumes, in chocolate milkshake covers, and a big furry My Little Pony Oonagh had bought herself when such things mattered to Alice. (Alice's tiny plastic My Little Ponies had all been instantly vanquished.)

'And I have far, far too much to think about at this particular moment in time.'

'Why don't you just take a paracetamol?' Alice asked. 'It's allowed now.'

Oonagh drew herself up. 'Just because something is allowed doesn't mean *my* conscience allows it. Haven't you read St Paul? What does he say?'

'"All things are lawful, but not all things are edifying."'

Exactly. All things are lawful, but not all things are edifying. Oonagh slithered under the duvet again and endured her cold without so much as a droplet of honey for comfort. She kept it up when the cold turned to flu. She lay shivering righteously for three weeks. With tears and supplications to God, she fought against a glasspaper throat and a ringing skull like a fire alarm. Creeping downstairs in her red satin Chinese pyjamas to make herself a pot of tea, she found she could hardly balance without the banister. God, she said, would be a lamp to her path and a light to her roadway. He would make her rise like an eagle and her limbs would not grow weary.

'Just a little spiritual flu, that's all,' she insisted. 'Perhaps I've been a little discouraged lately.'

Then she got seriously ill.

The strangest things happened.

She ate a ham and tomato sandwich and found she could hardly breathe. Later she managed a few mouthfuls of bolognese sauce but, within minutes, was retching minced meat meteorites into the lavatory bowl. Oonagh determined to restrict her intake to banana purées (pleasanter to vomit) from then on. She began to feel as though she were liquid only. The wardrobes in the bedroom loomed like skyscrapers. The clothes she'd left hanging over the cornflower corduroy chair writhed as though they were living. That was possible.

Everything seemed to be living except her. She felt like a corpse warmed up by the odd cup of Complan.

Oonagh started to wonder if she would ever be well again. So did Alice.

If sickness and death were spiritual diseases, Oonagh must be a sinner – headed for the hottest bits of Armageddon. This explanation was unacceptable. Maybe her conscience was overfine. William P. Pope always knew best. She decided to see a doctor.

Dr Sulakahn, however, was mystified. Oonagh, who had not seen a medic in almost thirty years, regarded him sceptically – like a witch doctor in the bush. He lifted her hand and listened to the music of her wrist. He shone a light into her eyes like a coal miner. He told her to poke out her tongue, asked various silly questions, then wrote on green paper.

'What did I tell you?' she said afterwards. Worldlings could not diagnose sickness.

'Yer've been down that fuckan route the once,' William counselled sagely. 'Stick with the doctor for a bit, huh?'

Meanwhile, Alice prepared healthy recipes, recommended by Jude's mother. One day she was grating carrots for a lentil and bacon soup. At least six large carrots were required. One arm grew weary with the labour, then the other. Swapping did not seem to improve the situation.

Potatoes slowly jostled in the cold water as she lifted the saucepan to the hob.

'How are we doing?' Her father came in to wash his hands in the sink.

'Good,' Alice replied without turning round. 'Soup's prepared.'

Suddenly, there was a loud bang and a cloud of smoke filled the kitchen. William cried, 'Ah fa fuck's sake!'

'What *the hell* was that?' Alice demanded.

'I was just trying to unblock the sink. I've got this stuff – whaddyercallit – that clears pipes and drains and that. *Jaysus.* Nearly lost me eyes there.'

William held a packet of white powder. The tap was still running. There were droplets of chalky water all over the draining board. Parts of the floor were wet. Alice turned with dismay to her soup. It looked undisturbed. But she could not be sure that it had escaped William's acid rain. It was too risky. Her mother was ill enough as it was. She took the pan-handle in both hands, shuffled across the patio and upturned the contents into the grass, where a freshly fallen fungus lay.

'Sorry, love.'

William put his hand on her shoulder and they looked at the remnants of the soup as though it were another burial.

'Had to be done,' Alice said, and then started crying.

'I'll help you make another one.'

'Will you,' she sniffed, 'do all the carrots?'

Every morning, there was a new development in Oonagh's disease.

Alice woke to wailing. Her mother had the answer to her troubles. She pointed a shaky finger at her kimono, hanging on the back of the door. It was black with a red lining and, on the reverse, the design of a great white snake, who was now Satan. There was also – Oonagh's finger indicated the dresser – a silver Charles & Diana celebration coin in a blue presentation box, allegedly given to William by a spiritualist aunt. Now the demons were using this corrupted coin as a medium to make her ill. Alice threw out the kimono and the coin, not in the kitchen bin, but taking them straight to the local parade of shops. She tossed the coin into the slit throat of a cigarette bin, and found a skip for the kimono.

'Don't let them back,' Oonagh begged. 'Whatever you do. They will wait. Then they will come.'

Unnerved, Alice began to question the wisdom of her garbage disposal choices. Knowing the council, the coin might never leave its last resting place. She'd no idea of the skip's provenance.

'I know they will come back for me,' Oonagh repeated.

The morning after, it was the pork chop she'd eaten twenty years earlier. There were worms in pork, she said, giving a confused explanation of trichinosis. These worms had been living in her all those years. They were eating her up from the inside. Alice thought of Darwin, who doubted the existence of a loving God when he learned how wasps reproduced. They laid their eggs in caterpillars. As the baby wasps grew, they survived by eating their hosts from the inside out. Nasty buggers from the beginning, then. They had to get all that aggression from somewhere.

Oonagh was frightened. So was Alice. William, however, was unperturbed.

'But yer haff to admit it,' he said. 'Yer mother is so much better when she's ill.'

'Is she?'

'Christ, yes. It gets her off my case, more or less completely. She's grateful now when yer do something for her. She needs yer. I can eat a bit of bread in the house nowadays.'

'Bread?'

'Yeah, yer know how it is. She's always fuckan creating whenever I eat summat in the house. Bread or milk or onions or any wee thing. Anythan I touch, she says, "I wanted that. That was for such-and-such. How *could* you be so selfish?" It's near enough a fuckan crime to eat anythan in this house. For a while I stopped altogether. Well, now it's her turn.'

'Couldn't you just – have separate groceries?'

'Tried that. Suit me if she stayed ill forever.'

'You can't mean that.'

'I bloody do.'

'That's not very nice.'

'Neither is she, me love, neither is she. The way it is, I get a bit of quiet now.'

'Well, I don't. Most mornings she's wailing. And I've got work to do.'

For the first time William looked concerned. 'Not interfering with yer studies, is it, love?'

'Not helping them, that's for sure.'

'I'll see what I can do.'

Later Alice heard her father talking to her mother.

'The thing is, love,' he said softly, ''tisn't hard to poison someone. 'Tisn't what yer'd call extremely difficult.'

Alice walked in and walked her father out.

'What the hell are you playing at now?'

'You said to quieten her down. Bit of fear, I thought, subdue her, like –'

'Not like *that*. She's bats enough as it is.'

Alice thought it was all in Oonagh's mind. She told Jude as much over the telephone. He was not allowed to visit because he had shingles. His chest bore a wiggly red line like a marked exercise book. Jude pointed out that Oonagh had been ill with flu before she turned loopy or William had started abusing her cerebrally.

'What's he giving his two pennyworth for?' William wanted to know when Alice repeated the conversation to him.

'But I *am* ill and it's *not* in my mind,' Oonagh pleaded, in turn, with her daughter. She was sitting in Alice's red chair. She might have been either man or woman. She might have been a Joshua tree: hair bristly, arms weakly supplicating. Below her eyes there were grey hammocks. Her lips were cracked. She whimpered about a man on the radio who believed, wrongly, that all his limbs were diseased and so proceeded to cut them off, one by one.

'I'm so afraid,' she added. 'I'm afraid because of my mother.'

One night her father had telephoned her at nine o'clock in the evening. Her mother was having an operation. Oonagh hadn't even known her mother was ill. Her father hadn't wanted to worry her, not with her having two kiddies of her own to think about now. He said it would be fine. When Oonagh got off the telephone, William said her mother was unlikely to make it. They didn't operate at nine o'clock unless it was an emergency. That night her mother died. Later Oonagh discovered what had happened. After her sixth child, Oonagh's mother had a hysterectomy. Cancerous weeds grew in the vacant lot. She was ill. But they packed her off to a mental institute instead. It was only when she started to bleed that they started to operate.

'They wouldn't believe her. You must believe me.'

Alice told Oonagh not to worry. A series of blood tests had shown nothing. However, Dr Sulakahn had thought of another test. A stool culture – aka: check the patient's shit for clues.

Unfortunately, Alice had to execute the plan.

First she had to collect the receptacle from the surgery. The receptionist inside the glass bubble was – Alice realised with a start – Jill.

'I thought you were a patient here,' Alice said. 'Like Dad. He told me –'

'How *is* your father?' Jill asked kindly. 'I imagine there was a lot of upset, when we . . .' She started again. 'I know your father must have been very hurt.'

William wasn't lying, then, when he said it was Jill who had ended the relationship. Immediately Alice felt anxious to protect him. 'Oh, you know my father. Nothing bothers him. He's a character. He doesn't take women seriously. You're all for recreational use. He's not got the addictive personality.' There was a pause. 'But I'm here for my mother . . .' And she began to explain.

'Package for a stool culture?' Jill repeated. Her green eyes widened uncomprehendingly. She processed *stool* slowly. As the solution came to her at last, she resisted it. Alice saw her eyes thinking of gleaming steel legs in an American diner. But this stool was shit and there was nothing for it.

Jill began to open drawers and close cupboards. She whisked about like the least useful implement in a deluxe blender kit. Defeated, she made enquiries with Dr Sulakahn.

'Ooh,' she said, back inside her bubble, 'apparently it's just like the urine sample pouches. Except there's – *a spoon.*' She took a moment to marvel at the small blue plastic spoon inside the plastic bag. 'Well, I've never seen one of those before.'

'Really?' Alice replied drily. 'I'm quite a seasoned user myself.'

Second and worse, it was Alice who had to obtain the sample. Her mother was willing to produce the batch, but Alice was in charge of selecting and sending the right bit for hospitalisation. Again, it was shit and there was nothing for it. It would be floating in the water, or sunk to hand-wetting depths. She'd have to harpoon it against the porcelain, and then ply her scoop with decision.

Oonagh emerged from the bathroom, her body doubled over like a suit in transit. Alice discovered she had a harder task than shit-whaling. Her eyes attempted to look into the bowl of the toilet without actually looking. It couldn't be done.

And the yule log she'd imagined turned out to be more in the nature of a chocolate mousse. Alice took her scoop easily enough, dispatched the spoon swiftly into the plastic bag, folded it over and sealed it with a sense of accomplishment using the pre-printed sticker. Then she took it to the hospital.

Chapter Twenty-Nine

Within days, Oonagh had joined her scoop.

Jude started to come round again – and with expectations.

The first day he turned up wearing a new three-quarter-length black leather jacket, a white T-shirt reading FCUK and dark navy jeans. He had no sooner been complimented than he was taking them all off. He said he was only showing her his shingle trail. To the observer, it was a crack in a fresco. Enticed, Alice put her hand out to it like Michelangelo's Adam reaching for God. God was unwilling, though.

'Easy, tiger,' Jude cautioned.

To the sufferer, the shingle rash was a magma line.

Then Jude removed his jeans. At this, Alice hesitated. She was very pleased to have been introduced to his beautiful appendages, but uncertain whether they should become a regular part of the proceedings. Her idea was that physical love between them would be all right so long as no penis was involved. The main reason for this was that she feared pregnancy. Sperm were her mortal enemy. Even Jude's underpants were a worry.

Jude looked at her squarely and replied, 'Well, you try swimming on cotton Calvin Kleins.'

In the interval since he had last seen Alice, Jude had seen Maria several times. Each time they talked frankly about the Plain Truth – and to do this felt more intimate and risky than to take their clothes off again. Jude, though, was sure he would not have minded. He began to feel uneasy once Maria insisted that only 'they' could talk to each other properly now. He refrained from telling her about the conversation he'd had with Alice about the Song of Solomon. Yes, it was only they, he agreed, who could penetrate the lie of the truth.

Now he turned Alice on her back, raised her T-shirt and pulled down her jeans. Licking his hand, he sluiced the vital part of himself, and explored the valley between her buttocks. In a whisper he promised his semen would land safely in the high mountainous regions of her back. Alice worried about pregnancy all the same. The pre-ejaculate dribbled on to her. Didn't streams trickle down valleys? Who'd ever heard of a stream trickling *up* a valley? She clenched her thighs firmly and willed her vagina shut.

Jude was moist now as a self-basting chicken, but her body wasn't helping either. She dribbled from both mouths. She remembered that sexual misconduct, in earlier times, was called *incontinence* and that seemed appropriate now.

As Jude climaxed, the sensations of Alice's skin reproached her. A burst of his come leapt and landed along her vertebrae like a locust. Then another like hot fat spitting out of the pan.

'Hold on,' he said, still panting, and taking a lemon balm tissue out of his pocket.

The tissue's fragrance had to do with his memory of the first time he came on the Italian woman. He could still hear her emphatic declaration, 'I hate the smell of semen.' When he asked where she'd smelt it before, she said there were tubes of it lying around the science labs at school.

As if.

How different could Italian schooling *be*?

Mopped up, sanitised, Alice stood. The movement pulled tiny hairs where Jude's semen had dried.

'You OK?' Jude asked tentatively.

'Uh-huh. You?'

'Me? I'm great.'

'I have a plan. Something much better than that.'

'You do?'

She did.

Alice's plan was her best and most long-lived idea about sex. The buttock business was far too dangerous. If Jude's penis had to get involved, she made up the rule that pregnancy could not occur so long as at least one of them always kept their jeans on. She felt there was also safety in distance and brevity. The relationship of her fingers to Jude's penis was like that of a brisk handshake in which the arm was stretched to its fullest length, elbow resentful of the notion that it should bend.

Jude said, as they tried it out an hour later, 'But I feel like you are in the bedroom and I am in the closet in the hallway. How can I make love to a woman who is in another room?'

It was a love triangle. There they lay – heads kissing (corner number one), bodies sharply diverging at forty-five-degree angles down to their bottoms (corners two and three), while Alice's arm formed the third side as it joined up with Jude's outstretched member.

But what about the legs? It was a love triangle with the legs dangling, far apart from each other. Like an A. Alice felt very pleased with herself on the whole. There were sacrifices, of course: fatigue in her arm after a while, worse even than grating carrots (which at least did not murmur when you paused to rest). Also anxiety in case the pre-ejaculate should be crawling up her arm and down her belly and somehow through the cervix after all. Then the trail of glue left to turn cold on her fingers.

Next Jude said he had a plan too. If pregnancy was her worry, he reassured her with no small amount of glee, then there were many ways around it. Sex was happening to Alice, one way or the other.

'Lie down,' he instructed.

Alice lay down on the bed gynaecologically. Jude's mouth took in the coral of her broken hymen and her sting ray labia. She was dinner, she was dessert. She was strawberries and ice cream.

Bliss. Then Alice panicked as she remembered reading, somewhere in the *Encyclopaedia*, that the entrance of air into the vagina 'may in some certain combination of circumstances precipitate *a fatal embolism*'. The words triggered a small earthquake. Death was surely worse than pregnancy. True, Jude had betrayed no desire to exploit her potential as a balloon. Nor any sadistic wish to pop her. But he was still breathing. Which was more than she might be, if this went on for too much longer.

She pulled away and said, 'I fear a fatal embolism.'

'A what?'

She 'explained'.

'Let's have a bath together,' he suggested happily.

'What's that?' he asked, pointing, in the bathroom.

That was a small wooden water-stained chair William had stolen from a primary school. Three folded handkerchiefs lay on it.

'Your father's bath towels? So that was true, then, what he told us that time?'

'Oh, yes. That's the trouble with my father. You never can tell.' She hesitated. 'Jude? You know what we've been doing?'

'Yes,' he said, wrapping his legs around her. She relaxed in the warmth of the water. Their greatest taboo wasn't sex. It was admitting to each other what they really felt about the plain truth of things. You could have sex and still believe in sin. The happier inversion of this statement they had not yet dared propose to themselves: you could disbelieve in sin and still have sex! Each one was too fearful to start the conversation, in case the other should be appalled. Alice did not want to mislead Jude. More particularly, she did not want the burden of a lifelong pretence. What, she asked herself, if he should be pretending too? It seemed foolish not to begin the conversation.

Alice crouched forward to twist the hot tap on again for a brief spurt. Her palms belly-flopped on the bubbles created by the falling water. The movement, the noise, the injection of warmth, allowed her to settle back and to say, as though her buttocks were the very foundation of confidence now, 'I may not – believe *everything*, you know.'

It seemed enough to say.

'I know,' Jude replied quietly, kissing her shoulder.

Chapter Thirty

Two weeks later, Alice feared she might be pregnant, after all.

She squatted and willed blood to pour out of her. Her cervix was a glass. It was simply a matter of tipping it. This was how unmarried girls and women with impotent husbands got rid of their babies in the old days. Surely a series of hectic squats could shake a period out of her too. Don't worry about the carpet, she counselled her cervix. Blood would hardly stain the bedroom's mangy dark pink carpet, anyhow. She repeated the action, then gave up. The cervix was an hourglass giving nothing away. Then she told herself it was persistence that won the day, and tried again.

Perhaps the setting was not right. Bedrooms were where you made babies. Bathrooms were more likely to get rid of them. She had come clean about the Plain Truth in there with Jude. Maybe she could come unpregnant in there too. Back in the salmon-pink suite, however, Alice despaired of the décor and her chances of infertility.

Half an hour later Jude arrived and, tapping his crotch, offered to blast the period out of her with his power tool – but that seemed contrary to the spirit of the problem. He had a

Swiss Army knife, too, which he believed could resolve any crisis of a practical nature. This time it stayed in his pocket.

It was decided that Jude would buy a pregnancy test. They waited all day. Under the cover of dark and his baseball cap, Jude drove through the streets. Unworried that Alice might be pregnant, which did not seem in the least likely, Jude was enjoying himself.

The tests were up near the cash desk. He made his way towards them.

'Jood!'

Jude put his basket down slowly, as though it were a weapon, and turned to face Maria. He would be bravely insouciant and, that way, the situation would be recoverable.

'I thought joo ignoring me.' It was the first time he had seen her in over a fortnight. 'I see joor cap, of course.'

'No. Just wasn't expecting to see anyone, that's all. Especially – not you. I heard you were in Spain.'

'I was. I was there, thinking many things. Should I come back, what should I say. And now – here joo are.' She paused. 'What joo buy?'

Maria lowered herself to Jude's basket and inspected three boxes of balsam-infused tissues for the price of two.

'Good for Alice's nose,' he explained.

'Alice, she is lucky to have joo. Pedrie, he never buy me tissues.'

Together they waited silently in front of packets of condoms, suppositories, pregnancy tests. Items that had to be bought under surveillance. Anadin and anti-itching creams, too. You couldn't have a scratch or a headache in private.

'Hey, Jood, you buy me a present?'

Maria waved her finger magically over the pregnancy tests. 'Which one would you like?'

Maria's finger circled, then pointed to a Clearblue box. '*Definitely* for a boy.'

They laughed nervously.

'I didn't know you were . . . ?' Jude nodded in the direction of the box.

'Oh no, we are not,' Maria replied defensively. 'But . . .' She searched for the words. 'If joo like we go for the drink and I explain to joo why . . . I fill sad.'

Jude hesitated. Maria replied for him. 'But I think – eh no.'

'I'm sorry,' he said.

Nothing more was said until they were outside the shop. Maria looked as though she was poised to say something momentous. Jude couldn't bear it.

'Listen,' he began, preventing her, 'I've forgotten something. It's kind of important. I'll have to go back.'

He returned to the shop and pointed out the blue box to the assistant.

An hour later, Alice was unwrapping the test.

Chapter Thirty-One

While Jude was in Boots, Alice was eating dinner with her father in the local pub. The landlady thrust the plates across the bar resentfully, as though they were unexpected and unwanted arrivals at her private family dinner. There were people brandishing notes, shouting to be served. It was more like the futures market at the Stock Exchange.

William found a table, and set down the drinks and the dishes. One beef: his. One turkey: hers. 'I'd have gone for the beef, messef.'

'I can see that,' she replied.

William split apart the Brussels sprouts, examining each one for worms. The landlady walked past, stared and seemed to take it as a personal affront.

'Slipp'ry wee buggers,' he said, 'Yer'll not get me.'

'They won't,' Alice agreed routinely. She had pregnancy on her mind.

'We're always thinkan of something else, us lot,' her father replied, undeceived. 'Ten things at once.'

'No. Well, yes. Lots of work to do.'

'I suppose there must be. Want a glass of wine?'

'No, I'm fine with lemonade.'

William paused to consider. 'A *nice* glass, though? How about that? Help you unwind.'

No, she said, she just wanted a lemonade. But trying to persuade people you really want lemonade is like trying to tell them you are not unhappy. They never believe you. Long experience had taught her that.

She capitulated. 'I'd love one.' She smiled fondly, because he looked so pleased to have made the breakthrough. He beckoned the landlady across and ordered a wine and a lemonade. She said they didn't have lemonade. They had 7UP. They had Sprite. They had R. White's. She put a ringed hand up to hair arranged like a loaf of chollah.

'That's what I meant,' Alice said. She was distracted, anxious. 'Any of them'll do.'

'I thought you wanted wine,' William remembered. His mind was elsewhere, too.

'Wine, then, whatever.'

Alice wanted to be at home, on the toilet, holding a test with a minus sign in the result window. The wine arrived. If she *was* pregnant, she should not be drinking it. She took the tiniest sip. The landlady walked sternly past, policing the room.

'She wants to watch it,' Alice said ironically. 'Once I'm divine – there's no knowing what I might do to her.'

'Listen,' William sniffed, cutting the last of the sprouts patiently. 'I have all this with yer mother. Yer here and then yer gone. We're only passing through. That's all it is. Is me mother still here? No, she's gone. She's in the ground. And she was a really good woman.'

He chinked his glass against Alice's.

'We're the same,' he emphasised. 'You and I. We're not good people. But at least we *know* we're not good. At least – we try.'

William loved altruism as only a deeply calculating person

can. To be doing something for nothing, when *everything* else was done with an eye to the main chance – the idea fascinated him. It was why he turned a blind eye when coke addicts stole JCB buckets from him. And why he got lists of people who had no visitors in hospital – and took them carnations and told them jokes.

'But I've never done anything like that,' Alice protested, feeling she had no right to shelter under the umbrella of his altruism. 'I haven't helped anyone.'

'Yer talk to the weak people in the church, don't yer? The old ones, and that. I've seen yer.'

'That's only so I don't have to talk to the strong ones.'

'Yer all right,' he said, and stroked her cheek affectionately.

William began talking about his financial scams. 'Jer think I'm a fool?'

'No.'

'People do. They think I'm a fool.'

Alice shook her head.

''*Tisn't* difficult, yer know, to poison someone,' he confided irrelevantly.

'No?'

'Happens all the time, actually. Can't think, messef, when it might have happened last.'

William was irreverently merry. Alice did not know whether he was boasting again about his crimes, or fantasising control of events beyond him.

'You mustn't say things like that.'

'No, I mustn't,' he mocked. 'Yer man Nielsen, know him?'

'The mass murderer?'

'Yup. He'd kill 'em and keep 'em. Propped the bodies up in chairs, then had cornflakes with the corpses. Cream teas in the afternoon. Talk to them.'

William regarded the criminal famous as friends he might have had.

'They don't be right, these guys, in the head. That's what yer've to understand. Ian,' he explained, as though they were on first name terms, 'sure he was jerst the same. *Ian Brady*,' he pronounced proudly and for the benefit of the uninitiated. 'But yer know my favourite?'

'Hitler?'

'Hitler. The man had vision. He had trains. Put the fuckan Worldwiders in the camps, anyway. Shame yer mother wasn't around then. She'd know all about persecution then. She's been persecuting me my whole fuckan life. What did he say? He'd raze yus all to the ground. Or freeze yer fingers off, anyway, in Siberia. Just like the Jews. Mother had relatives in Dachau, yer know.'

'Actually, not just like the Jews. There was a difference.'

'*Was* there, by Christ?' William waited eagerly.

'Worldwiders could sign a document saying they would renounce their faith. That way they could get out. The Jews had no options like that.'

'And did they? Sign?'

'No. Or very rarely.'

'Fuckan ejits.'

It seemed patronising to agree too enthusiastically with this judgement. Alice thought the martyrs were brave but credulous – and pitied them. She'd read their letters, saying they were sure they would feel no pain at death. She'd seen videos documenting the history of the Worldwiders in the camps. She suspected guiltily that William P. Pope was grateful to Hitler. The Führer had given Pope's Church a place in history. Members of the local Church (including Oonagh) were armchair martyrs modelled on these World War II resisters.

It was common to talk of how, as The End of The World approached, your fingernails would be pulled off by tormentors, and yet you would not reveal the names of your co-Saints. Alice hadn't any nails to be pulled off, but she would have told them the names anyway. Especially of the Smiths, the Jellys and that Italian woman.

As she saw it, the problem wasn't the martyrs. It was the whole concept of Christianity. Christianity praised, not the ordinary, but the mediocre. The more unambitious you were, the more ignorant you were, the more boring you were, the more likely it was that God would save you. What was this but an encouragement to be vain about nugatory achievements? It was arrogantly complacent. The Worldwiders took their unremarkableness as positive *proof* that God must prefer them to people who were remarkable. Alice could hardly bear to hear them praise themselves in church for being so very humdrum. For being 'sheep' not goats.

'What are sheep?' she asked. 'Sheep are stupid animals who follow the crowd and bleat when they get caught in barbed wire. If you were God and you had *the whole world* to choose from, *surely* you wouldn't pick Mum, or me, or Peter to save? Surely you'd pick someone useful and innovative – Dr Sulakahn. Even *I* wouldn't pick me.'

'Don't be talkan like that,' her father said crossly, as though criticism of the Church was his monopoly. 'Who'd jer get this from?' he asked, not having heard of Nietzsche. 'Jude? Yer need yer faith.'

'But you called them *ejits*.'

'So? I think Jude's a bad influence on you.'

'No he isn't. And anyway,' she hesitated fractionally, 'I love him.'

'You can get in the way of lovan anythan. You can love a

turd from the arse of Henry G. Shepherd if yer not extremely careful and don't keep all yer wits about yer.'

'Don't you love Sarah?'

William paused. 'See this hand?' He extended five prime-pork-and-leek fingers.

Alice nodded.

'Sarah is the tiniest piece of dust on this hand. And I could blow it off any time.' He demonstrated. 'See?' He puffed. 'See?' He puffed again. 'Anyway,' he pronounced, 'she's a funny one.'

'Is she?'

William looked round for the landlady, crouched forward and lowered his voice. 'Asked me to shave the hairs on her arse a few times. Said I was fuckan lucky to be doing it.' He sat back emphatically.

'What's she want you to do that for?'

'I don't really know.' William shook his head.

'And anyway,' Alice added, 'I thought you said you weren't sleeping with her? She wasn't "like that"?'

William was still answering the first question. 'It's just a thing, like, right, that she wants.' He leaned forward again. 'Then she said that if I was *ever* to try anythan on with her back *there*, right, yer know, we wouldn't be seean one nother again. That'd be it.'

'But I'd have thought the shaving thing was a, kind of, *prelude* . . . to . . . the other?'

'I know. So would I. But yer never can tell.'

Alice took another tiny sip of wine as she contemplated this unexpected revelation.

'She's just a child. She thinks she's all grown up. She keeps sayan to me things like, "a woman a thirty's been round the block". But when she . . . well, at a particular moment, right, when she . . . well, anyway, what happens, right, is she sucks her thumb.'

'Right.'

'Sometimes,' William added, 'I be very good in bed, and sometimes I be very bad. I can't . . . judge it.'

These confessions fascinated Alice and she waited to hear more.

'Yer mother,' he said, 'I realise it now. How old-fashioned she is. She jerst won't do a thing . . . Are you going to drink that or just play with it?'

William's red face was jovial as he offered to take the glass off her. He gulped it down in one. They got up to leave.

Once outside, Alice asked, 'Can we – not go there again?'

'Wasn't *that* bad, was it?' There was surprise in his voice.

'It wasn't the food. Or,' she added quickly, 'the wine. Nice glass of wine. I just don't like the landlady.'

'Her. Yes. She's like yer mother, that woman. Terrible intolerant. It all has to be *perfect*.' He pronounced the word facetiously.

Back home, William settled into the mushroom whiteness of the sofa, where, between him and a bottle of Napoleon brandy, he tried to understand why his wife didn't appreciate him. He took a telephone call, and then settled again to ponder this mystery.

Chapter Thirty-Two

The pregnancy test was smuggled in the free box of tissues.

'Just had a call from Maria,' William told Alice.

Jude tensed.

'What's she want now?' Alice asked.

'Reckons she wants to go back to Spain. Reckons there's nothan for her here now.'

William turned to Jude. Jude concentrated on not looking guilty.

'Says Peter isn't attentive enough,' William continued. 'She's off again for a bit, next month, without him. I think she's got some fella on the go. Sh'ever bend your ear about it?' William asked Jude, who promptly shook his head.

'Thing is, right, to find out who's the little fucker she's been messan about with.'

'And tell Peter?' Alice asked.

'Christ, no. Yer can't tell Peter anythan. Yer know what he's like. Loves her, don't he. It'd destroy him. No, yer'd get rid of the man she's been messan with. Get some guy, give him five hundred quid or so, and one day, when the little bugger's leavan the pub, get him smashed up.

Pavlova face. He'd think twice about it again, I can tell yer.'

'But why the man? Why not her?' Alice asked.

'She's beautiful. Yer can't be fuckan up a face like that. It wouldn't be right. Anyhow, that was my idea of it. I was wonderan. Reckon yer might trail her a bit for me, yer know, like a detective?'

Alice laughed. 'Don't be ridiculous. This isn't a film.'

'What about you, lad?'

Jude cleared his throat. 'Erm. Don't think I can.'

'It would save me havan to pay someone,' William continued. 'Yer could wait in the café opposite her shop. That kinda thing.'

Alice said they would think about it. Anything to get away.

She made for the bathroom. Jude waited in the bedroom. The test lay inside the box, wrapped in many tissues. It tumbled out like Cleopatra from the carpet. Or the concubines of the Chinese emperor in the Forbidden City.

The tester looked like a tampon. Which idiot of the design department had thought of that? she wondered. Just then, she could feel her period starting, after all. She wiped herself with a tissue, examining it like nuptial sheets displayed, in olden times, as proof of virginity to the parish worthies. Menstruation was confirmed. So was virginity. She rushed out of the bathroom with the good news.

'I'm so pleased for you,' Jude replied.

'For me?'

'Oh, *Alice*. If I could impregnate people that easily, I could make a living out of it.'

'But these things happen.'

'No they don't. People just say they do. Remember that girl, what was her name? Said, "It happened the first time." Why?

She didn't want to make it sound as though she'd done it a lot of times before. They were calling her the village bicycle as it was.'

'And had she?'

'Well, how should I know? But I expect. You be at the practice tomorrow?'

'Yes.'

'I'll keep you a seat.'

'Practices' were Armageddon 'waiting' surgeries: weekly Bible meetings conducted in the living rooms of private homes. Lately Alice had started going to the one at Jude's parents'. He answered the doorbell, parents on either side as if he needed restraining. They had painted the interior of their house sanatorium white. The walls were white, the doors were white, even the floors were covered with white vinyl tiles. The furniture had white washable plastic surfaces. There was a meagre allowance of magnolia gloss on the skirting boards and cornices – as though, where you might expect white paint, it was disallowed deliberately. Alice stood like a blot in the hallway.

'Lydia!' Jude's father Theophilus spoke excitedly, his arms describing wild monsters in the air.

'Her name is Alice,' Jude corrected.

'*The*-o.' His wife's voice assumed a warning Doppler effect.

'Alice? Is it *really* Alice? Have you thought of Lydia?' Theophilus asked, as he chivvied her down the hallway. 'Lydia is a good Greek name. And a biblical one. Lydia was a seller of purple who became a Christian. Acts 16.' Theophilus always conversed with his fellow Saints as though they had not read the Bible. 'How lovely it was in those times,' he continued. 'It was not like now, when technology has ruined man. In those days, you could simply sell a colour for a living. Purple, red, blue. Myself I would sell yellow.'

'OK, Pop,' Jude said. 'That's enough.'

'I think purple means purple dye, doesn't it?' Alice replied politely.

'Not die, no, we don't die. A living, I said.'

Alice found herself in the living room. Folding white plastic chairs were ranged confrontationally round the walls. The 'waiting' in this spiritual surgery happened before the meeting. People sat silently, or else talked cautiously, glancing at the practice leader who occupied the sole armchair in the room and made such decisions as whether to begin at 7.29, 7.30 or 7.31 p.m. Every week, he looked at his watch and remarked insightfully, 'Well, as we know, time only moves in one direction. So let's make a start.' Waiting also happened when the practice leader asked a question of the assembled Saints. Not that these questions were unpremeditated. Nor were the answers difficult to find. Everyone held between thumb and forefinger an open copy of Pope's latest book – at this time, a thin mauve volume entitled *Christian Life on Other Planets*. All the questions the leader was going to ask were printed, like footnotes, at the bottom of the page. Ideally, everyone would read the relevant chapter for discussion before coming to the practice, and underline the answers.

The chapter provided all the answers.

The underlinings gave all the necessary verbal and visual prompts.

Saints were encouraged to practise for the practice – by trying out their answers in front of a friend. Or, failing interpersonal skills, a mirror.

And still, there was a great deal of waiting.

The situation was tense, the room so dazzling and cuboid in its whiteness that Alice, staring at the title of Pope's book, feared she might be falling through space, already on her way to Christian life on other planets. Theophilus read the chapter – a paragraph at a time – before the relevant question was asked. Despite his general mania and a nationalistic disposition to stop and offer unsolicited etymologies for all English borrowings from the Greek, he could not read very well because he was dyslexic.

There were plenty of good readers in the room, but they were all women. Women could not read if men were in the room. Even when men were not in the room, women had to show they were not divinely intended to read by wearing a covering on their head. A hat or a scarf would do. Some, like Oonagh, staged a token rebellion by wearing a token Kleenex.

Jude was there, too, but the pastor had instructed the practice leader that he was still in the probationary period. He was not yet in good enough 'standing' with the Church to read again. Good readers in a good standing, or bad readers in a good standing, could read, but never good readers in a bad standing. So it was that Jude's father read about the moral code of Christian aliens, which was remarkably similar to the moral code of William P. Pope and the Ten Commandments. In fact, all three were identical. This was because God had spoken personally to the prophets Moses and William P. Pope – and the greatest among the saved aliens, whose name was Greene.

At each mention of *fornication* and *fornicators*, Alice's armpits grew moister and her body faintly shook. She felt the need to swallow – as though this reflex would rid her of discomfort. Or perhaps because it would demonstrate to her that she was still in control of her bodily functions. Then, in mid-swallow, she feared this swallowing would be audible and thus a sign of her guilt. As a result she choked on her spit and had to cough. A couple of people looked up. Alice was red-faced. Jude fetched her a tumbler of water.

Yet she had not committed full fornication.

Fornication in fact occurred, shortly afterwards, as a result of rather contradictory logic. First, though relieved by the absurdity of Pope's all-encompassing definition of fornication, Alice began to argue that, if she was 'guilty' now, she might as well be properly improper. Second, she reasoned that she was actually *less* likely to get accidentally pregnant by having sex than by not having it. Sod's Law applied with particular vigour in her case, so she decided to thwart it bravely. Also, they could take precautions. These thoughts occurred when Jude was moving on top of her with particular yearning.

This first attempt was, in fact, just that – an attempt. Oonagh was in bed next door. Alice and Jude were being quiet on the carpet. They were allowed to be alone together because Oonagh assumed that brick walls masked nothing. She also thought that Jude would not have the nerve for another sexual misdemeanour.

When desire took off, it did not concern Alice that Oonagh was – like a rat in London – only three metres away. But when desire wavered, the loudness of her breathing was like an oxygen mask. Just now, though, breathing was moderate and Alice was settling herself back on the rug with lifted skirt and the thought that the virgin's experience was not too bad after all, when Jude whispered that he wasn't actually *in* – and could she possibly help out? Alice tried, but it was impossible. She couldn't be a fornicator, no matter how hard she tried, or Jude tried. Copious quantities of spit didn't help either. Half an hour later they had another shot. This time the rubber tip of Jude's pencil made it. Alice was pained but relieved. It could only get better from now on. She remembered a line from Laclos's *Les Liaisons Dangereuses*, 'the shame is like the pain – you only feel it once'.

But Laclos turned out not to be writing about Alice. It got more painful with every subsequent attempt. She argued that the rubber tip was obviously as far as things were meant to go, anatomically speaking. Jude was unpersuaded. He was twenty-four years old and if this was sex, then his name was William P. Pope. Neither of them were fornicators yet, he was sure.

Alice refused to let him in at all after that.

Domestic circumstances were, in any case, becoming less suitable. Oonagh now managed short upright periods several times a day. The sex life of Jude and Alice was consequently conducted on a two-minute unit: the time it would take Oonagh to get from her bed to theirs.

'We could try my parents',' Jude suggested.

'Or not.'

Instead they started doing things out of doors. These out-of-doors experiences were so fearful they might as well have been out-of-body experiences. Jude's car was little protection. In car parks, late at night, all would be going well until another vehicle's headlights changed Jude's Fiat Punto into a Chinese lantern. Hands were withdrawn. Jude laid a map over his groin and flicked on the internal light, pretended to read.

'Your penis is a book rest,' Alice giggled.

'You ought to like it, then.'

With nowhere to go, on one of these stalled occasions the would-be lovers started to imagine another world. A utopia for the bed-starved. There would be private booths for sex, rather like automatic toilets. In each booth, a modest double bed, made up with freshly pressed white sheets, a shower with rainforest, mist and massage functions, and two thick cotton bathrobes. These items were immediately cleaned, dried and reinstalled each time a pair of lovers exited the booth.

Utopias are like fundamentalist churches, however. They have very strong rules. An element of coercion entered the fantasy. The booths were there, not because the utopians necessarily loved sex, but because it was the law. The laws were decided by Jude. Jude being an accountant, his law said that sex was a tax. Each utopian was obliged to pay their sexual dues to society. In hard terms, this meant they had to perform at least fifty sexual acts per month. Since people still had to work, the booths were there to allow people the chance to copulate when out shopping, or after paying their other bills at the bank. A utopia for the sex-starved, then, for fornicators, adulterers and the randomly randy – but a dystopia of orgasmic drudgery for everyone else.

Jude became increasingly concerned with the penalties for those who failed to make the satisfactory tax returns. Offenders, always beautiful young striplings, were sent to sexual dungeons, where thirty-stone men and women with police batons and garlic breath forced them to make up their scores.

In this way, a month passed.

Chapter Thirty-Three

Maria returned from Spain with sangria – and spirit. She kept on her sunglasses by Chanel when Peter picked her up in the Arrivals hall at Luton. They were still on as she lay on the sofa. In sequinned sandals, her sepia feet dangled and jigged as she smooched down a monster-size beef and chilli pizza, and drank two pints of Coca-Cola. The glasses were still on when she got into the bathtub. She grinned grimly.

'I think I go in Espain again soon.'

'You know what people are saying?' Peter paced the tiles.

'Noh.' She was admiring her bloated belly, stroking and cupping it.

'They say you're having an affair.'

'Well, me I say *fuck* the peoples.' And, farting into the bathwater, she laughed.

Peter rang his father and arranged a mutual grumble about the state of women.

In William's back-room office, a diminutive wall-heater ('Only costs me a penny an hour,' he bragged) competed against a penny-sized hole in the single pane of glass.

'People say she's having an affair.'

'What people?'

'Isabella.'

William was dismissive. 'Well, I wouldn't worry then, she's just a jealous little bitch.' He paused. His eyebrows contracted. 'She mention who with? Some Spanish buck, is it?'

'No . . . It wasn't that. She was hinting it might be *Jude*?' The statement took on a dubious interrogative quality. Sitting side-saddle on the desk, Peter pursued the hypothesis doubtfully. 'But it couldn't be – could it?' A piece of the leather top had come unstuck. He fiddled with it like a scab.

'Oh,' William replied with artful casualness, 'leave that alone, will yer?' he asked irritably, indicating the desk. 'Yer don't want to make it any worse than 'tis already.'

'Sorry.'

William pushed his swivel chair back a metre. Old, weathered invoices climbed up the spike like poppadoms.

So *that* was who the little fucker was. And the discovery hadn't cost him anything. No private detective needed. 'Well, maybe, now yer put it like that. In actual fact I thought the same messef at one time.'

'And you didn't *tell me*?' Trembling, Peter got to his feet and kicked an absent football furiously. 'I will never –'

William waved him down crossly. 'Chrissake, lad. Just listen to me for a minute, will yer? I *thought* it. But there was nothan in it, right. I had her followed, yer see,' he explained. 'A private detective by the name of Jonathan Hunt. He was workan on it for two months. The first bill came to eight hundred and fifty-nine pound and sixty-one pee. After that I stopped counting.'

Peter wasn't at all mollified by this fabrication. William had to find another argument quick.

'This isn't just about *you*, yer know,' he added huffily. 'There's Alice to be considered as well. D'yer think I'd be letting Jude marry her if I thought for one minute –'

'They're getting *married*?'

'Oh, yes,' William lied confidently. 'I've been encouraging it. 'Course if y'ever spoke to yer own fuckan mother or yer sister, yer might find these things out. Sure Jude's a grand lad.'

'*Marry*?' Alice repeated, surprised and pleased, an hour later. William was wearing his overcoat indoors, as he often did. 'But I thought you disapproved? And what about my degree?'

'Finish it in married quarters,' her father suggested. 'They must have them in that university. Yer can't stop people marrying.'

'What about the vacations?'

'Live with us. We'll be moving back to Westwood soon.' When he rubbed his hands, she heard the slight sound of trowel in cement. Her father was full of solutions. He had pulled off a successful insurance fraud: he could do anything now. He beckoned Alice into his bedroom. His briefcase sat on a metal safe, draped with a spare bed sheet that served as a tablecloth. He showed Alice, as though it were a certificate, a letter that said the insurers had reached their final decision. He must inform them in writing whether he was willing to accept the sum of £259,000. A cheque would be posted within ten days.

'Yer know what the beauty of this is?'

Alice waited.

'The beauty of this is where the money comes from. The insurance companies I'm using, right, they were in that fuckan stocking stock exchange whaddyercallit conglomerate that lost me me money. The Pretty Polly people. If it wasn't for them, we'd never have had to leave Westwood. I'm just gettan it back now, yer see. The fuckers *owe* me it. It's bloody compensation.'

This payout would reduce his mortgage on Westwood sufficiently to make it manageable again. And he had other plans for retrieving the further hundred grand still 'owing' to him. His fleet of JCBs was also now insured by associates of the former conglomerate. 'Come with us to Westwood,' he persisted. 'I'll give yer the master bedroom suite, huh?'

'Oh, but we couldn't.' Alice could picture herself all the same. On the bed at one extremity of the seventeen-foot room. Jude in front of the rubber-wood chest of drawers at the other. She waved to him. Or they each hid behind the shuttered doors of their own built-in wardrobe. Or one used the avocado bidet while the other sat in the corner bath. 'That's yours.'

'Doesn't worry me, love. Yussef and Jude can have it. I insist. No wonder Mother's ill, what with this house being so small.'

'It's a four-bedroom detached house.'

'She's used to five. These things have a way of havan an effect.' He paused. 'Wrong sort of windows here, as well. They made her ill before.'

There was an opaque window in the porch the colour and thickness of a Lucozade bottle. The rest of the windows – narrow horizontal paranoid slits – had been designed for a world in an oil crisis.

'Remember the windows in Westwood?' her father asked.

Alice remembered the triptychs of windows, each with a cathedral curve. The middle one in the sequence had a vent like a hairdresser's clip.

'Yer'd never get ill with windows like that.'

'And what about Mum? She'd be too ill to come.'

'Yer mother,' William replied emphatically, 'will right herself for this. Trust me. I'll pay for that too.'

'Pay who?'

William surveyed Alice warily, his expression ironically

uncertain. He continued, after a long pause. 'Oh, so yer *are* still me daughter, then, and not some bleedan idiot who just happens to look like her. Pay who? Pay Mother, a course.'

'How will that help? Give her a hundred quid and she'll perk up?'

'Yer've a point there. More like five hundred, yer think?'

'*I mean*, money doesn't come into it.'

William smiled pityingly.

'Money always comes into it. What yer haff always to remember, Alice, is I've known yer mother for far longer than you. Says she doesn't care about money, or the house she lives in, because of God. It's *all* she fuckan cares about. That woman's a terrible liar.'

'But she says she's never told a lie. She says she speaks only the plain truth now.'

'That's only because,' William smacked his hand down on a windowsill and looked at it, faintly puzzled, when it smarted in return, 'she told so many fuckan lies afore she was a Saint, she's no *need* to tell lies now.'

'Maybe it would be better if she did. I think it's far worse when she tells the truth. Remember when she told Peter I typed that letter for her? Then she told me that he wanted nothing more to do with me. Now I suppose he wouldn't even come to the wedding.'

'She said that?'

William was angry now, and Alice was afraid. She could feel the heat of his rage. For him, it was as if these statements had been her own, just because they were now on her lips. This was the inevitable assumption of the serial liar: all reported speech was the fabrication of the present speaker. All quotations were inventions.

'Yes,' she admitted.

'Don't get involved,' he said, 'in yer mother's ideas. She's just tryan to split yus kids up. She doesn't want yus being friends.'

'Why not?'

'That's just the way she is. Selfish. Not family-minded. Look at where she comes from – lot of nutters. She's the best of them. But they're all a job lot.'

'I don't understand. And anyway – you haven't the highest claim to sanity yourself.'

'But Alice, you know what the difference is with us lot?'

'No.'

'We *know* we're mad. Yer've only got a problem when yer don't know yer mad. Like yer man's father – what's his name?'

'Jude.'

'No, the father.'

'Theophilus.'

'Yeah, Jude's father. Doesn't know he's mad, that man. And that's his problem. Then, yer in fuckan trouble. Yer'd just want to watch the son doesn't go that way, that's all.'

'Get *married*?' Jude repeated William's suggestion. He hadn't forgotten the threat of a Pavlova face. 'I thought he didn't like me.'

'Well, there you go,' Alice replied happily.

'I didn't know we were even an item. I thought they said we couldn't be?'

Alice returned his gaze amazedly. 'But I'm – *kissing* you, aren't I?' she asked simply. 'And things?'

'Alice – do you know how naive you sound sometimes?'

'I'm only a small girl,' she explained in a baby voice.

'I know.' He paused. 'You know what my father said to me

the other day? He reckoned I should take you swimming – you know, to see you're all there, to see there aren't any missing legs, before we get married or anything.'

Alice contemplated herself one-legged in a one-piece. Or a bikini, with shorts to hide the stump. A Manuel Blasco beach scene, maybe. She would be leaning against a wall licking a 99 in the bottom left-hand corner of the painting.

'So he's not *all* mad, then.'

'He isn't *mad*,' Jude replied touchily. His head flushed as he rubbed it and shed micro-flakes of fish food. 'Labels like that are very easily thrown around. If he was mad, he would be diagnosed mad.'

'I'm sorry. I didn't mean to –'

'Forget it.'

Things were easier for them already. Oonagh's illness had stabilised. She was less given to wailing, although her health had failed to improve significantly. On balance, she thought it better not to push it – and so remained in bed. As a result of Oonagh's continuing illness, the lovers recovered their former freedoms. They began to empathise with the ethical position of the (free-range) poisoner. Reinstalled in Alice's room they lay about on the rug or the bed and wondered how William was doing it. Bleach in grapefruit juice? Tablets ground into her packet soups? Or maybe it wasn't a poison. Crushed glass? There was a case of a man, Alice said, who'd ground it so small that his unharmed wife voided it from her person for months without incurring a haemorrhoid let alone a haemorrhage.

Jude laughed, and in that moment Alice decided to forgive him for failing to make fornicators of them and relented in a way that would make the event more probable.

Relenting, together, behind the red armchair, there was the same pain as before but Alice felt it differently now. This was

Chapter Thirty-Five

William brought his face close enough to kiss his daughter-in-law.

'I'm telling yer –' he threatened, 'yer stay away from that Jude.'

Maria continued cleaning the ceramic hob. Another squirt of Jif, more busy circles. She wiped froth up the walls and under the extractor fan. Finished, she turned and held her head high over the Edwardian collar of her thin black jumper.

'Me, I am like the wife of Potiphar. There are men like Jood, they are everywhere. They are like Joseph. They want my body but I say *eh no*.' Maria squeezed the dishcloth. 'Always I am *r*unning away. *R*unning.'

Each time she rolled the *r* with deliberation, like a slowing roulette wheel, then turned her face away and sighed.

William frowned.

'But I thought yer man Joseph was the innocent,' he objected. 'I thought it was Potiphar's wife who was givan him the eye. I thought that's why he went to prison.'

'Well,' Maria replied, 'maybe you have seen more of this Anjou Lloyd Webber *rrr*ubbish. Jes? Joo tell me once, remember?, how *The Phantom* is so, so *stupido* that es unbelievable.'

William said never mind the Bible, in musical versions or any other, he didn't believe a word of what she was saying. 'Listen, love. Do it again, and I'll be taking yer both out.'

'Oh, jes?' Maria replied uncomprehendingly. 'Taking us where?'

'Pinner Cemetery.'

Maria laughed, but her eyes were afraid. She rinsed the cloth and hung it on the Pinocchio nose of the mixer tap. 'Es not my fault. Joo don't understand. I don't want this boy. Jood – in my opinion – he is compleeterletly juicerless for me or any woman.'

'It's true,' William conceded, 'that yer don't get many men like me.'

He was pleased with the way everything was turning out lately. He went home and lit some cigarettes, though he did not smoke, because he liked burning them. He reread his letter from the insurers and turned the gas fire on as August glared outside. He recorded a documentary about forest fires and played it twice.

That night he dreamed of four men, assassins, sitting on the dry, albino grass. All wore mirrored sunglasses and rotated their heads like solar panels as he approached. He said he had a spot of business for them.

'Ten grand,' the nearest man replied quickly.

'*Ten grand?*' William repeated crossly. 'How would it cost that?'

'Mr West,' the first man replied quietly. 'Or John? John, first there's your straight job. The labour alone's four grand. But then there's your body disposal fee. Your rumour fee.'

'Your snitch fee,' the second man added.

'And you want it done soon, right?' the first man continued.

William nodded.

'Then an express service fee may apply. Weapon replacement fee. It's like this. You got to think of it like a funeral. Or a wedding. It's an event. It's got to be right. If you're spending so much money on the casket, are you going to skimp on the flowers?'

'Or the nails,' the second man suggested.

'Or the nails,' the first man repeated solemnly.

'What's dearest?'

'Disposal. That's five grand, easy.'

'But I don't need disposal. I told you. I've got this incinerator, right, that'll do the job.'

'In that case . . .' The first man conferred with the second. 'Corkage applies?'

The second man nodded. 'Corkage applies.'

'How much is corkage?'

'Three grand.'

'So that's seven grand.'

'Not seven, exactly, no. Rumour fee's five hundred. A man goes missing, you want there to be a story not connecting it to you, right? And we offer an optional snitch service as well. That's a grand. Someone feeds a line to the police, pinning it on whoever you like. We want to make this process as smooth and painless for you as possible. That's our job. But it does cost. I can shield you from the action. I can't shield you from the cost of it.'

'I don't need a snitch either. I've got lady friends in the police.'

'OK,' the first man replied sceptically. 'I'm only trying to advise. If you don't want to take it, that's your look out.'

'And this fuckan corkage lark,' William objected. 'I'll do a deal with yus.'

William suggested they drop the fee in exchange for one free use of his incinerator.

'I could charge five grand for an incineration,' he claimed. 'Ten grand, even, if I had to deal with the body messef. Yer'd be getting a bargain.'

The first man hesitated. 'I'd want to use it three times.'

'Twice,' William bartered.

'Done. Twice, plus the four grand. And if you should change your mind . . .'

'I'm not going to change me mind.'

'People do. So. As I was saying, if you change your mind giving at least seventy-two hours' notice, you'll get a refund on your deposit. In your case, that'll be the four grand. Any later, we keep the deposit. Whatever happens, I want to use that incinerator. And,' he added slowly, 'if you turn out not to have an incinerator . . .'

'*Course* I've got a fuckan incinerator.'

'. . . then you'll find you've dug yourself into a hole you can't get out of. You got the deposit?'

William put his hand confidently in his pocket. There was nothing there but his handkerchief. The Indian restaurateur Ahmed Mahfooz appeared and giggled. William woke just as the third man in shades and the fourth raised knives to stab him. His pyjamas were drenched.

Chapter Thirty-Six

There was a service in the church the following night. Jude arrived ten minutes late.

'How's your mother?' he whispered to Alice.

'So-so.'

'And how are you?'

'Fine.'

Jude smiled so sympathetically, Alice felt that she might laugh out loud. There is a hysteria that comes with too long a period of gloom. That's why, in *Madame Bovary*, the chemist and the cleric laugh together over the heroine's dead body. It is why Alice now stared at things that were not really funny, and found she could not stop shaking.

The pastor used the overhead projector to show graphs and architectural plans for a new church. The grey screen wobbled. He could not get the designs in focus. One of the transparencies went fluttering off the side of the stage. Alice gasped tensely. Then two transparencies got stuck together. She felt sure she would laugh this time. Jude pointed to parts of two words in his small maroon Bible. The first was *con-*, prefix of *-gregation* in the next line. Jude pointed instead to *dom-*, after *king-*. Alice snorted and turned it into an improbable cough.

Jude nudged her and she knew she should not look again. But she did. Now Jude had found *a horse of strong testicle neighing*, and a *Nazi* (pressing his finger firmly over *-rite*) who ate *a cake of raisin*. Alice begged him, as if he were tickling her, to stop. She couldn't look at him, not at his face, his smile, his finger.

'Now,' the pastor continued, 'we come to a smaller project. More modest but no less vital. The redecoration of the living room of one of our most cherished Saints, Mabel Day. Who would like to volunteer for this worthy assignment?'

There was a pause.

'Will none here . . . ?' the pastor asked reproachfully.

Wildly Alice raised her hand. It felt like sticking out her tongue.

'Is that Alice?' the pastor asked.

'What are you doing?' Jude whispered.

'Something,' she replied and went out to the toilets, where Sally Jelly's mother accosted her – bacon-cheeked, with a large orange dress that added to the overall breakfast effect.

'Is your mother any better?' she asked Alice.

'Not really.'

'We just never know what Satan has in store for us in this old world, do we? Do they know what's wrong with her yet?'

'No.'

Illness was big news, in a world where nothing ever happened, because the sick person was unable to congregate. This could spiral off into spiritual death.

'Well, it does happen,' Sally Jelly's mother said, 'that some-times a person just loses their health for no apparent reason and they have to lie in bed for the rest of their life until The End of the World comes.'

Alice thanked Sally Jelly's mother and made her way back to her seat. Now the pastor was speaking about the dangers of Internet dating. You might end up marrying someone on the basis of a false description they'd given about themselves. The last speech was about how animals, in the forthcoming paradise, would no longer kill each other but would all be herbivores. They had the stomachs for it. They had been designed with all the right resources. Everyone was to pick up a new folding A5 leaflet about it on their way out of the church.

'Oh, yes,' said Jude, as they walked towards his car. He always walked with such a quick irritated stride, it was hard for Alice to keep up. 'Obvious, isn't it? Cheetahs – they were *designed* to run at seventy miles an hour just so they could *catch grass*, were they?'

In the safety of the car, Alice looked across at her lover and at last was able to giggle in earnest.

Oonagh's night light was on and they gave her the leaflet. It was entitled *An End To Suffering: How?*. She folded it into a pouch and studied the picture. On one side, Armageddon – a terrifying graph of red mountain ranges. The wicked were, judging by their agonised faces, the constipated. Armageddon was probably a great relief. On the other side, a pastoral scene. In the foreground, a woman knelt beside a huge basket of fruit. In the middle distance, a stag with great antlers stared.

'Bit against the spirit of things, a stag, isn't it?' Jude suggested lightly. 'What's he going to do with those antlers but fight?'

'Ah,' replied Oonagh, 'that's the point. Only paradise will beat those antlers into ploughshares.'

Those antlers were why The End of the World needed to happen. Soon they would be harvesting wheat. Inside the leaflet, there was a picture of Jesus dying slowly.

'Poor bugger,' Jude added, in the safety of Alice's room.

'Was he?'

'Yeah, suffocated to death, didn't he?'

'Did he?'

'Why'd you think the Roman soldiers broke his legs? *He* wasn't going to run away, was he? It was so he couldn't pull himself up to breathe.'

'Oh.'

Briefly Alice felt her throat constrict.

Cautiously, the next morning, Alice pushed back her mother's door. It cracked like a firework and two bright eyes blinked above the satin duvet. Dr Sulakahn was expected.

'We've got the results,' the doctor told them, half an hour later. 'And it's good news. It's nothing serious. You have too much H. pylori, that's all. *Helicobacter pylori*. Like a helicopter, we call it, because it rises up from the chest and flies . . .'

Dr Sulakahn propelled his hand from his heart to his throat. 'That's why you felt you couldn't breathe sometimes when you were eating.'

'How it is cured?' Alice asked.

'I'm prescribing a course of antibiotics. Your mother must take them, three tablets a day, for a month. We'll see how it goes after that. And avoid eating fish. Or tomatoes. The bug breeds in them.'

'But fish is good for you,' Oonagh said.

'Not in this case.'

'How did I get it?'

'Oh, it's in the air, it's in everybody. I'm just surprised it's made you so ill, that's all.'

Like being bedridden with thrush. Not a life-threatening condition at all, as it turned out. Showing the doctor to the door, Alice slipped him the forty quid her father had advised.

Dr Sulakahn was embarrassed but willing. Oonagh was chirpy and holy.

At Oonagh's first service since her illness, the pastor began by reading a letter, addressed To All True Churches in Great Britain. It explained that a television documentary would be broadcast that night which slandered the Worldwide Saints of God. There would be accusations of paedophilia – covered up by deacons, and pastors, and even William P. Pope himself. It was not for the Church to decide whether a Saint should or should not watch the programme. Each would make his own decision. Each would 'carry his own burden', the Bible said. Each would be a donkey arriving at the judgement seat of God with his or her justification for watching telly at nine o'clock on Saturday, 22 August 1997.

'Will you watch the programme,' the letter asked, without prejudice, 'or will you show your confidence in God's true Church? Will you allow the lies of Satan's media to distort your grasp of the Plainest Truth? Do not forget: the word *devil* means, in Greek, *slanderer*.'

Jude's father and others nodded contentedly. The letter explained what the Plain Truth was, in relation to paedophilia. Accusations were easily made. The World was full of vicious six- year-olds pointing fingers at adult innocents. Sadly, some children in the Church were copying the practice. Therefore, an accusation of paedophilia could be accepted only if . . . At this point, everyone was invited to open their Bible and turn to the book of Matthew.

'Let every case be determined at the mouth of two or three witnesses,' the pastor read.

Jesus had said this. So it had to be right. Two, or preferably three, adult Saints must have witnessed the act of paedophilia personally in order to corroborate the child's claim. Why these non-participators would have stood around and not intervened at the time was unclear. Perhaps they were too busy doing the washing-up. Perhaps they had half an eye on the football results. But that they were worthy witnesses of events was certain. Why the paedophile would have risked trouble in this way was equally mystifying, especially as paedophiles were well known to pick on children who would not utter a peep, but that was by the by.

At nine o'clock the battle music began. A red jagged fracture opened across the television screen. A camera swept through a dark empty corridor. A masked girl sat in a chair. Her voice broke. The camera waited patiently for her to cry.

How limited the media were. For years Alice had been waiting for a media exposé of the Worldwiders – for outside intervention to rescue her. Why weren't they more specific? Why didn't they talk about *The New Truthful Children's Book of Bible Stories*? On one page children were told that it made Satan and the demons happy if little boys and girls touched their own private parts, or each other's. Why didn't they talk about the terrors of Armageddon?

Instead the programme assimilated Pope's Church to stereotype: it was improbably described as a paradise for sexual abusers. Still Alice watched – gleefully, guiltily, sadly, angrily. She wanted the Church to be wrong, even stereotypically, so that she could be right to despise it.

A well-mannered boy of seventeen, wearing a huge protective yellow cagoule, shook on his own sofa. A Saint who used to give him lifts to the services had abused him for years. But the case could not be determined without two or three back-seat passengers.

Then William Pope's spit slid down the camera lens as they repeatedly asked him for an interview. Neither he nor any other prominent member of the Church would give an interview, unless the programme was broadcast live. This was because they feared their comments would be edited prejudicially. If only they could explain, live and in full, the Church's position on paedophilia – so satisfactorily given in the letter – all doubts and fears would disappear.

Oonagh trembled to this programme. It was a point of pride to her, and to many of the Saints, that the clergy of mainstream Churches were composed principally of paedophiles – while William P. Pope took a strong expulsive line of all forms of sexual offence. Alice watched her mother's reaction closely. She hoped this might be the way to raise some serious doubts about the Church.

'Makes you think, doesn't it?' she suggested.

'It's a test,' Oonagh replied without hesitation.

A personal test for Oonagh, the former victim of abuse, the new enjoyer of her regained health. How sad if Satan should succeed in this way. He might have gone to the trouble of an entire *Panorama* episode, but still he would not have her soul.

'Some of the people in that programme were ridiculous,' Jude added. 'That woman from Sedona with the long hair blaming the Church for her husband abusing their children. It was up to her to do something about it, not the Church. It'd have happened whichever Church they were in.'

Oonagh nodded, pleased.

'But don't you think,' Alice said as her mother withdrew to make a pot of tea for one, 'they're missing the whole point? It's our *minds* that were abused as kids. We're all fucked up.'

'Speak for yourself. I thought you didn't want to get all "psychological" about it?'

Alice gnawed her lip. *Mightn't* the Church's revolted denunciations of illicit sex have caused her own dysfunction? Was that it?

She could not stop thinking about the programme. She was

disgusted when new issues of *The Plain Truth* slithered through the letter box saying that the celebration of birthdays and Christmas was now permissible. Even the Sabbath need not be kept. A concession to those who had stuck with the Church. A cynical bribe. Alice pitied the younger version of herself who had tried so hard and believed so much – for nothing. All her sacrifices were in vain. It was unjust. As though balloons and marzipan could make up for things!

Some things never changed, however. Fornication, of course, was still wrong. The Bible said all true Christians must *abstain from blood, and from things strangled, and from fornication*. The FTSE index of sins in the New Testament: no eating of black pudding, no watching of the last act of *Othello*, and no premarital sex.

'Never hear them mention gluttony, though, do you?' Jude mocked.

He always noticed things Alice hadn't, and she was interested.

'Stands to reason, doesn't it?' he continued. 'All those fat people up the church. Smiths and the Jellies. Can't knock out the main supporters of the religion.'

Alice laughed. 'Maybe gluttony isn't as bad.'

'Oh, c'mon! One of the seven deadly, isn't it? And why do you always curl up your toes?' he asked.

Alice inspected her bare feet. She tucked her toes under the balls of her feet whenever she was not wearing shoes in case the blade of a passing ice skater might happen to slice them off.

'No more of that,' Jude said. 'Everything's going to be fine. What time do you want me tomorrow?'

'All the time,' Alice replied saucily. 'But I think we should start about eight.' They were going to decorate Mabel Day's living room.

Chapter Thirty-Seven

Ever since she had suspected that she might be mortal, Alice had struggled against sleep. Inclined to think that time slept was time lost and that the recommenders of camomile baths, Horlicks and bedside anthologies were diligent squanderers of the last remaining moments of consciousness, she used them to think. This practice she considered not only economic but bold. It recovered the ancient freedoms of reading books by torchlight under the bedcovers. Or, when it had been love poetry, by moonlight on the sill that had the condensation problem and the refillable tissue box.

Tonight's thoughts were to be psychological. She would regard her pillow as the headrest of a black leather couch. She would abandon her prejudice against the psychoanalytical view of her sexual condition. She would undertake A Brief Comprehensive History of Her Mental Life in Relation to the Zones Erogenous.

Item one was her glimpse, aged three, of her mother's sex, red raw as she pissed.

Gawd. Alice shifted her weight impatiently in bed and noticed that she had begun to dribble on to the pillow. She turned it over for the dry side. *Gawd.* Your mother goes to the loo, just the once, and you grow up dyspareunic? Surely not.

She turned to item two. Squeezing, aged maybe five, an aunt's left breast as it reposed under a cream chiffon blouse with a large neck-bow. Alice was sitting on her lap. Her mother rebuked her. Her aunt laughed awkwardly and said it didn't matter, but Alice was mischievously certain that it did. She had the idea that she was inflicting pain – but whether this was before or after her aunt had winced she could not say.

This aunt was not the infanticidal sister of Oonagh, but a sister-in-law of William's. She was eventually divorced because she was frigid. It was said she had a childlike idea of marriage as a husband, a brick house, and a garden with a long over-looked narrow lawn and daisies. Like a Victorian bride, she was unable to admit coitus to this combination of ingredients. She was receiving counselling while William's brother courted her. Chivalrously he used to give her a lift to the hospital: he had not thought to enquire why she was going. Oonagh main-tained that he deserved what he got. He'd engaged himself to a long string of pearly girlfriends before – lovelies like the one who wore a twirling pink minidress in Oonagh and William's wedding photo – only to let them all down. And when he finally married, the wedding took place in his tiny home town under the snivelling nose of the last and loveliest girlfriend he had jilted. He got, Oonagh said, what was coming to him.

And then little Alice had squeezed the woman's unrespon-sive breast. No wonder Oonagh was mortified.

In Elizabethan times, and much later, wealthy women did not breastfeed their own babies but put them out to 'wet nurses'. If the children turned out bad, sometimes people said they had imbibed it from their nurse's milk. Alice wondered briefly if she had squeezed frigidity out of her aunt's breast that day. Superstition not psychology, of course. Was it even remotely possible that hearing the story of her aunt – when she was, what, eighteen? nineteen? – had frightened her? Again, the effect seemed curiously disproportionate.

Alice returned to her own story. Item three was the stool incident, aged ten, when her cunt was cut. She had been thinking about it when Jude first asked her why she wore towels not tampons. She had been trying *not* to think about it only the other day. She could not remember clearly what had happened. She could only remember what her father had told her mother at the time.

She had been standing on the stool, when it collapsed. She fell on to the broken shards of wood. That was how she cut herself. It had happened in the bedroom, *this* bedroom, in fact. She sat up in bed and stared into the gloom. The stool had been a child's picnic seat in pine, with a slatted seat and criss-crossed legs. If she peered hard she imagined she could see it – whole. She couldn't remember it broken. She sank back into bed. Then there was more conversation. Her mother crying what was she to do! Her father said there was no problem about that – he had thrown away the stool already. Her mother replied crossly that she didn't mean *the stool*. She meant *Alice*. They couldn't take her to A&E. It wasn't allowed among the Saints in those days. Alice remembered her father telling her mother to give the child 'one of them things' to absorb the bleeding. The sodden thing had sat bulkily in Alice's knickers like a large shit.

A stool for a stool: that was all. Memory's vanishing trick.

Now she asked herself, why should the stool have vanished with the alacrity of a murder weapon? It was true that her mother was highly impatient of mess: toddlers who spat out their vegetables were beyond the pale. But what else might be true?

She felt hot. She turned over the pillow to lay her cheek on its cool side. It wasn't so much cool as wet from the earlier dribbling, and she was obliged to seek a patch on the far left-hand side.

Images of the teenagers interviewed on the paedophilia programme: they sat on things that could not hold them up either. The girl on the chair broke down. The boy on the sofa shook. And then there was Alice, her younger self, falling on the stool.

Imagine *she* had been abused.

In that case, the stool was quickly hidden from Oonagh's sight because it had never been broken. Because it wasn't the stool, was it, that had been broken. It was Alice's hymen that had been broken. That had bled. A literary critic and a psycho-analyst would tell you the same thing – the stool was the penis that had cut her up. The stool 'stood for' the penis. (There was even a Freudian pun in Alice's alleged 'standing' on it.) Momentarily Alice was carried away by the brilliance of her theory. Never mind a chapter in *All About Dating*. She was now holding out for a salient paragraph in *The Interpretation of Dreams*. Her father's tale about the stool, his expressed concern to get rid of it, was an attempt to cover up what he'd done. And it would suit him that Alice couldn't be taken to a doctor. No one would ever find out. No swabs for sperm would be taken.

So there had been no falling on to a stool. There had only been a falling on to her father. Alice remembered many occasions (these counted as item four) when he lay in bed, drawing his knees up like hills. On the modest summit she would perch. And then he would open his legs all of a sudden and she would fall on to him and they would both laugh. They would do it again and again.

If you explained items three and four like that, then it was easy to make items five and six add up to paedophilia too. You could say, for item five, that Alice hadn't cut her thigh with a pair of scissors in the sewing class and run home to her mother.

She had been abused and tried to tell her mother, who had not listened.

Nor had she begun menstruating early, when there were those pale brown stains in her small cotton knickers (item six, exhibit A). She hadn't even been producing vaginal fluids. No, her knickers were swimming with sperm. The brown in the stains could have any number of explanations beside menarche. Fissures. Tearing. Mingled with sperm, either would present a pale brown discharge.

And this would explain her parents' odd comments at the time, once they thought she might be menstruating. William had been anxious about pregnancy. Oonagh about the biblical ban on copulation during menstruation. Alice had always thought these comments typically absurd and overemphatic. And quite irrelevant to her situation as a ten-year-old child. What ten-year-old girl would be at risk of getting pregnant, for Gods' sake? Answer: a menstruating ten-year-old girl who was being abused.

It would also explain why her father used to say it wouldn't be a shock to his wee girl when she got married. No, because she'd been initiated already.

And an explanation for her nervous breakdown in her twentieth year (unlucky item seven) would emerge with monstrous clarity too.

The 'lost' tampon, which no one could find, was her displaced attempt to recover the truth that had been repressed for many years – that her father's penis had once been inside her. It was traumatic that no one would corroborate her fear – ostensibly, that there was a lost tampon; latently, that she had been abused. The nurse said yes, but the doctor said no. The person in authority said it had never happened. That would be enough to cause her breakdown.

In fact Alice could write the whole equation without too much difficulty. Three factors remained.

Item eight, William didn't want Alice to have a boyfriend – sexual jealousy.

Item nine, he mentioned that Sarah sucked her thumb in bed – displaced paedophilia again.

Item ten, the sex life of William and Oonagh was nearly non-existent. Oonagh the abused child had married an abuser. It was textbook.

And it was nonsense.

Alice turned over, and over again. Her father wasn't against Jude. He was the one who had suggested they marry. Plus William was a *woman*iser. You didn't catch him in Woolworths Pick and Mix. You caught him in the changing rooms of Next.

And if it wasn't nonsense?

Alice could hardly begin to acknowledge the possibility. What she had conducted was a mental exercise. In the abstract, she was pleased by how many pieces of her story slotted under the theme Paedophilia. It was like writing an exam essay: once she got going, fine pertinent quotations and arguments popped into her head and out of her nib onto the wide-ruled page of the answer booklet. The ones that occurred to her while she was writing were always more exciting than the ones she had planned on from the outset.

Had her father abused her? Alice refused to believe it. Feeling hotter than ever, she was reluctant to cast the safety of the duvet aside. No. Absolutely not. Definitely it was not a thought to be entertained. And that was her final word. Yes it was.

The last thing she heard was the click of her father going out the front door.

Chapter Thirty-Eight

William dragged open the yard gates. He was meeting a man at midnight. He waited behind the workshop at the base of an electricity pole. From this side the yard resembled a quarry. There were chalky basins and slag heaps. No one around. He listened to the motorway traffic. He could make out the gasps and sighs of coaches and passing lorries like bursts of aerosol. He clambered up a steep verge, hauling himself up with tufts of grass. A hundred metres on, in the middle of the field, he stopped and knelt beside a metal disc. Gently he worked it out from the hard earth to expose a small cylindrical hollow. The space was waiting. He was expecting a delivery from Ahmed Mahfooz, Balti City. How he liked Mahfooz, who called him my so special Mr West even after he'd stopped driving the Bentley.

William refitted the metal lid and slid down again. He checked on the incinerator, a huge metal can with a front door like a Smeg fridge and a skylight exit. He could hear a vehicle making slow progress up the laneway. There were potholes and pebble mounds. Impatiently the car sped the final few metres through the gates, on to the concrete road, and halted abruptly, absolutely, like an ice skater. William beckoned on the driver. The car was a Ford Focus. It did not look like the right sort of car. He had expected mirror windows at least. As it stopped again, out of the rear left door, a man put a foot.

'John,' he said.

'How are yus doing?' William replied nervously.

The man walked past William without answering and round to the boot. Inside was a large navy bag. A body delivered like a bulky item of dry-cleaning.

'Who was he, then?'

'You want to see?' The man grinned.

William watched as he unzipped the bag in a single movement. Like a trail of gunpowder. He felt he must say something strong and violent.

'Little fucker,' he declared.

The man paused, looked at William closely and grinned again.

The dead man was an Asian, in his sixties. The dead mouth gaped with surprise. Or it might have been pleasure. There were no eyes to guide interpretation because the lids were pulled down.

'Christ!' William was shocked. 'It's Mahfooz. I thought *he* was gettan rid of someone.'

'He was.'

'Jaysus.' William was wistful. 'It gets to this. Yer don't know what to do in the end. Yer get too old for the whole game.'

'If you say so, mate.'

William sharpened up. 'Where's my stuff?'

'In the back.'

William checked the metal Thermodyne case. Then, with the driver's assistance, they picked Mahfooz's body up and fed it slowly to the great fire monster. A great grey brain of smoke issued from the top of the incinerator and climbed to the landing lights of tiny planes on their final descent to the runway on the other side of the carriageway.

'Say a little prayer for him,' William appealed.

'Not really my thing, mate,' the man replied, walking away, his hands deep in his overcoat pockets.

'No, no,' William said. 'Yer don't get it. It's not about it being "your thing". It's very important.'

'Oh, fuck off,' the man said, without animosity.

The Ford Focus made its way irritably back down the lane – like the action replay of a rodeo. Bucking, shrugging, stopping, lurching, starting. Some beast bent on unseating its rider – and failing – in slow motion. William sat on the top of an upended JCB bucket, and watched earth turn to air. Then he took the metal briefcase up the hill and carefully placed inside the waiting hollow, a silvered upright copper canister of nitroglycerine. There it waited in the cool earth like a bottle of Purdey's.

William waited too. At 7.30 a.m. he was sitting on the edge of the small front-garden rockery at Jude's parents' house. Jude was unlocking the porch door from the inside when his mother appeared in a fleecy peach dressing gown. 'Don't forget your hat!' She handed him the item to preclude amnesia. 'It's cold!' She stood waving and saw William. 'Oh, how lovely! He's come to help you.'

'I think it was this way yer wanted to go, lad.' William's finger beckoned.

With hypnotic helplessness, Jude followed. He was afraid to go with William. He was afraid to seem ridiculous by refusing. William's van was parked three doors down. The rear doors were already open like a wing-case.

'Hop in.'

There was a concrete breaker and a small drum of diesel

on the gritty floor. William slammed the doors shut. 'Yer got that Swiss Army knife on yer?'

Jude felt his trouser pockets and shook his head. William took out a flick-knife with a chewed handle. 'See this?' he said. And he held the knife out to Jude. The blade ejaculated a centimetre away from Jude's nose. Calmly, dementedly, William explained what he wanted. Jude was to call off the wedding – on the grounds that he was homosexual – or else William would cut him into fun-size pieces.

'And I don't want it to be no "theoretical" arse-banditry. None of that –' William spoke *falsetto*, his words on point – ' *"I might be, I might not, I just need to find messef"* bollocks. I want yer to tell her how yer've been putting yer cock up other men's arses and that. How yer've been doing little boys in school toilets. Takan a job as a janitor. Whaddever yer can think of. So there can't be no doubt about it. Yer got it?'

Jude nodded. No spit to speak with.

'Good. Now. This is what yer do. Go away, think about it for a bit. How yer gonta tell her and that. Because if yer don't get it right, I'll fuckan kill yer. And yer mum and yer dad. Even if yer mum is nice and yer dad is mad. I'll fuckan burn down the whole lot of yus in yer beds one night.'

Half an hour later at the kitchen table, Alice glanced apprehensively at her father. It was so strange. The most ordinary things seemed suddenly theatrical. The way he walked in. His jaunty stage wink. The way he made himself a boiled egg and offered her one too.

He was also a man of fire. A heat-sensitive camera could record the tarnished stencilled ectoplasm that billowed round his body with every movement. She could feel the danger on her face.

And yet he had no way of knowing what she'd thought the night before.

No list of items, no essay points, now. She had this image: a blue-black hole in her chest, the diameter of a pencil. A large maple leaf exit wound, puking like a gargoyle.

She could imagine it – accusing her father. She could imagine his casual admission: 'Chrissake, girl, it never did yer any harm, any of that.' He might discuss it quite calmly. Or perhaps he would be very angry. She visualised his one-sided smile, the facial fishhook appearing and disappearing in his left cheek. In a rage he had once raised a saucepan to Oonagh's head. What was he capable of, after all?

Alice was mid-row with Oonagh over the breakfast things. The truth, Alice explained, was things like: Mabel Day was an old woman. She had lived, she would soon die. The best that could be done was to make her living room pleasant. And that was what Alice was hoping to achieve this morning.

'And you think that's *it*?' Oonagh shook her head. 'That we live and die and that's the end of it? There'd be no *point* to it, Alice.' She applied her plum nail varnish.

'That is exactly the point. It's precious because there isn't much of it.'

'And you *choose* that?' Oonagh was incredulous as she fanned her left hand dry.

'I don't *choose* it. It's the fact and we have to get on with it. Every person who has ever lived on this planet has died and that's the end of it.'

'What about Jesus Christ?' Oonagh asked with a note of triumph, as though Jesus Christ were the point irrefutable, and started on her right hand.

'Jesus Christ,' Alice replied, half diplomatically, half facetiously, and without the faintest belief in the resurrection of Jesus Christ, 'had a head start. He was born the Son of God. He must be the exception.'

'Exactly.' Oonagh claimed her daughter's argument with dogmatic uncertainty. 'The resurrection of Jesus is the start. Because he is resurrected . . .'

'Just tell me' – Alice cut across the unbearable theology – 'can you help with Mabel or not?'

'Not today.'

Alice turned to her father instead. He *ummed* and *aahed* as she explained she'd volunteered to decorate an elderly lady's living room. She needed his help.

'I thought Jude was helping yer.'

'He was.' She put two spoonfuls of sugar in her herbal tea to steady herself. 'But he hasn't turned up. I keep ringing his mobile and there's no reply. Now it's on answerphone. And I said I'd do it this morning. She's an old lady. She'll be waiting. I can't let her down.'

'Lazy little bastard,' William replied. 'Not to worry, love. Yer old dad's never failed yer yet, has he?'

They left ten minutes later. William did not really expect to have to stop at junctions. He kept going as though optimism would preclude the need and, on the occasions when it was unavoidable, mildly whiplashed his passengers. They drove along the main road. On the left, Alice noticed that the black squares of her old school had new cream cladding. After the roundabout, she saw a new road sign reading *The Church of the Worldwide Saints of God*. Everything said: this is your past, and it is changed. The high street was a Monopoly board of recently acquired and recently dashed property interests. William was thinking of buying a couple of shop flats cheaply. A farm with horses disappeared quickly on the right.

Alice kept glancing at her father. Was it possible it had happened? Was it possible they had agreed on the stories about stools and scissors they would tell other people? Or had he simply told the stories with such conviction that it was impossible to disagree – and disagree so disagreeably, so embarrassingly, so impossibly?

Alice felt as if her memories were corroded silent-film stock.

At Mabel's, they moved all the living-room furniture into the garden and lifted up the carpet. Alice painted the walls with a quick-drying barley-white emulsion. William went to the shop and chose a new carpet. Mabel wanted plain biscuit, no pattern. What if she shouldn't like it? she asked Alice. Alice reassured her that she would like it. Mabel waited in the bedroom, steadying herself on the ferrules of two rosewood walking sticks. The fitters arrived with a peach carpet with a white stripe. Alice looked on in dismay.

'And that's *biscuit*?' she asked her father reproachfully. William faltered.

'Haven't you ever seen a Rich Tea?' she pursued sharply. 'Underside of a chocolate digestive?'

'Not familiar territory, love, in our house.'

This was true. Oonagh never bought biscuits in case someone should eat them. So Alice watched nervously as the fitters laid the carpet – pushing and lopping and stapling. She stood with her father in the garden, watching through the patio doors.

The carpet wasn't so bad when it was down. Alice told her father not to walk on it in his muddy boots, and began to ask another question.

William did not let her finish. 'The weddan? Great idea, love. Terrific. I'm all for it, me. Yer know that.'

'But you don't like him?'

'Who says I don't like him?' William sniffed defiantly with his left nostril, and stepped forward. She failed to restrain him. He walked on the new carpet in his muddy boots. Just to show he could, it seemed, and that she couldn't stop him. What wasn't he capable of, after all? There were footprints all over it now. Fortunately, the fitters had gone. It was a symbol and it was literal too. He would sully anything he liked. Alice burst into tears.

'I've never seen yer like this,' her father said uneasily. 'Don't be like this.'

He stroked her cheeks and Alice cried. For herself. For the old lady who wanted her last carpet and her walls whited so that she need not be ashamed, any more, to have visitors. Alice wiped her face and put the offcuts over the worst of the tracks. She took the old lady by the hand and promised the marks would be cleaned just as soon as the mud had dried. Mabel smiled and said nothing was perfect and that Rome was not built in a day. She had not yet given up hope of her engagement to a young man who had died in the Second World War.

'Who yer calling now?' William asked as Alice dialled her mobile.

'Jude,' she replied, a cold monosyllable to wound her father with his redundancy, and turned away.

'Go ahead,' he instructed her redundantly. 'I've to get back to the yard anyway. Lot on today.'

Alice listened to the answerphone message again.

'Yer've always got yer old dad,' William said gently. 'No one's reliable like me. I'll take yer to the bus.' He added, 'I'm thinkan of getting shot of Sarah, yer know,' as though he expected her to be pleased.

'Is that so,' Alice replied without interest.

Then he said he had another plan. One that would save his wife from the mortal threat of ever having to live again in a house that was too small for her. Another insurance job, this time on the Bentley Mulsanne and some of his old JCBs. He'd already bought their replacements. He would show her. They would have to stop briefly at the yard first.

'It'll help her come round to yussef and Jude, like,' he explained, 'when the money comes in. Pound notes are always the way. I know yer mother like no man mortal.'

'But she isn't ill now,' Alice objected flatly.

'But she could be,' William replied. 'Anyway. You ready?'

They got into the car. William started the engine. She wanted to stop him, to shout: first I have to know first.

The moment had escaped. She'd failed. She worked herself up for another attempt. Each time she told herself that this was the moment, William overshot a junction, mounted another curb corner, went through the lights on amber.

Again she was faintly surprised that her father, there with her in that same slight breathing space, knew nothing about what was happening inside her mind. This was the great advantage of thought and this was the great disadvantage of thought. She thought of asking him to go for a drink, except there would be an audience.

'Could you just pull over?' she said in a choked voice.

'Are yer sick?' William asked, puzzled.

Alice felt the end of her nose redden and her eyes smart with the pepper of new tears. 'I don't know. I'm not really sure.'

Tending the travel-sick was one of William's eccentric pleasures. He pulled smoothly on to double yellows, set his hazard lights blinking, nipped out the door and opened hers. Smiling encouragingly he squatted on the curb, and offered a plastic bag from Tie Rack.

Alice held it to her chest. Her father had been doing this for her since she was tiny. There were countless long-distance journeys when he had looked after her, without her mother, because her mother didn't want to come. If Alice wet herself, William never complained but drew on to the hard shoulder, opened the boot, and got her a new pair of woollen tights. 'But I need a skirt too,' she might protest. 'Don't worry about that,' he would say. 'Yer fine.' So she would turn up at the houses of great-aunts and great-uncles with tights and boots and a coat but no skirt – and everyone would think it was odd but no one would say anything. Instead they put her in a bath with two yellow plastic ducks.

William was remembering too. 'It gave yer great confidence, when yer left yer mother and come with me all by yussef. Yer were only three the first time. Christ, yer thought yer was going to the moon!'

What was he capable of, after all? Tears budded again. Alice wondered if she was getting herself upset so that she would be able to say something – or upset so that she wouldn't have to. And she wondered, if she was doing the wondering, where in her brain it was all getting decided. Perhaps she hadn't gone far enough with Freud. Perhaps Freud was like bird shit on the windscreen – ubiquitous but no aid to vision. And she was tired of thinking.

William got back into his side of the car.

'I remember when I was ten,' she said quietly.

'Do yer by Christ,' William replied encouragingly.

'I fell on a stool.' Falteringly Alice described everything she could remember. '*Did* I? Would it, would it, have – broken?'

William scrutinised her doubtfully. 'Didn't know it was Civil Engineeran they had yer doing up at that university.'

He didn't understand. She would have to be direct. She saw the thoughts she would have to speak. Words she could send out of her mouth. Then they would be visible. *I think you abused me. Did you abuse me?* She didn't know how to say them. It was like trying to think how to move your limbs. What was automatic became impossible.

When she spoke, her voice was detached, as if she were not really speaking at all. There were words in the air. She was just watching her father's face.

He told the rear-view mirror a story. 'I had a relative once, right, she was about yer age. She went schizo. Yer know how they knew?'

Alice did not reply.

'They knew because one day she started accusan her lovan and devoted father a interfering with her, and that. It's in the early to mid twenties it normally starts. I only pray to God,' William shifted his gaze to the grey cloth ceiling, 'yer don't go that way yussef.'

Still she watched him. His cold brown eye. His great hooked profile. His small lipless mouth. He held his pose unblinkingly, and then convulsed like someone being given electric shocks. He turned his face away. When he raised it again, it was red with pain. She thought of the day of Paddy's funeral, when he had performed his own grief. Her father was a man who could forge his own signature. He was a real fake.

This weeping might simply be real. This weeping might simply be fake.

You could never know with a liar. And everyone was a liar.

You could never know. She felt *dull*. That was the word she saw now.

'I –' William's words got stuck. He coughed up phlegm, wound down the window and spat clumsily. 'Why yer'd be sayan this . . .' He bowed his head again and gripped the steering wheel.

'I never done nothan,' he said at last and raised his hands briefly from the wheel. 'The thing yer've to try to understand, right, is it's not an exact science, being a dad. Yer do yer best and yer still don't get it right.' He paused. 'Now then,' he announced, *herrumphed* commandingly into his handkerchief, sniffed, and turned the ignition.

And he began telling her about a substance called nitro-glycerine obtained from an old IRA contact, about three assassins in a car with mirror windows, and about his disappointment that no body had met its end, yet, in his incinerator.

But he was hopeful.

And it was hopeless, he knew now. He could hear distant politeness in each of her replies, in each of her questions about his plans. Like a ripple she was receding from him.

In the old water tank he sat down and cried. Nitroglycerine spurted from the pipette, the match rasped against the box. It wasn't an exact science, love.

He never meant to kill *her*.

Because he really loved her. And that was the truth.